Reunification

Two Worlds Book #1

By Timothy L. Cerepaka

An Annulus Publishing Book

Annulus Publishing, Cherokee, Texas, 2015

Published by Annulus Publishing

Copyright © Timothy L. Cerepaka 2015. All rights reserved.

Formatting by Timothy L. Cerepaka

Contact: timothy@timothylcerepaka.com

Cover design by Elaina Lee of For the Muse Design
(www.forthemusedesign.com)

ISBN-13: 978-0692498293

ISBN-10: 069249829X

Acknowledgments

I would like to thank my uncle, James Wilhite, for helping me get this manuscript into publishable shape. I'd also like to thank the rest of my family for supporting me while I wrote this novel. You guys rock.

Chapter One

How different the city of Xeeon was from the city of Ra-Dela back home from whence I came. The sun shining above was harsh and unyielding, like the open oven of a baker, whilst large telescreens blared such raucous advertisements for things such as some useless toothpaste that made me wish to plug mine ears and never hear another sound in my life. Even the news reports—one of which currently showed footage of some monster-like robot with a gaping maw attacking another group of robots on the border between the city and the Dead Lands—were so loud and boisterous that I had no idea what they were trying to show me. That I could not read the words on the screen, either, made my stay here that much less enjoyable.

And the loud engines and exhaust ports of the Spear hover vehicles flying above to and fro like busy bees assaulted mine ears at every turn. 'Twas madness, I tell ye; madness!

That was not even counting the hundreds and hundreds of people in the streets, all speaking in Modern Xeeonish, an ugly, practical language that I understood not one word of. They bustled along the crowded streets, talking and laughing and joking, shoving aside strangers without so much as an 'Excuse me' or 'Sorry,' and discarding their garbage everywhere. Their collective stench was like oil and concrete, a combination that made me wish to vomit, though I held it down, for I had nowhere to puke it.

The children were the worst; whereas Delanian children were as meek and quiet as the music of the Old Gods, Xeeonite children were loud and dirty, crossing the streets at random, causing vehicles to blare their horns when they got in their paths, even mocking the robotic law enforcers that protected this city from crime. Where were their parents? Did all Xeeonite parents abdicate their parental responsibility once their children reached a certain age? Mine own parents certainly would not have tolerated such rudeness.

Not that my opinion of the robotic law enforcers themselves was much higher. As I sat in a pathetic wobbly chair outside the Crossways Cafe, a ram-shackled cafe that was somehow still in business (despite their main product, what they referred to as 'genuine' South Delanian tea, which tasted more like dwarf piss), I kept a careful eye on the J Series Law Enforcement Robots. Only two such robots were out in this part of the city today (at least that I could see), overseeing the hundreds of scurrying people with those cold mechanical eyes that reminded me of Sir Alart's replacement eye.

In particular, the robots seemed to be focusing on me, likely because my dress—a simple brown tunic, with humble green pants I had bought from a kind old seamstress back in Ra-Dela prior to coming here, and rough leather shoes that were as good as

I could afford based on the wages I made—pegged me as a Delanian. Though Dela and Xeeo had not been at war for over a century now, still there existed animosity between the peoples of both worlds. Most of the Xeeonites passing in the street before me paid little attention to I, but every time one glanced at me, I saw disgust and distrust in their eyes, whether they were human or Rathonian or some other Xeeonite species.

No doubt the clickers looked upon me as a possible threat, even though their records ought to show that I was Rii, a Knight of Se-Dela. The Knights of Se-Dela had worked with the J Series Law Enforcement Robots many times over the years, yet I would be telling stories if I were to say that I trusted any of those dead machines with so much as a cup of water.

Look at them. Cold eyes, with no sign of emotion or a soul within them … metallic skin, freezing to the touch and reflecting the light of the sun in a way that hurt the eyes … and the way they watched over the people like predatory birds, ready to eat up any lawbreakers their eyes fell upon. Oh! How cruel they can be to any they deem worthy of their attention! Even the Knights of Se-Dela, as ruthless as we are toward criminals, barely come close to meeting the sheer brutality of the J series robots.

Yet I would admit, though without any happiness, that the bots were indeed effective. Whispers through the Portals asserted that the low crime rate of Xeeo and its many countries was due to the widespread adoption of these machines, and certain whisperers even suggested that King Waran-Una and the Mystical Alliance of Dela were thinking of replacing us Knights with these automatons.

What a disgusting thought. True, 'twas only a whisper, one

which none of us Knights believed, but 'twas a whisper which popped up every so often. It was such a regular occurrence that at times I believed King Waran-Una himself was the source of these whispers, simply to keep us Knights on our feet. Whatever their origin, I pushed them out of mine mind for the time being because today, I had more urgent matters to worry about.

My eyes flew over the crowds, searching for the Jikorian merchant who had agreed to meet with me on this day. The seller of goods had said, in his letter written in rough Delan to me, that he had the knowledge I sought, but would only meet me in a public place. He had specified the Crossways Cafe, but I had been sitting here for half an hour already and yet the merchant was still nowhere to be seen.

My tongue grew dry with thirst, yet I was loathe to drink my 'genuine' South Delanian tea. It tasted nothing at all like actual South Delanian tea, but when I complained to the waitress—a young bald woman, an ugly style that was apparently popular among the young women of this city—about it, she brushed off my complaint like I was nothing more than an annoying bug buzzing in her ear.

Looking at the tea more closely, I wondered how anyone with working eyes (or mechanical eyes, in the case of many of these Xeeonites) could mistake this for the real tea. True South Delanian tea was a rich, deep brown, like the bark of a sama tree in full bloom. This was a muddy, ugly brown, and it smelled like a dead rat.

I considered asking for water, because the other drinks they offered on their menu—among them something called 'mechanic's delight,' whatever that meant—sounded as appealing as dwarfish beer, but then decided against it. If the owner of this restaurant served such terrible, deceptively-named tea in the first place, their water was likely fit only for the dregs of society, if even that.

Where was the merchant? I did not know. I kept glancing at my watch, which ticked as steadily as the rising and setting of the sun every day, and wondered when the merchant would get here. I did not have all the time in the world to sit and wait; today was my only day off this week and I would have to leave before sunset, because by the time the sun set here, it would be morning in Dela and I would be expected to show up for duty at first light.

Though no matter what time I left, I would not be in a good mood. Whilst Dela and Xeeo were similar in some ways, the two had different time zones. When the sun was high in Dela, it was midnight at Xeeo; when the sun was shining merrily over Xeeo, Dela was ruled by the night.

To wit, I was tired and more irritable than usual. To make this trip, I had had to disrupt my normal sleep schedule. That meant getting up in the middle of Dela's night. 'Twas hard on me; being a Knight of Se-Dela was a herculean task, thanks in no small part to having to lug around a heavy suit of metalligick armor and a skyras sword all day. I valued mine sleep highly, but I valued the information that this merchant promised me even more, though as he still seemed unlikely to show up, I began to wonder if I had made a foolish sacrifice.

Mine thoughts were interrupted when a shrill, annoying voice croaked, "Hi!"

I looked up from my disgusting drink to see who had spoken to me. Striding up to my table from the street was a being I had never seen before in my life. He was humanoid in appearance, but his head was much larger than any human's, with a massive forehead to go with it. His skin was a light green, almost appearing painted-on, though if the stories about the Jikorians were true, this was his natural skin color.

The newcomer also wore a loose leather jacket, which looked as old as the foundations of Castle Una, and by his side was strapped one of those silly laser guns carried by almost all citizens of Xeeon. Slung over his shoulder was a large white sack, perhaps carrying his goods, though secretly I hoped it would instead contain the knowledge I sought from him.

Without thinking, I stood up and extended one hand in his direction. The newcomer stopped and reached over the table, grasping my hand with his own. His hand felt slimy and sticky, like mud in a swamp, and an awful stink of wet grass flowed from his body into my nostrils. I would have gagged and declared that I had not smelled such a terrible stink in all my years, but I did not wish to offend the merchant, so I kept my silence.

We sat at the table, opposite each other. The merchant rested his bag on the ground near his chair, which wobbled under his weight, and he then clicked his fingers. Not snapped; nay, that was not the right word. The merchant's fingernails were long and sharp, allowing him to click them together like the chirping of a cricket.

'Twas not a second after he clicked them that the disrespectful waitress from before appeared, like a spirit summoned by the gods. She held in her hands one of those strange tiny little handheld computers, a stylus in her other hand, the stylus's tip hovering over the screen of the computer as if she was a scribe recording the Revelations of Waran-Una.

REUNIFICATION

"What da ya want, sir?" the waitress said.

The merchant smiled at her, revealing blunt, short bluish teeth that looked like candy. "Whatever my associate here is having, miss."

'Twould have rolled mine eyes at the use of the word 'miss' to describe this woman, because I could think of no women less of a mistress than she. Wench, perhaps, or whore, for I suspected she slept with many men, based on how she initially flirted with me before I made it clear I have zero interest in romance or sex at the moment.

The wench simply noted that order in the computer and was gone again, the back of her red shirt disappearing through the Cafe's front doors.

I shook mine head and said, "Brother merchant, I would have advised against this 'genuine' South Delanian tea. It is a mockery of the true concoction, a deceptive advertising ploy."

"But I like it," the merchant said. He sniffled loudly, like he was taking in all of the smells around us. "It smells so good. Besides, what does it matter if it's the real thing or not? Taste and smell are the only things that matter to me."

Under ordinary circumstances, I would have berated the merchant for continuing to support such deceptive business practices. His attitude toward the subject confirmed what I had suspected about the decadent Xeeonites; so long as they got their fill, they were happy, like pigs in a pen.

But now was not the time to discuss this. I leaned forward 'cross the table and said, "Now, brother merchant, the letter ye gave me said you know something about my missing sister, Kiriah. Correct?"

The merchant leaned back in his chair and folded his hands behind his head. 'Twas an annoying thing, what he did, because it seemed highly disrespectful to me, but Jikorians were said to be an easy people, so I tried not to take offense.

"Yep," said the Jikorian, nodding. "That's right. When your friend showed me those pictures of your sister with that man, I recognized her. That's pretty good for me, because all you humans look the same to me. Not trying to be a bigot or anything; I just don't think you humans are very distinct."

I should have taken offense to that, but I cared not for his own nonchalance, for there were more urgent matters to attend to. Perhaps before this was all over, however, I would chide him for his inability to distinguish betwixt us humans.

Yet to be certain we were talking about the same woman, I withdrew from mine pocket an envelope containing the photographs showing my sister. As I did so, the merchant grimaced.

"Wow," said the merchant, blinking. "I forgot that you Delanians are so … quaint."

I scowled. 'Twas true that we in Dela still used paper for most of our dealings, whereas those in Xeeo relied mostly on digital and electronic gadgetry to conduct their business. Hardly mattered to I; Xeeonite tech was clumsy and brutish, aside from their Diamusk vehicles, which we Knights use to traverse Dela.

I placed the three pictures on the table and pushed them toward the merchant. He leaned forward to look over the pictures, which caused his stink to get even closer to me, but again I did not show mine annoyance because I did not wish to offend him.

The pictures showed my sister, Kiriah, sitting outside this very

8

Cafe, sipping from an emerald cup, similar in color to mine. She was alone in the first two, but in the last one, she sat across from a large bearish man whose back was to the camera. I had already seen these pictures before, of course; had pored over them for even the slightest detail that might explain why my sister was here or who this man was, but I had found nothing, hence why I was speaking with this merchant.

The merchant's beady eyes scanned the pictures before he leaned back in his seat. "Yep. That's her, though I don't really know her name."

"But she looks like my sister?" I said.

"Yep," said the merchant, nodding. "She doesn't come here too often, but she's hard to miss because she's sometimes with that man in the third picture."

The merchant tapped the third picture with one of his thin fingers, leaving tiny blotches of that disgusting gunk on it. I made a mental note to clean the photographs with the purest water I could find after this discussion was finished.

"What is that man's name?" I said. "Do ye know him?"

"Yeah," said the merchant. He looked over his shoulder so quickly that his head was a blur before he returned to looking at me. "I mean, it's hard to tell from this picture, of course, because if you humans look the same while facing forward, you are indistinguishable from the back, but even I wouldn't mistake that large back for the back of anyone other than who it belongs to."

"Delay the revelation no longer, merchant," I said. I glanced at mine watch. "I have little time to waste going in circles like this."

"Fine, fine," said the merchant, holding up his hands as if to calm me. "He's Xacron-Ah. Ever heard that name before?"

I frowned. "Nay. 'Tis a criminal?"

"Actually, he's the Mayor of Xeeon," said the merchant. "'Course, you wouldn't know that, seeing as you don't live here, but that's who he is."

I glanced down at the third picture again. "How can I be sure ye are telling the truth?"

"Let me show you a picture of the Mayor to back up my claims," said the merchant.

I expected him to pull out a little device to show me the picture; instead, he tapped his right forearm, like a pianist tapping a key, and the skin of his forearm slid back, revealing a small screen the same size and shape as his forearm.

How grotesque. The Xeeonites were absolutely obsessed with using their technology to 'enhance' their bodies, but I considered these aberrations to be nothing more than disgusting abominations that ruined the beauty of nature. Though again, I kept that opinion to mine self, because I was more interested in seeing this Xacron-Ah fellow than in sharing mine thoughts.

The merchant must have noticed my disgust, because he said, "What? It's an arm screen. Every Jikorian merchant has one. Those little phones and tablets that humans carry are so clumsy. Makes more sense to have this embedded in your body where you can't lose it, right? Well, unless a mad man cuts off your arm, of course, but that happens pretty rarely."

The merchant laughed uproariously at that joke, as if it was the most humorous crack on both Xeeo and Dela. I found no humor in it, for I was too disgusted by the sight of the tech built into his arm to find it humorous.

The merchant then tapped the screen, swiped to the left a few times as he went through a multitude of pictures I could not see due to the speed at which he swiped his screen, and then said, "Okay, here's a picture of Xacron-Ah. Notice any similarities?"

I leaned forward to get a better look at the Mayor of Xeeon. The photograph showed a large, bearish man standing in front of a podium, perhaps delivering a speech to an audience that was not shown. The man wore a navy blue suit, reminding me of the ocean, though his fingers were metallic, as if they were robotic replacements, though they could just as easily have been covers for all I knew. 'Twas hard to tell with this picture, as clear as it was.

His eyes were orange, an unusual color for certain (though I had heard rumors that Xeeonite humans often used chemicals to change their eye color, which might have explained it). 'Twas hard to tell for certain if this Mayor was the same man as the one in the third picture, but their body sizes were similar enough, as was their hair, which fell to their shoulders in locks.

I sat back, scowling, while the merchant pulled the cover back over his arm screen. "I will admit that the two look similar. Does the Mayor have an identical twin brother?"

"Nope," said the merchant. "Far as I know, the Mayor doesn't have any family. If he does, they're back in Dela."

"Why would they be back in Dela?" I said. "Xacron-Ah is a Xeeonite, is he not?"

At that moment, the wench waitress exited the Cafe and strutted over to us, as if she was a queen. She placed the merchant's red cup on the table between us, but before she even asked, the merchant said, "Here you go, girlie," and swiped his hand over her money scanner before she even asked. The scanner beeped and the waitress, apparently happy with that sound, turned and left without saying another word.

"What?" said the merchant, looking at me in confusion. Then he clicked his fingers. "Oh, right. I just paid for my drink. I know you Delanians use actual paper and metal to pay for your stuff, but here on Xeeo, almost everyone has payment chips embedded under their skin. Way more convenient than lugging around an unwieldy purse, for sure."

Under other circumstances, I would not tolerate this attitude from someone like him. Xeeonites were always arrogant, boasting about their technological prowess as if they were superior to us Delanians. 'Twas the main reason I rarely visited this world; I did not need to be chided for my 'primitive' practices, especially from individuals who regularly mutilated their bodies with technology.

"Anyway, Xacron-Ah actually isn't a native-born Xeeonite," said the merchant. He took a swig from his cup and sighed contentedly, as if he had just taken a sip of the wine of the Old Gods. "He came from Dela about twenty years back, had his citizenship changed from Se-Delan to Xeeonian, and then won the mayoral election about six years back. I didn't vote for him, by the way; always thought he was an idiot."

"Six years ago?" I repeated. "Why, that is the same time my sister vanished."

"Maybe there's a connection between those two events," said the merchant. He tapped the third picture again. "We know your sister and the Mayor have met together at least once."

"For what reason would the Mayor take up an interest in my sister?" I said, staring at the photograph glumly. "Mine sister never mentioned knowing any Xacron-Ah, nor did she ever show any interest in going to Xeeo ever."

"So she just up and vanished one day, completely out of the blue?" said the merchant. He leaned back in his chair again, this time holding his cup close to his large lips. "What a great sister you've got there, just off and running away on her own like that without telling you where she was going."

I slammed my fist on the table, causing my emerald cup to shake. The movement was so sudden that the merchant nearly fell backwards off his chair, but he caught himself at the last minute and brought all four legs of his seat back onto the ground. It gave me some satisfaction to see that he had spilled some of that disgusting South Delanian tea on his shirt, though the satisfaction only lasted for a little while, like a burst of sunshine in the middle of a storm, and was quickly replaced by anger.

"Speak not ill of my sister, merchant," I said. "Kiriah was a noble woman who would not simply run away without telling me. We were as close as any brother and sister duo could be; hence why her disappearance has plagued me like a sickness for the past six years."

"Right," said the merchant. "Well, I apologize for that accusation. Since I don't know Kiriah, I guess it's not my place to say what she is or isn't like, eh?"

He did not sound at all apologetic. No doubt his bigotry towards humans was the cause of his false apologetic tone. I wanted to challenge him to a duel right here and now, but I knew that duels were illegal in most Xeeonite cities, so I refrained from doing so.

"Apology … accepted," I said, though I did not level my tone much. "Now, ye said ye have seen Kiriah here at this cafe sometimes. How often is 'sometimes'?"

The merchant sipped from his cup again. "About, oh, every three or four months I guess. She doesn't stay very long; just long enough to speak with the Mayor, or occasionally, one of his servants."

"Where does my sister go when she finishes conversing with the Mayor?" I asked. I looked around at all of the towering skyscrapers around us. "Does she have an apartment in one of these buildings?"

The merchant shrugged. "How am I supposed to know? I'm not some creeper who follows around human females. I never gave her a second thought whenever I saw her. Never even spoke to her before. I only notice her because she talks with the Mayor sometimes; other than that, she's pretty discrete."

I grabbed my heart and gave a long sigh of despair. Oh! How I had wished I would find my sister today! Here I thought I would be able to speak with her at long last, but suppose this merchant was honest—and despite his terrible taste in drinks, he probably was—then my eventual reunion with mine sister was to be put off yet again, though for how long, I knew not.

"You okay?" said the merchant, perhaps noticing how I clutched mine heart so. "Are you having a heart attack or something?"

"No," I said, lowering my hand from my chest as I sigh deeply. "No heart attack has struck me. I am simply disappointed that I will not be able to meet my sister today."

"Okay," said the merchant, though he eyed me warily still, as if he expected me to suffer an actual heart attack any moment.

"Well, I've told you all I know about your sister. Don't know anything else, so pay up."

The merchant held out his free hand, flexing his three fingers like the heads of a trinity snake. As he did so, he loudly slurped his drink, making me cringe at the noise.

"Didn't we agree on fifty delanes for my information?" said the merchant. "Because right now I *should* be back at my stall preparing for the rush hour, when all of the office people are getting off work and aren't thinking straight enough to question the prices I set for my goods."

I frowned. The merchant spoke the truth. When I first contacted him a week ago, when my friend Sir Alart told me that the merchant might know more about my sister, the merchant had told me he would tell me what he knew only if I paid him seventy-five delanes. Of course, that was highway robbery, which was to be expected from Jikorian merchants, so I negotiated the lower price of fifty delanes, which was still far too much, as I was paid only one-hundred and fifty delanes a week. Still, 'twas a small price to pay if it meant I would get to see my sister again.

Nonetheless, unlike some individuals, I was a man of honor. Hence, I pulled my purse out of my pocket and withdrew ten five delane notes, ten rectangular pieces of paper that bore the image of King Waran-Una upon them. His face looked like a lion, with a large gray mane of hair to go with it; having seen Waran-Una so many times, however, I paid no attention to the notes.

The merchant returned his chair to the ground and took the notes from my hand. He counted the notes with the speed and efficiency of a seller who did not wish to be tricked, but I was not worried, for I knew better than to swindle anyone out of money I owed to them.

The merchant must have been satisfied, because he rolled up the notes and stuffed them roughly within the pocket of his jacket. "I would have preferred you sent me the money electronically, as that would have saved me a trip to the bank to get this money put into my account, but that's fine. Now, if you will excuse me, I must go. Business awaits."

The merchant stood up, the legs of his chair scraping against the pavement, and swallowed the rest of his drink in one gulp. He then burped loudly, though the sound was almost drowned out by the constant bustling of the city all around us.

But before he left, I reached out a hand and said, "Hold on a moment, brother merchant. I have one more question to ask of ye about my sister and the Mayor."

The merchant looked over his shoulder, like he wanted to leave right away. "Well, I really don't have the time—"

"Please," I said, putting my hands together like a priest of the Old Gods. "I want to know if you know why my sister would meet with the Mayor."

"No idea," said the merchant as he placed his now-empty cup down on the table 'tween us. "I've never actually spoken with the Mayor, but if you want to meet him for yourself … well, actually, I doubt you will be able to, seeing as the Mayor only ever meets with people of higher social standing than a Knight of Se-Dela."

"The Knights of Se-Dela are …" I shook my head. "Mind not my protests. I will figure out my next move on my own. Thank ye for your aid."

The merchant nodded as he picked up his bag and slung it over his shoulder in one smooth motion. "No problem. If you need anything else, just come on down to Mackar's Miscellaneous Stand of Treasures and Antiques. It's located just south of the Xeeon Parliamentary Building, near the Central Office Park. Can't miss it."

I looked at him with disbelief. "Do ye try to fool me into buying your wares with your petty advertising?"

"I didn't say you had to *buy* anything there," said the merchant in a false innocent voice. "I just wanted to let you know where my business is located, so that if you need me, you can find me. Do you Delanians just not advertise or market *your* businesses or something?"

"Never quite so awkwardly or abruptly," I responded. "How brutish."

"You say 'brutish,' I say 'taking advantage of every opportunity that comes my way,'" said the merchant. Then he frowned. "Wait. Those two aren't exactly the same. Oh well. You get the idea."

"As certainly as the sun rises and sets every day, I do," said I. "Perhaps we will meet again someday, if I ever require need of your services once more."

"Looking forward to it," said the merchant. Then he produced a card from his pocket and slapped it down on the table. "There. That's my business card, just in case you need to contact me again."

Then he turned around and left. I watched him go until he disappeared into the crowd of bustling Xeeonians. Then I picked up the card and looked it over briefly. It was a tiny little thing, very poorly made, and it was written in Modern Xeeonish, which looked like little more than gibberish to I. That meant I could not use it to contact the merchant again even if I wanted to, unless I first found someone who could read and translate it for me.

Nonetheless, I pocketed the card anyway, even though no thought of ever meeting him again currently dwelt in my mind. Whilst he had given me much good and useful information about my sister, I did not like having to pay him fifty delanes. At the very least, I doubted I would return to him for quite some time.

Yet what did it matter, whether I did or didn't meet him again? I had more important things to think about, such as why Kiriah was meeting with the Mayor here at this Cafe every few months, and what mine sister was doing here in Xeeon at all.

Because prior to her disappearance, Kiriah had never shown any interest in visiting Xeeo at all. Always she had told me that she wanted to stay in Dela for her whole life in order to serve the Old Gods, a dangerous, yet brave, undertaking, considering how little tolerance the current government showed towards worshipers of the Old Gods.

Now, however, I knew not whether my sister even worshiped the Old Gods anymore. I leaned back in my chair, scratching my chin, as mine eyes surveyed the busy streets of Xeeon, though in truth, I wasn't looking at the passersby at all. I was looking at mine memories, thinking about the mysteriousness of this situation and trying to decide my next move.

'Twas an easy decision to make: To solve this mystery, I would need to speak with the Mayor. Though if the merchant's words were correct, the Mayor would ignore any requests on my part to meet him, which may be for the best, because a feeling of illness came over me whenever I thought about this Mayor Xacron-Ah. There was something about the man that I did not like, though I did not know what.

Mine next move, then, was to speak with the owner of the Crossways Cafe. Though I loathed to talk to the proprietor of such a disreputable establishment, I knew it was the only way I could get the information I needed on the Cafe's patrons. After all, I reasoned, the Cafe's owner likely knew the face and name of every man, woman, and child that visited his establishment and would hopefully be willing to share that information with one of his customers.

Standing up, I left my half-empty cup where it was and made my way into the Cafe itself. The door opened before I could even lay one hand on it, surprising me and causing me to step back, suspecting some kind of evil afoot, before I remembered that Xeeonite doors opened on their own due to some kind of technology, not due to the wicked or nefarious enchantments of a decadent wizard.

Nonetheless, I walked through quickly, not wishing to get caught between the doors, which closed behind me as soon as the heel of my left foot passed beyond the threshold. I spared not a glance over my shoulder at the closing doors as I looked around at the interior of the dingy cafe.

Oh! How terrible this place was. The ceiling was low enough that 'twas like walking into the home of a dwarf, rather than a restaurant for humans. The old floor creaked under mine feet and was stained with a kind of liquid I could not identify, but which I strongly suspected to be dried blood. Of course, it could have been nothing more than spilled beer, but either way, it was nothing less than a total and complete example of the unprofessionalism of the cafe's owner.

The dinginess of the place was in sharp contrast to the rest of Xeeon, which, whilst not as beautiful or majestic as Se-Dela, was nonetheless a clean city. The tables were scattered about randomly, like die blocks, while the chairs were made of some kind of old plastic, for they were as cracked as the earth during a drought. One of them was even missing a leg, which had been replaced with a tall bucket placed upside down 'neath it.

The stink of the place assaulted my nose. Did remind me of their 'genuine' South Delanian tea, which made me wonder if that was their most popular drink. If so, then that told me all I needed to know about the tastes of the general Xeeonian public.

Leaning against the counter was the waitress from before. Her face might have been beautiful if she had not been frowning in boredom and picking at some kind of ugly scab on her skin, while she clicked through a holographic projection rising from her hand like the water from a geyser.

Above her, to the left of her head, was one of those bothersome and ungainly squares otherwise known as telescreens. This screen showed a news robot that looked like a mockery of a human being, with its finely-pressed suit and red tie, talking about a parade that was happening in downtown Xeeon at the moment. I paid little attention to it because I cared not for the recent news in this accursed city.

Aside from the waitress, there was no one else in this cafe. 'Twas not even a cashier to take orders, though I supposed that the large, boxlike machine behind her, with a device that resembled a touch screen, might have taken peoples' orders instead.

"Waitress," I said. "I demand to see the owner of this establishment right away."

The waitress's eyes flicked up from the holograph and I caught a hint of annoyance in them, like she was bothered that a paying customer was asking her anything.

"Da boss?" she said. "Mr. Ryun?"

"If that is the name of the owner, then yes, I would like to speak with Mr. Ryun," I said. "It is of utmost importance that I speak with him right away."

The waitress returned her attention to the holograph. I could not tell what the holograph showed her, but whatever it was, it could not have been so important that she had to treat me so rudely and disrespectfully.

"Sorry, Mr. Ryun doesn't talk to random people like ya," said the waitress, though she hardly sounded apologetic to I. "He gave me strict orders never to give out his personal number to anyone. Not even to customers."

"But …" I struggled to think of something to say. "But I have a … a customer service issue, I believe is the term ye Xeeonites use. It is an issue that can only be resolved by speaking with the owner."

"Didn't ya just hear what I just said?" said the waitress, looking up at me, her blue eyes shining with annoyance. "Are ya deaf or something?"

"I can hear as clearly as the day I was born," I replied, gesturing at my ears. "It is ye, I dare say, who does not understand the urgency of my request."

"All I understand is that I'm not being paid to get Mr. Ryun angry by going against his orders," the waitress replied. "Now, why don't ya get out of here? I know ya hate our drinks anyway. Wouldn't be a loss if ya never returned."

"What disrespect," I snapped, pointing at her. "Why, I will make sure to tell all of my friends and family to never bless this establishment with their delanes, unless they wish to be treated with disrespect by a waitress who is less of a waitress and more of a—"

I was interrupted by something I saw on the telescreen out of the corner of mine eye, like the shadow of a stalking predator. I looked up at the telescreen, wondering if I had seen what I thought I had seen, while the waitress lowered her holograph and said, "What were ya going to call me, mister?"

I paid no attention to her at all, however, because I was too busy staring up at the screen above to care about her anger. I could hardly believe what I was seeing, but mine eyes never deceived me.

The telescreen still displayed that parade in downtown Xeeon I had noticed when I entered this restaurant earlier, though I could not be sure how far away it was from here because all of the text on the screen was gibberish to me, being as it was written in Xeeonish. For that same reason, I could not read the signs that might have told me what this parade was about, but that mattered not. For among the hundreds of faces of individuals from every species on Xeeo crowding in the street, I saw one that I recognized with no trouble at all:

It was my sister, Kiriah, wearing a long brown cloak that did not look Xeeonite in origin, and she was standing there with everyone else, watching the floats and bands that paraded down the street in celebration of something I did not know.

Chapter Two

I looked at the waitress, urgency rising within me like lava within a volcano. I pointed at the telescreen. "Miss waitress, where is that parade taking place?"

The waitress glanced at the telescreen above and then looked back at me. "Ya mean the Annual Unification Day Parade? It's in downtown Xeeon."

"What's the quickest way to that parade from this restaurant?" I asked, already prepared to run.

"Just go down the main street, take a right when you get to the Police Center, and keep going down that alleyway," said the waitress. "Should take ya there no problem, though I doubt ya'll get a good spot. Why?"

"Many thanks, miss waitress," I said as I turned and headed for the doors. "Perhaps I will return someday to give ye a tip for helping me so, assuming I do indeed find the person there I am searching for. Farewell, and may the Old Gods be with ye!"

The doors opened just as I approached them, but that no longer startled me so. Indeed, I was pleased as a pygmy when I crossed the threshold and headed down the main street, just as the waitress had suggested, praying to the Old Gods that I would get to the parade in time to see my sister again for the first time in six years.

Run! I told myself as I fought through the crowds of Xeeonians traveling along the crowded streets. Run! Do not let your sister get away! Do not hesitate, nor tremble, nor allow doubt or fear to fill your muscles with lead or freeze your bones to the marrow.

How thankful was I for the waitress's simple directions! Down the main street I ran, heading for the Police Center, which was distinctive among Xeeon's many buildings, for it was shaped something like a castle, with turrets and towers rising up out of the corners. 'Twas even easier to spot, for those bothersome robots flew from and onto its turrets, perhaps reporting in or coming to charge their energy from a long day's work.

Though it mattered not to me what they were or were not doing. Once I spotted the building, I turned right down an alley, dashing past a couple of youngsters who looked at me as I ran, like they had never seen a real live Delanian before. My dress was unusual, but I was in such a hurry that I did not dwell on their possible opinion of me.

The alleyway I ran down was narrow and dingy, a stark contrast to the clean street I just left. Ahead, I could hear the sounds of strange music bellowing, that horrid electronic mess that sounded to me less like music and more like broken wires hissing through the air. Under normal circumstances, I would have been running the other way in order to escape this terrible music, but knowing that my dearest sister was there, watching the parade, I kept going.

Just as I reached the middle of the alley, something jumped down from the roofs nearby and landed in mine path. I skidded to a halt, almost tripping over a discarded beer bottle on the street, and righted myself as I looked upon the newcomer, who stood up to his full height.

No; not 'his,' but 'its.' The figure standing before me was a machine; not one of those J series robots, but a completely different kind of robot I could not identify. 'Twas humanoid, but whereas the J bots had at least a semblance of a human face, this thing had no facial features at all. Its face was as blank as a canvas, which made it resemble Falnoth the Old God, which was so uncanny that it made me shiver in my clothes.

Yet that would not have deterred me from going around it, if only the robot had not drawn a long, silvery sword—with blinking lights running along its flat—from its waist. It drew the sword with the same expertise as the Knights of Se-Dela drew theirs, which made me wonder if this bot had somehow been trained in the way of the Knights.

Whilst the robot drew its weapon, the sounds of the parade grew fainter and fainter, which told me that I had no time to waste if I wanted to reunite with mine sister in time.

Thus, I pointed at the machine and said, with as much authority as I could muster, "Foul clicker, get out of mine way. I do not have time to waste talking with a pitiful machine like yourself."

"Talking?" said the robot, its voice as metallic as the sword it carried. "I am not here to talk."

My eyes darted to the blade it held, which looked even sharper than the blades used by the Knights. "So ye wish to fight me. Is that it?"

The robot raised its sword until its tip was pointed at me, like the arrow of an archer. "How could you have ever guessed? I can see that you are an intellectual of the highest order. I wonder if your intellect matches your skill in combat."

"I did not know that robots were capable of such biting sarcasm," I said. "But it matters not, because even if ye wish to fight me, I still have more important matters to attend to."

"Not unless I challenge you to a duel," sad the robot, its sword never wavering in front of my face, "which, according to the Knight's Code, means you must accept, if I am not mistaken."

I looked down at mine clothes. I had not brought my sword or any other weapon with me when I came to Xeeo today, mostly because I had not expected to get into a duel with a faceless machine. 'Twas a decision I started to regret with great sorrow, despite knowing Xeeonite laws preventing Delanian citizens from bringing weapons with them through the Portals.

So I looked up at the clicker again and responded, "I must decline this offer for the moment, machine, because I am unarmed. If ye are such an expert on the Knight's Code, ye would know that no Knight of Se-Dela can challenge an unarmed foe unless he is willing to offer that unarmed foe one of his own weapons."

"Good thing I'm not a Knight of Se-Dela, then," said the robot. "I only made that offer to see if you would be naïve enough to accept it."

"It matters not whether or not ye were serious," I said. I

pointed at the bot sharply. "Who are ye and why do ye stand in mine way like a rock wall? 'Tis an annoyance, which is all ye bots are."

"My name and identity are unimportant," said the robot. "I was given one mission, and one mission only: To keep you from reaching the Annual Unification Day Parade. Any way I can."

The robot charged at me, sword swinging before it as wildly as the claws of an angry big cat. The clicker moved faster than any machine should have been able to, but I was able to jump out of the way to avoid its attack.

Or would have been, if the robot had not come to an abrupt halt and slashed its sword toward me in the direction I had jumped to avoid it. The blade was coming at me too fast, like a wasp flying in the air, and I tried to step back to avoid it.

But, whilst I avoided getting my gut cut open, the sword blade did indeed cut through my shirt and skin. 'Twas nothing more than a flesh wound, perhaps, but the pain was as real and burning as any, making me curse as I clutched my bleeding stomach, which began to stain mine clothes.

Yet I was afforded no time to focus on that problem, for the robot was upon me again, mine blood coating its blade, and raised its sword to strike once more. I staggered back, trying to stay out of its reach, but the bot kept advancing, its faceless plate preventing me from seeing what it was thinking. Perhaps that was not necessary; I already knew what this monster wanted, which was hardly a great mystery at this point.

Whilst I tried to avoid getting hacked to pieces like fresh meat under a butcher's knife, the electric music blaring from the parade, along with the cheers of so many different peoples and

27

species watching it, grew fainter and fainter with each passing second. How much time the Old Gods had given me before the parade ended entirely, I knew not; therefore, it was imperative that I end this conflict quickly.

I nearly tripped over something and glanced down to see it was a metal trash can lid, lying in the street as though discarded like it was itself trash. I quickly picked it up and held it before me in the same manner I would hold a shield of the Knights of Se-Dela, though I was fully aware of the futility of this action, particularly with mine still-bleeding gut.

"Reduced to using a trash can lid for a shield," said the robot, shaking its head as it drew closer to me. "How pathetic."

I still backed up until I hit something solid and metal. I had backed into one of the buildings which formed this alley, but before I could do anything, the robot swung its sword at my head again.

I ducked immediately. The robot's sword collided with the wall, sending sparks that bit at the back of my neck. The impact of the blade against the wall caused the sword to fly out of the robot's hand. The robot looked over its shoulder, watching its sword fly away through the air like a bird flying for freedom, whilst I took advantage of this opportunity and charged at the robot behind mine makeshift shield.

Yet 'tis not as successful as an attack as I hoped, for when the lid crashed into the robot's body, the robot held its ground and did not so much as budge one inch from its current position. Amazed by this, I forgot to dodge the robot's incoming fist.

Oh! How it hurt to be hit in the face by this machine's fist! Stars flashed in mine eyes, while my jaw felt like powdered mush in my mouth as I staggered to the side, still clinging to the trash can lid in my hands. Hot blood trickled down the side of mine face, rolling down from my temple, though I had no time to deal with that at the moment.

I shook my head and recovered in time to see the robot advancing on me again, although it had not bothered to retrieve its sword. But I highly doubted that the machine needed any sort of weapon to kill me; indeed, a weapon likely would have gotten in the way of its mission. Its hands alone looked strong enough to break my neck like the neck of a chicken.

By now, the sounds of the parade had grown perilously faint indeed. Deep in my heart, I feared that Kiriah had already left, returned to wherever she lives in this damn city, but still I clung to the hope that she had not yet left, that today would indeed be the day I reunited with her.

Whilst I was a brave Knight of Se-Dela, I knew I was no match for this mechanical monstrosity. It would keep going no matter what, even if I did mine best to beat it; 'twas one of the worst qualities of Xeeonite clickers, doubling also as one of their best. 'Twas only so long I could go before my wounds caught up to me and forced me to give up.

Nonetheless, I hurled my makeshift shield at the machine. It did not bother to so much as duck; instead, it knocked the spinning lid out of the air with one hand, causing the lid to crash onto the pavement under our feet.

Though I barely paid attention to that, because the second I had thrown mine makeshift shield, I turned and ran, ran as fast as I could, down the alleyway toward the street where the parade was being celebrated. Perhaps a foolish attempt, for I was still bleeding and in pain, but I was too desperate to care at this point.

I heard the quick, light steps of the robot behind me, coming after me as swiftly as a swift hunting cat. I did not even look back, for I feared that looking back would only result in my end coming that much more quickly.

But then I heard something flying through the air behind me and I tripped. I fell on my face, hitting my head against the pavement and making my head bleed even more. A quick glance at mine feet showed me that they were bound together by a metal chain that was attached to the robot's hand.

The fiend! It caught me with its chain, but I did not have time to free myself, even as I rolled onto my back. For the robot was upon me once more, raising its sword above me, ready to hack away at my flesh with it. The sun shined off the robot's face plate, reflecting so brightly that I had to squint to protect mine orbs from being damaged forever.

But I was not about to let this clicker kill me. I kicked out with mine feet, striking its own and knocking the machine to the ground. As it fell, it dropped its sword, which clanged against the pavement next to me, loud in mine ears.

Yet I did not hesitate. Instead, I reached over and grabbed the sword, wrapping my fingers around the blade as tightly as I could, and then tried to raise the sword.

'Twas almost too heavy for me to lift, but I was strong and I raised it nonetheless. Sitting up, I swung the sword at the chain around my ankles, snapping it effortlessly and allowing me to scramble back to mine feet as the robot rolled away from me. It jumped back to its feet and held its hands before it in a fighting stance, like it had been trained by a professional fighter of the highest caliber.

"Run, machine," I said, holding the sword in both hands, though it was hard to maintain such a posture due to my bleeding gut. "Or I will use your own blade against ye."

The robot jerked one of its hands toward me, like it was pushing air at me. 'Twas a puzzling gesture, but then the sword flew out of my hands back toward the robot. The blade landed on its outstretched hand, and as soon as it did, the robot closed its fingers around the handle and held it in both hands like how it had before.

"Magnetism," said the robot, no doubt in response to my confused expression. "Very useful for when I lose my weapon like that."

"'Tis like the magic of Dela," I said. "Are ye certain ye are no wizard in disguise?"

"It's not magic, but science," said the robot. "Though I suppose that's to be expected from you Delanians, who couldn't tell the difference between the two even if it slapped you in the face."

The pain in my abdomen burned, causing me to grab my stomach. It was not a conscious reaction; I was simply reacting on instinct to the pain which harmed me.

This turned out to be a mistake, however, because the robot charged at me again. It jumped into the air, swinging its sword wildly, while I staggered out of its path.

Luckily, I managed to avoid the sword; however, when the robot landed, it swung the remaining chains hanging from its hand at my face. The metal chain struck me in the face, a hard, sharp blow that sent me staggering to the side. I almost tripped over my feet again, but caught myself before I could do so.

Yet I had little time to recover, because the robot was coming at me again. I backed up as quickly as I could, because there was no hope in the two worlds that I could possibly win this fight.

"Technically, I don't have to kill you," said the robot, its metallic voice as menacing as ever. "Just keep you from getting to the parade. Nonetheless, I can tell you will be a bigger threat in the future if you're allowed to live. Killing you is the only way to deal with you permanently."

"But the J bots will find mine body," I said, walking backwards as fast as I could, holding mine hands over my bleeding wound to stem the flow as best as I could. "Murder is illegal in Xeeo and Dela. They will eventually track my murder back to ye, and then ye will be dealt with like any other criminal."

"A naïve thought," said the robot, shaking its head. "Haven't you wondered why no J bots have yet to intervene, despite our fight not being in the center of Xeeon? If you understood the answer to that, you would understand why you're going to die today."

The answer did come to mind immediately, but 'twas so horrible that I dared not utter it. Nor did I need to; the robot raised its blade again, and this time, I knew there was not a thing I could do to stop or avoid it.

Yet before the swordsrobot could bring its blade down on my head and end my life, it froze like the ice sculptures of the Winterlands. At first I thought it was some kind of trick, one final ploy to make me give up in despair, but then the robot collapsed onto the street, its sword clanging against the pavement beside it.

What in the names of the Old Gods was this? Was this divine

intervention? Was I—

"Hey, Rii!" shouted a feminine, shrill voice I had not heard before. "Stop standing around like an idiot and get over here!"

I looked around in shock, trying to locate the source of that voice, when I noticed a young woman—Rathonian, based on her large, apelike frame and the antennas sticking out of her head, though truth be told, I did not know my Xeeonite species as well as I should have—standing at the other end of the alley, gesturing for me to come toward her. In her other hand, she held some kind of small device, but what it did, I could not tell from this distance.

"What are you waiting for?" the Rathonian woman asked, speaking in remarkably clear Delan, despite the fact that she was clearly not a native of that world. "Come on now! He won't stay down forever. Or do you want to die?"

What a foolish woman. I did not want to go with her, nor did I wish to stay here and die. Though the sounds of the parade were farther away now than ever before, I still believed, with the faith of a priest of the Old Gods, that if I ran now, I might finally be able to reunite with my sister.

But then the pain in my wounded abdomen burned and I grabbed it with both hands. The blood was hot and sticky, as blood always is, and I suddenly felt far woozier than I did before. 'Twas like getting punched in the face by an angry dwarf, a feeling I knew well, for I had once been assaulted by such a dwarf when I and my fellow Knights were attempting to capture a well-known criminal who had a penchant for punching those he disliked in the face.

I staggered toward the woman, but I had lost too much blood, which made even that basic movement as difficult as if I was swimming through a thick chocolate river. Blood dripped onto the pavement underneath me, but I was so absorbed by the pain that I barely noticed. All I was aware of was that my consciousness was fading … fading … fading …

Chapter Three

How my death came so early in my life! For I was only thirty-years-old, not even half as old as Sir Lockfried, and yet today I had met my end as abruptly as the sudden appearance of sun in the middle of a stormy day. What a pathetic way for me to die, bleeding in the street like a dying rat, without ever seeing mine sister again.

At least, that is what I believed had happened. Truthfully, I had no idea if I had actually died or not; having never died before, I did not know what that might feel like. The stories that my older brother Sura, a priest of the Old Gods, used to tell me about death always described it as an excruciatingly painful ordeal, an experience no one ever wanted to repeat. I vividly remembered the story of Garla and the Pepper, a story that ended with Garla's untimely death at the hands of the aforementioned pepper, which was said to have burned his innards and his very soul.

Yet the more I thought about it, the more I realized that I was not in very terrible pain at all anymore. That might have been another clue that I was dead, for it was said that those who pass beyond death cease to feel pain.

If that were so, it did not explain the soft mattress I felt under me. 'Twas as comfortable as—no, more comfortable than—the springy mattress of mine bed back in Dela, except that this one did not feel quite so springy at all. Indeed, it was more like a soft cushion for me to lie on, which made me only want to sleep and rest on it forever.

But now was not the time to rest. For I now realized I was alive—Hallelujah! Praise to the Old Gods!—but I did not know where I was or what I was doing. My eyes were closed, but I managed to open them, slowly, in order to discover just where I was.

The room I had awoken in was small, but clean, as far as I could tell. The walls were a calming white, like the garb of the priests and priestesses of the Old Gods, while a metal chair stood beside my bed. The room was made even whiter by the florescent bulb above, which made me squint it was so bright.

As for the bed I lay on, it was large enough only to hold one person, and even then, I could easily roll off it if I wasn't careful. The sheets were blue, a deep, dark blue that contrasted sharply with the starkness of the white walls. And they were the softest blankets I had ever felt in my life, perhaps made of those synthetic fabrics that the Xeeonite scientists were said to have designed, though at the moment 'twas not much of a problem to me.

For a moment, I thought I was in one of those Xeeonite healing centers, which the Xeeonites referred to as 'hospitals,' but this seemed too small to be the room of a hospital. There were no windows, either, though about ten feet from the foot of mine bed was a closed metal door. The door had a smooth surface, without a doorknob or keyhole to be found, which told me it was another one of those infernal automatic doors that the Xeeonites seemed to love more than life itself.

Aside from myself, there was no one else present in the room. I pondered why that was so until I remembered the wound in my abdomen. The stink of blood was still strong in my nostrils, causing me to throw the blankets off my body to see how it was.

To my surprise and relief, the wound had been sewn up and cleaned, but why and by who, I did not know. 'Twas no longer a bleeding, disgusting mess; instead, a white bandage had been wrapped 'round my body, wrapped so tight that it almost hurt. I touched my forehead and no longer felt that bleeding as well, although I felt no bandages, either.

Thank the Old Gods! Here I was thinking that I had indeed bled to death, yet if this meant anything, I had been saved by a goodhearted fellow in my time of need, whoever it was. I only wished I knew who had done it, for I wished to thank them a thousand times over and pledge my life to theirs.

But as I noticed before, there was no one else in the room. I tried to sit up and walk toward the door, but despite my wound being bandaged, my legs felt too heavy to move. It was like someone had tied cement blocks to my feet, making it impossible for me to even budge them.

Then I noticed it. In the upper right corner of the room, to the door's right, was a mechanical eye that watched me as unblinking and still as the eye of a corpse. The florescent light reflected off its surface, which did little to ease my soul.

What was this monstrosity? I pulled away from it, staring up at the eye uncertainly. It was elongated and attached to the ceiling via some wires that reminded me of the snakes of the Lower Panhandle. I could not recall seeing anything like it before in my life, which made me all the more frightful.

Mine first impulse was to think that it was some kind of guard meant to prevent me from escape. It reminded me of the unliving eyes of the J bots; cold, calculating, without any hint of human compassion and emotion beneath.

Unfortunately, I was still unarmed and could not get up and check out the eye for myself. Not that I wanted to, seeing as this thing was clearly a creature of evil, but I despised sitting here in this bed because there were still so many questions I had that I did not know the answers to, questions that were extremely important for me to discover the answers to.

Naturally, then, I decided to ask the eye these same questions. I doubted it would hurt. Whilst the eye was clearly not a kind creature, it did not seem to have any sort of weapons or anything else with which to hurt me. The worst that could happen was that the eye would not answer my questions.

Thus, I asked, "Great Eye, creature of evil, where am I? How did I get here? How long have I been out? Do ye want something out of me? If so, what is it?"

As I suspected, the eye answered not one mote of any question I asked. It simply stared at me, stared at me as if it had not heard anything I just said. 'Twas an infuriating thought, that this machine had heard my questions but had decided not to answer them; yes, I had expected this silence, but it was still infuriating nonetheless.

Just as I wondered whether I should try rephrasing mine

questions in order to get a response, the door at the other end of the room slid open with a screech. The sound almost made me jump out of mine bed, but I recovered my composure quickly as two beings stepped through the door, allowing the door to slide shut behind them once they passed over the threshold.

I blinked. No; not two beings, but one. It was an elvish woman, with some strange machine attached to her waist like a belt. Rising up from the machine was a writhing, snake-like metal creature, though its face was less serpentine and more humanoid, with a simple nose, bright blue eyes, and a speaker for a mouth. 'Twas the oddest thing I had seen in my life so far, which was saying much, for I had seen many, many odd things in my life, particularly during my time as a member of the Red Ring Smugglers.

As for the elvish woman, she looked like most elves I knew: Tall and fair-skinned, with pointed ears, though she was as bald as the waitress of Crossways Cafe, which I suspected must have been a trend among the women of Xeeon. Yet another mystery of the fair sex that I would likely never know the answer to.

Her clothes were by no means elvish. She wore a drab, colorless jumpsuit, which I thought was odd, for elves were known for their love of extravagant colors and designs in their clothing. Then again, I could tell already that this elvish woman was by no means a normal elf; she must have been raised on Xeeo, though I did not know that for certain.

"Who be ye?" I demanded. I pointed at the eye. "And what is that eye up there? Is it a thing of evil?"

The elvish woman rolled her eyes and nodded at the strange machine attached to her waist. A clipped, mechanical-sounding voice issued from the machine's mouth, saying, in clear Delan, "That is a security camera, not an eye, Mr. Knight. And it's not evil, either. We set it up in here to keep an eye on you until you awoke."

Security camera? I vaguely recalled Sir Alart telling me about something like that once. He had told me that the Xeeonites had found ways to record crimes as they were being committed, often without the criminal knowing, and without using the skyras magic that we Delanians used for similar purposes. At the time, I had not believed him, but perhaps I owed my brother in arms an apology, assuming I ever saw him again.

Regardless, I said to the machine, "Oh. I had not known that."

"No surprise there," said the machine. "Most Delanians are ignorant of Xeeonite technology."

I nodded at the elvish woman, who still had not said a word during this whole conversation. "Machine, why does your mistress not speak? I'd rather speak with a fellow living being than a dead piece of metal like yourself."

"But I *am* talking to you," said the machine. The elvish woman gestured at her throat. "I lost the ability to use my vocal chords a long time ago. Therefore, I have to use this speaking snake to communicate."

"Speaking snake?" I repeated. "What sorcery is this?"

"It's not sorcery, it's science," the speaking snake replied. "But that's irrelevant right now. I came in here because Coga saw you awake through the camera and told me. I was given the job of taking care of you, which is why I decided to come and talk to you."

I did not like how that 'speaking snake,' as she called it,

sounded at all. It didn't look like a friendly helper to me; to me, it resembled a dangerous serpent, ready to strike and kill when you least expected it. I could not understand why the Xeeonites would even design such a thing after a snake; then again, there were few things about the Xeeonites I did understand, so perhaps it wasn't as puzzling a mystery as it first seemed.

Nonetheless, I pointed a finger sharply at the woman and said, "Then tell me your name, woman. I have never laid eyes on ye in my life; nay, not even once."

"My name is Lanresia," said the speaking snake (though I perhaps should have thought it as Lanresia, but to me the snake and the elf were still different entities). "It's an old elvish word that means 'kind one,' if you didn't know."

"Lanresia?" I repeated. I scratched my chin. "I seem to recall knowing another elf with that name once, a fellow Knight of mine in the Order. Though perhaps not; I sometimes have a hard time distinguishing between you elves."

Though the speaking snake's expression did not change, I noticed a shadow of annoyance cross the elf's face, as though she was offended by mine words. Though I cared not; after all, I did not know whether she be friend or foe, so why should I care if I offended her or not?

"Yes ..." said the elf, though I could tell based on the way her ears twitched that she was trying not to be highly offended by my words. "It's a common name, but it is my only connection to my home, so I wear it with pride just the same."

"Ah ha," I said, stroking my chin in satisfaction. "I knew it. Ye are not a native-born Delanian elf at all; rather, ye are one of the Xeeonite elves. Tell me, did ye move here or were ye born here?"

"How I got here doesn't matter," said Lanresia, shaking her head. "Nor is it any of your business. All you need to know is that Xeeo is my home. I will tell you only what you need to know when you need to know it."

Though the speaking snake's mechanical voice seemed incapable of changing its tone, I could tell easily that Lanresia was quite offended by my questions. 'Twas not something I understood, though in truth, I barely understood elves as it was, even the ones I worked alongside with in the Order. They were a strange people, the elves, with their focus on the more mystical aspects of skyras magic and their odd dances.

Still, I conceded that the question was an irrelevant and trivial one, which could be answered at a later point if necessary. I had more urgent questions, then, that I knew she would have to answer, unless she was trying to keep me in the dark, though why she would, I did not know.

Thus, I spake, "Very well, then, she-elf. But I have other questions to ask, such as, where am I? How did I get here? And how do I know I can trust ye? Among countless others, of course."

Whilst I said that, I kept a careful eye on the she-elf. I could not be certain if or when she was lying to me, but having worked alongside several other elvish Knights for some time, I had learned to understand some of the physical clues elves displayed whenever they lied. A lying elf usually shuffled their feet unnecessarily and sometimes twitched their ears as well.

This she-elf, however, displayed none of the usual signs of a lying elf. That may have meant she was not going to lie to me, though I kept mine guard up anyway, for I was unarmed and in an unknown location. Indeed, for all I knew, she was going to kill me in cold blood and dispose of my body where no one would ever find it, despite not seeming that psychotic.

"Where are you?" Lanresia repeated. She gestured at the room. "You are in a secret place near Xeeon. I can't disclose its exact location to you just yet, but rest assured that you are safe here."

"I care not for mine own safety, she-elf, if that is what ye believe my main concern to be," I replied. "I want to find mine sister, Kiriah, not hide underground like a rat."

"You don't want to find your sister," said Lanresia. "Trust me. It's better that the two of you stay apart."

"Stop speaking in riddles," I said. "I have spent six years searching for mine sister and ye are telling me that I should not see her? She-elf, ye do not know my sister or I. Kiriah would be overjoyed to see me again. This I know with the certainty of the sun."

"You're right," said Lanresia, her speaking snake's eyes glowing. "I don't know you or your sister very well; however, I do know that trying to get involved with her is the quickest path to death. As you almost found out yourself when that assassin bot tried to kill you."

"But why?" I said. I threw the blankets off my legs and tried to stand up again, but my legs were still too weak to support me, so I simply stayed where I was. "Ye have yet to explain that to me. And if ye continue to speak vaguely, I shall draw upon the power of the Old Gods and teach ye how to speak plainly, she-elf."

That threat of mine did not mean much, because I truly could not draw upon the power of the Old Gods. I said it only to frighten Lanresia, who probably did not know of my bluff.

Lanresia held up her hands, as if to calm me. "Don't get angry. There's a good reason for all of this, I can assure you. We are not holding you down here for no reason."

"'We'?" I repeated. "So there are more of ye? How many more?"

"I can't disclose the exact number to you yet," said Lanresia without hesitation. "We're not sure if we can trust you with that information. Still, I will do my best to answer your questions as honestly as I can."

I snorted at that. "Oh? I doubt it. I imagine if I asked ye what the position of the sun in the sky was right now, ye would say ye could not trust me with that information."

"We're running a very delicate operation right here," said Lanresia, tapping her foot, which I recognize as an elvish movement that most elves used to show their frustration. "Very delicate. I'm sorry you can't handle the fact that we won't just disclose all of our secrets to random strangers like you, especially strangers who aren't even native Xeeonites in the first place."

"What *can* ye tell me, then?" I said. "No, wait. Do not answer that. I want to speak with your leader, whoever he or she is, not with a simple peon like yourself."

"The Head is currently too busy to talk to you at the moment," said Lanresia. "Besides, speaking with guests is my main job in the organization. We have a very strict hierarchy here; no one ever does anyone else's job for them except in extreme or unusual circumstances."

"'Tis seems like an unusual circumstance to I," I replied. "But very well. I know when I cannot win, so I shall instead ask what organization this is."

"Now that is information I can share with you," said Lanresia. She gestured at the tiny room in which we stood. "You are currently inside the headquarters of the secret organization known as the Foundation."

"The Foundation?" I repeated. "What kind of foundation is it? And how come I have never heard of it?"

"You've probably never heard of it because very, very few people outside of our circle have," said Lanresia. "We've worked hard to keep it that way, for we answer to a much higher power."

"King Waran-Una?" I asked. "The Old Gods? Who?"

"That is another thing you don't need to know," said Lanresia. "At least not yet. All I can tell you is that we are working hard at uncovering the lies and deception of Xacron-Ah, although that we do many other things as well."

"Xacron-Ah? I remember that name," I said. I patted my body quickly and was relieved to feel the envelope with three pictures were still in my pockets. "That is the name of the man who was in that picture with my sister."

"We know," said Lanresia. "We've been keeping a careful eye on your sister ever since she first appeared in this city. And we think she is working with him, though what their ultimate end game for this city is, even we don't know for sure."

"Hold on," I said, holding up a hand. "I confess to being greatly confused. Why would my sister be working with the Mayor? How do you even know he's corrupt? My understanding of this situation is as opaque as the polluted oceans of your world."

"Xeeo's oceans aren't *that* polluted," said Lanresia, rolling her eyes. "But you're right. I should probably start at the beginning. I can't tell you everything—I'm not allowed to tell you all of it— but I can tell you enough that you can be confident that you know what's going on."

Lanresia gestured at the chair next to my bed. Wheels, as round as the sun, popped out of the chair's legs, allowing it to roll over to her across the smooth floor. Whilst that might have shocked me under ordinary circumstances, I was not quite so surprised to see that her chair could move; after all, Xeeonite technology could do almost anything. 'Twould not be surprised if at some point I ran into a robot that could cast magic, though to my knowledge, such a feat was beyond the current limits of their technology.

The chair stopped behind Lanresia, allowing her to sit down on it. When she did, the wheels popped back into the legs, thus assuring that she would not go sliding across the floor unnecessarily.

"Where should I start?" said Lanresia, putting the tips of her fingers together. "Ah, I know. I will start with Mayor Xacron-Ah himself. He's at the center of all of this, so he's the best place to begin."

"I was told he came from Dela," I said. "Is that correct?"

"All our sources say so," said Lanresia, her speaking snake nodding along with her. "More importantly, though, is the reason why he moved from Dela. Do you know?"

"No, I do not," I said, shaking mine head. "The merchant I spoke with did not tell me why."

"He has told very few people why," said Lanresia. "It's pretty obvious, of course, why he's keeping it a secret, but that still doesn't make it any less scummy on his part."

"For what reason did he move to Xeeo?" I asked. "I am tired of you going on like this; please just get to the point."

"All right," said Lanresia. "Xacron-Ah used to be a super speed drug dealer. He would arrange huge shipments of the drug to be illegally distributed from Dela's Lower Panhandle to Xeeon and the surrounding countryside. He says he's reformed, but considering how corrupt he is, we tend to doubt it."

"If he says he has reformed, why did you say he has kept it a secret?" I said, folding my arms over my chest.

"I didn't say that was what he kept a secret," said Lanresia. "Xacron-Ah ran a successful campaign six years back on the premise of absolute honesty, so he didn't deny the allegations that he had once illegally distributed super speed drugs to the general population. He apologized for it, and as a result, everyone thinks he's an honest man, which is how he won the election despite not being a native Xeeonian. What he kept a secret was why he came here in the first place, which has nothing to do with honesty or truth."

"What was his reason for doing so?" I asked. "Was he escaping the law?"

"We believe so," said Lanresia. "He left Dela because his former drug dealing friends turned on him. We think he sold out his gang to the authorities, which is why he moved to Xeeo, where he thought he would be safe."

"That seems an odd thing to keep a secret," I remarked. "I am no expert in Xeeonite elections—for I find democracy an ill substitute for a good monarchy—but I would think the people would be more attracted to the criminal who turned in his comrades, not less."

"That's because it's not as simple as it seems," said Lanresia, shaking her head. "He didn't have a simple change of heart, from ruthless drug dealer to noble statesmen. He sold out his fellows because he made a deal with the International Delanian Alliance of Law Enforcers to get some good money out of his deeds."

"I see," I said, stroking my chin. "So this Xacron-Ah fellow betrayed his friends because he saw more green in the words of the law than in the spoils of crime."

"More or less," said Lanresia, her speaking snake nodding as it spoke. "All of the guys he sold out to your government are currently behind bars, but they have friends on the outside who have been hounding Xacron-Ah for a while now, which is why he moved here."

"How come I have never heard of Xacron-Ah, if what you say is true?" I interrupted. "I used to be a member of the Red Ring Smugglers before joining the Knights about a year ago. I don't recall ever hearing about this Xacron-Ah fellow."

"Wait," said Lanresia, looking at me in surprise (which I could read easily, as she still had normal facial expressions despite being mute). "You were a member of the Red Ring Smugglers?"

I hesitated to answer that. That information had slipped from mine tongue like quicksilver; 'twas knowledge I usually kept to myself. I had thought this she-elf had already known about my past, but perhaps these Foundation people were not quite as knowledgeable as they appeared.

In any case, I could not see any reason to deny it, for I was an honest man who believed in the virtue of truth, no matter the consequences. Though I made a note to be less frank about my past from now on, for such information could be used against me quite easily, a tactic I knew from mine Smuggler days quite well, for I had seen the Smugglers' leader use it to blackmail many individuals into aiding us.

Thus, I nodded and said, "Yes, I was. 'Tis a time I now so deeply regret with mine deepest heart and soul, but it was true for a time."

"Interesting," said Lanresia. "Well, I'm not going to ask why you were a member of the Smugglers. Mostly because I don't care."

Her ears twitched when she said that, though it was a subtle movement that she no doubt believed I had failed to notice. But notice it I did, which told me she was lying, though why she would lie to me, I did not know. Likely she truly did care about my past; if so, I would have to be more careful than ever with what I shared with her, or anyone else who was a member of this 'Foundation,' as she called it.

"Anyway, Xacron-Ah wasn't a very big-time dealer, even at his prime, so that's probably why," said Lanresia. She snapped her fingers and a holographic screen shot out of the speaking snake's eyes and hovered before her, glowing blue as the ocean. "Let's see … yes. According to this, the Red Ring Smugglers are active mostly in Northern Se-Dela, whereas Xacron-Ah's gang was on the tip of the Lower Panhandle. That explains it."

"This makes no sense to me," said I. "Why would Xacron-Ah become the Mayor of a major Xeeonite city if he was trying to escape his former comrades? 'Tis similar to painting a red target on one's back in the middle of a war zone and hoping that it will deter a sniper's aim."

"True, but it's not quite as vulnerable position as you think," said Lanresia.

She waved at her holograph, causing it to spin around and show me an image of Mayor Xacron-Ah. The image closely resembled the one that the merchant showed me before, with the Mayor standing at a podium delivering a speech to an unseen crowd like a priest of the Old Gods, but I noticed several armed J bots standing 'round him like the walls of a fortress, whilst a vaguely glowing red energy field seemed to cover him like a dome.

"The Mayor of Xeeon always receives an entire squadron of J bots whose sole purpose is to protect the Mayor from enemies and assassins who would like to kill him," said Lanresia. "And those are just the visible ones. Often, before Xacron-Ah appears in public, he will have his men scout out the area for any possible hiding assassins or enemies that he cannot see, such as hidden snipers on top of nearby buildings, for example."

"Ah ha," I said. "I see now. The Mayor is the most protected man in the entire city; therefore, it is unlikely that his former smuggler friends will be able to get him, as he is protected at all times by those infernal machines."

"Exactly," said Lanresia. "Not to mention that if he was attacked or killed, then his squadron of J bots would hunt down and arrest whoever did it. It was a brilliant move on his part, one which has served him quite well."

"Still seems to me a silly move, however," I said, stroking my chin. "There must be some other reason why Xacron-Ah ran for Mayor."

"You're right," said Lanresia. "There is. But that ties back into information I'm not allowed to give you yet, such as the true purpose of the Foundation, so don't ask."

I frowned. I hated working with such tight-lipped people, but 'twas no way for me to make her tell me the truth. I would figure out someday, however, though for now I would ask her other things that she might be allowed to tell me.

"Was that assassin bot that attacked me one of his bodyguards?" I asked. "The one with the sword from earlier, which fought like a true Knight of Se-Dela?"

"Yes," said Lanresia. "That robot is called Assassin and is the only one of its kind that we know of. We think Xacron-Ah had it specially designed for his own needs; most likely, he ordered it from Annulus Robotics, Inc., the largest robotics company in Xeeo, even though we haven't found any evidence of that yet."

"But why did it attack me?" I asked, scratching the back of mine head in confusion. "I was not going to attack the Mayor. I merely wanted to see my sister."

"Protecting the Mayor isn't Assassin's only job," said Lanresia, shaking both of her heads. "It also protects your sister and keeps away anyone the Mayor doesn't want talking to her. It must have recognized you as Kiriah's brother, maybe considered you a possible threat to Xacron-Ah's life, so it tried to end you before you could get too close to her."

"Vile machine," I said. I shook my fist at the ceiling, even though Assassin was not there. "Why must ye keep me from reuniting with family? For what purpose does that serve? Do ye enjoy seeing siblings remain separated and apart? What perverted pleasure must you take from indulging in such evilness?"

"He's not here," said Lanresia. "You are talking to the ceiling."

I looked back at Lanresia and said, "I know that, she-elf. I am merely expressing my anger and frustration at this revelation. Once I leave this place, I will find that machine and dismantle it piece by piece."

"That's a nice thought, but not very realistic," said Lanresia, leaning back in her chair. "Especially, you know, after you were almost killed by that same robot just a few hours ago."

"So I've only been out for a few hours now?" I said. "Tell me, the parade—"

"Is over," Lanresia finished for me. "The floats have been put back into storage, the onlookers have gone back to their homes, the performers have moved onto other towns and cities to entertain their audiences, and the streets are clear. That means your sister is gone again, Apakerec. I'm sorry."

I slammed my fist on the mattress under me, which did little, as the bed merely absorbed the force of the blow under me; nonetheless, it felt good to do so, for I needed a way to release mine anger constructively.

"Falnor's luck must be upon me, for that is the only explanation for why I was unable to reach mine sister in time," I said. "Tell me, where did Kiriah go?"

"We don't know," Lanresia admitted. "Despite our best efforts to keep an eye on her, she always manages to disappear every time she leaves the public. We suspect she's staying in the Mayor's Mansion, as it's the only place we've been unable to search, but we still don't know for sure."

"I had hoped ye would be able to tell me where she had gone," I said, my shoulders slumping in disappointment. "Tell me, what is the point in having a secretive organization like yourselves if ye cannot locate even one woman in one city?"

"Don't blame us," said Lanresia in annoyance. "Your sister, in case you didn't know, is working with the Mayor. For whatever reason, Xacron-Ah is keeping her out of the public eye. He clearly doesn't want anyone to know of her, because he's gone to great lengths to hide her mere existence from everyone else."

"That does not tell me *why* my sister is working with him," I said. I leaned forward, ignoring how tight the stitching in my stomach became when I did that. "According to the merchant I spoke with, Xacron-Ah was elected to Mayor six years ago, which is the same time my sister disappeared. Yet my sister has only been seen and photographed recently, which means there is a gap between the time my sister disappeared and when these photographs were taken."

I drew out of my pocket the envelope with the three photographs I had been given by the Knights of Se-Dela, pulled out the photographs, and held them up before her. The robotic eyes of Lanresia's speaking snake and her own organic eyes scanned my photographs, though something in the way Lanresia looked at the photos told me she had seen these before.

"We don't know for sure why your sister is working with the Mayor," Lanresia said. "We've been keeping track of her, of course, but so far she has not done anything except occasionally meet with the Mayor at Crossways Cafe for lunch. Even then, they don't talk about much; mostly they discuss the weather, sometimes recent political happenings, but not much else."

"It sounds as though this Mayor Xacron-Ah fellow is not quite as devious as ye make him out to be," I said. "Now ye haven't explained just what this 'Foundation' is. Ye have only said that ye are against Xacron-Ah's lies and deception, which I know nothing about."

"Right," said Lanresia. She briefly exchanged looks with the speaking serpent, like she was asking it a question, before looking back at me. "The Foundation is a secret organization founded by … well, I can't tell you that. What I can tell you is that we have been around for a very long time and have done many things. Our current objective is stopping Xacron-Ah's plans, which will hurt the people of both worlds if we fail to stop them in time."

"Yet ye told me that ye do not know what he is trying to do," I pointed out. "How, then, do ye know that he is up to no good?"

"Our founder says so," said Lanresia, as if that was obvious. "And our founder is always right. Not to mention all of the evidence that incriminates him, although we still don't have enough yet to expose his true nature to the public."

"What government are ye affiliated with?" I demanded. "The United Federation of Xeeonite Nations?"

"We're an independent organization," said Lanresia. She gestured at her shoulder. "As you can tell, we have no symbol, no insignia, nothing to signify who we are or who we work with. That's intentional, because we can only be effective by working in the shadows, beneath the foundation of Xeeo, where no one can see us."

"I do not like shadowy organizations acting behind the scenes," I said. "Even if your intentions are pure—which I doubt, but I shall play along with ye anyway—I find your unwillingness to tell me the truth about your actions to make ye out to be especially untrustworthy."

"You don't need to trust us," said Lanresia. "Just listen and understand."

I thought that was an exceptionally silly thing to say, but I was getting bored of the subject, as it was quite clear that Lanresia was not going to tell me much more about the Foundation or its history. 'Twas time to change the subject.

"Ye said it was better that I try not to contact my sister at all," I said. "Why is that? Do ye think my sister would be unhappy to see me?"

"Because you'll get killed if you try," said Lanresia, as if I was being intentionally dimwitted and stubborn. "Assassin doesn't just protect the Mayor. It also protects Kiriah and anyone else who the Mayor wants to keep safe. Whether or not your sister still wants to see you, I don't know, but I do know you are better off here, where Assassin can't get you, than up there, where it can."

"Give me a sword," I said, holding out mine left hand. "Any will do. I will then use it to slay this machine like a dragon."

"Not a good idea," said Lanresia. "Assassin is the strongest robot working for the Mayor. It's never been defeated by anyone before. You'd be a fool to fight it now, especially since you're still recovering from your last fight with it."

I rested my hand on my abdomen, which was still covered with that bandage. I rubbed my fingers against the cloth as I said, "You are right, but I am still a Knight of Se-Dela. We are supposed to fight no matter how badly we are injured, especially when our family is in danger like this."

"Your sister isn't in any danger, from what we can tell," said Lanresia, shaking her head. "Every time we've seen her, she's always been protected by Assassin. She doesn't seem to be held against her own will, at least."

"Nonsense," I said. I lowered the photographs onto my lap. "My sister would never willingly work with a criminal like this Xacron-Ah fellow. I knew Kiriah. She was a righteous woman, even more so than I, for she never worked for any sort of criminal gang even once."

Lanresia held up her hands again. "I don't know everything that's going on. I'm just saying that it seems like your sister is not being held captive. Can you think of any reason why she might willingly work with Xacron-Ah? As you are her brother, you should know her better than anyone."

"No reason for this behavior of hers comes to mind," I responded. "Assuming, of course, my fair sister is even doing that. Ye have lodged nothing but baseless accusations at her, offering not even the flimsiest of evidence with which to convict her."

"Well, could you tell us any reason she might have for disappearing in the first place?" said Lanresia. She swiped at her holograph, turning it back around to face her, and then swiped across its surface before placing one finger on it, as if to catch a bug that had landed there suddenly. "According to our records, your sister disappeared from her home in Northern Se-Dela on the third day of the fifth month six years ago. At the time, there were only three other people in her home; you, your older brother Sura, and a family friend called Hajan."

I tensed. My memory returned to that fateful night. Even now,

I could still remember the sounds of the rain pattering against the roof, the rolling of thunder across the sky, and our own frantic attempts as my brother, our friend, and I searched for Kiriah, who we had thought might be hiding somewhere in the house.

But I pushed away those memories. They were too painful for me to focus on right now; indeed, I had spent many a year ignoring these memories, for on that night something else terrible happened, something I had done my best to avoid remembering. I had done much a good job of avoiding its memory so far, but Lanresia's words were starting to jog that memory and I did not want that.

So I said, "All of that is correct, but irrelevant. My sister had no reason to disappear or run away. She never even mentioned Xacron-Ah around us before. I stand by my belief that she was kidnapped, but by who, I cannot say."

I hoped that Lanresia did not notice how I refused to elaborate on the facts she had just read to me from her hologram. Granted, what I remembered was unlikely to be very useful to her, but knowledge was power and I was not going to give her any more power over me, not when I still knew so little about her.

"I guess we'll see which one of us is right soon enough," said Lanresia. She stood up, the hologram flashing back into the eyes of her speaking snake as she did so. "Now, Apakerec, I think I have told you as much as you need to know for now. I am going to leave, but don't worry, because we'll send someone soon with some food for you to eat."

"Ye are leaving?" I said. I tried once more to lift my legs, but the action 'twas in vain, as always. "I shall join ye. My sister is still out there. I cannot simply sit here and rest, as if I was on vacation in the Sunny Isles."

"Sorry, but we can't let you do that," said Lanresia. She nodded at mine legs. "You still need to rest. Your fight with Assassin took a lot out of you and it's clear that the medicine is still affecting you. It would be incredibly foolish to go looking after your sister again; next time Assassin finds you, it will definitely finish the job it started."

I scowled. As much as I was loathed to admit it, the she-elf had a point. Whilst I did not feel quite as bad as I had when I had fought with Assassin earlier, I believed her when she said that I would not survive long if I fought it again, at least in mine current condition.

But I still did not like being here. Despite Lanresia's reassurances that this 'Foundation' she belonged to was a good organization, I deeply distrusted anyone who held me in captivity and refused to tell me their true motives. The she-elf was hiding much from me, but sadly I did not think I could get her to tell me what.

Then an idea occurred to me to convince her to let me go. It was a brilliant idea, as brilliant as the sun that shone over Dela and Xeeo, far more brilliant than I ever was. Perhaps the Old Gods had given me this idea, though whether they did or did not, I would still use it.

So I said, "There is another reason ye cannot keep me down here forever, Lanresia. I imagine ye know this already, but I am a Knight of Se-Dela. Tomorrow, I am supposed to return to work, and if I do not, then my fellow Knights will notice and begin to search for me. They will find ye, and once they do, your precious Foundation will come crashing down all around ye like building blocks stacked on top of each other."

"Your fellow Knights couldn't find us if we opened the front door and placed a giant 'WELCOME' sign in neon lights outside it," Lanresia replied, with more than a hint of sarcasm in her voice. "But you are correct that we can't keep you down here forever. Don't worry; we'll send you back home soon, once all of this is over."

Lanresia snapped her fingers. My eyelids became as heavy as a sack of potatoes and my muscles began to relax. My conscious rapidly began slipping away even as I realized what was going on: she had cast a sleep spell on me, the witch. I had not noticed any skyras rings on her fingers, but perhaps the Xeeonites could use magic without needing those, or maybe she had some other way of doing it.

I reached out toward her, but it was no use. Sleep was coming upon me like a falcon flying over a field mouse. I tried to fight it, but it was like trying to fight the winds of a tornado.

Just as sleep conquered me, a loud explosion rocked the room, causing Lanresia to stagger. The chair was knocked over, as if someone had thrown it, and my bed shuddered and shook with the explosion.

But I did not have a chance to find out what was going on, because the comforting darkness of sleep claimed me at last.

Chapter Four

Mine dreams were as frightening and bizarre as the wildest tales of the story scribes. 'Twas like I slept in an iron oven, burning like an everlasting flame, with the groaning and clanking of the metal booming in my ears. My skin seemed to melt before my very eyes, like butter on a hot pan, but I could not scream because mine mouth was burned shut and my tongue flew above my head, circling my crown like a vulture.

Even worse, strange creatures crawled along the ceiling, growling and howling like the wild dogs of the Fertile Lands. Some of them did not have eyeballs, while others only had fire leaking out of their empty sockets like a leak from a dam.

Such horrifying visions made me cry out, which was strange, because mine mouth was still sealed shut. Nonetheless, I cried out, unable to believe what my eyes showed me, and I thrashed about until I rolled off the oven rack and onto the floor of the oven below.

Yet when I landed on it, I did not burn into pieces. Instead, like the flip of a switch, I found myself lying on the soft mattress of the bed I had been sleeping on inside the Foundation, but it was nigh impossible to see because of the darkness of my room. I did not see any sign of those strange imp-like creatures, nor did I hear the oven's creaking and groaning anymore.

That is not to say that I was well, however. The room was unnaturally hot; 'twas like a hot summer day in the Fertile Lands, though without the cool breeze that usually accompanied that heat. Sweat ran down my temples and a strong stink of smoke entered my nostrils, burning them and making me feel as though I was trying to breathe toxic gas.

I pushed myself up on my hands and looked around at my surroundings more closely. The room was almost too dark to see in, but every now and then the florescent light bulb above would flicker on, giving me glimpses of what the room was like now.

It looked essentially the same as I remembered it, except that a chunk of the ceiling had fallen at the foot of mine bed (explaining the weight I felt near my feet) and it smelled like smoke and fire, even though I saw neither. Lanresia was nowhere to be seen; not even her annoying speaking snake was present. This disturbed me greatly, especially when I saw that the door had been blasted off its hinges and lay, a smoldering heap, at the foot of mine bed. As for the camera, it hung loosely from the wires connecting it to the ceiling, though that did not disturb me quite so much as the way the rest of the room appeared.

What had happened here? I did not know. Did remind me of a photograph I once saw, of a Xeeonite hospital room after a mad bomber had blown himself up in it. Only, in the photograph, there had been more blood and corpses.

My body was so sweaty that it made my clothes stick to my

skin like a second layer. I sat up, pulling at my sleeves and shirt to loosen them around my body and allow air to flow through, though the air in this room was so stifling that I felt even more sweat coming from my pores.

It might have been wiser to simply sit back and wait for one of the Foundation's members to return and tell me what happened. Though I still knew nothing about what caused the explosion, I knew enough to say that this was not a normal occurrence down here. Unfortunately, I was unarmed and not certain how much of the Foundation's hidden underground headquarters was left, which meant it would be foolish for me to search for answers on my own.

Indeed, for all I knew, the explosion might have completely blocked off all escapes routes from this place. Perhaps it had even cut off our air supply, which meant that I would soon run out of air and when I did, then I would truly die.

But it was not in mine nature to simply sit back and let others act in dangerous situations. I had to find out for myself what was going on in here, even if there was nothing I could do about it. Besides, despite the heat making mine clothes stick to my body, I felt as though I could stand up and walk, at least, which 'twas all I needed to do.

So I sat up and threw mine feet over the side of the bed, but when they touched the floor, I pulled them back up quickly. The floor was hot, almost too hot to touch, and I had no shoes nor socks nor boots nor any other footwear covering my feet. It burned with the might of a thousand fires, but if I was to find out what had happened here, I would need to brave it anyway.

Gritting my teeth, I lowered my feet onto the floor again. It still burned hotly, but not quite as before. Maybe the floor was cooling or maybe I was just getting used to it. Or maybe—most likely—it was my own bravery aiding my feet in resisting the heat that had been left over by the explosion.

Although, now that I thought about it, why did the floor burn if the explosion had not happened in here? 'Twas like someone had set the entire headquarters on fire, yet the flickering of the florescent bulb showed little evidence of flame anywhere. What a strange mystery.

But before I went any further, I knew I needed a weapon. Assuming the explosion was the responsibility of a vile enemy, I would need to defend myself. Yet when I looked around the room, I saw no sign of any weapons I could use, not even so much as a rock to throw.

Thus, I picked up the plaster that had fallen from the ceiling onto my bed. It was hot and crumbly between my fingers, which made me doubt it would be good for more than one hit, but sometimes all ye needed was one good hit to the head to defeat even the mightiest foe.

With my trusty chunk of plaster at mine side, I advanced toward the open doorway. The closer I drew to the doorway, the worse the smoke became, though it was nowhere near as thick as it could have been. Praise be to the Old Gods, who must have somehow kept me safe from the worst of the smoke during the initial explosion, for aside from some scratchy lungs, I had not choked to death due to the smoke.

No noise emitted from beyond the doorway. I peered through it and saw a long hallway stretching down both ways just outside mine room. 'Twas a dark hallway, though as with the florescent light in my room, a few bulbs here flickered on and off.

What the flickers showed unsettled me greatly. Corpses lay in the hallway, ones I did not recognize. The corpses appeared scorched by fire, as did the walls and floors, which told me that the explosion must have come through here at some point. The combined stink of blood and smoke entered mine nostrils, making me gasp from the horribleness of it all.

The corpses, from what I could tell, were mostly human, though I noticed an ape-like Rathonian that appeared to be missing its head. The explosion might have killed them ... or maybe something else entirely had done so.

For that matter, I could not tell if they were Foundation members or perhaps belonged to whoever had started the explosion. Considering how light the stink of blood and smoke was, and how cool the floor was in comparison to the floor of my room, I wondered just how long I had been out. Was it already the next day?

Surely my fellow Knights must have noticed that I had not returned by now. Perhaps they had even sent a page to my bed to find out why I had not yet awakened, though I could not be sure even of that much, for mine sense of time was thoroughly off. For all I knew, I could have been sleeping for years, like the Heavy-Eyed Man of that old children's fairytale my mother used to tell me when I was little.

In any case, I did not have the luxury of hiding in mine room forever. There were still many questions I did not have an answer to and the only way to find those answers was to move bravely forward, regardless of what threats awaited me in the darkness.

Thus, I inched out of my room as carefully and slowly as I

could. I was not moving cautiously out of fear, but because I did not want anything to jump me when I least expected it. In my younger days, I would always run headfirst into these kinds of situations, but several lessons from Sir Lockfried—my mentor—and a few beatings of his had removed that habit from me fairly quickly. That I lacked any shoes also made it prudent to go forward only cautiously, for I did not wish to step on anything that could draw blood or stick into mine feet.

Still, it seemed like the hallway was abandoned, as though whoever had come through this way was long gone. I might very well be the only living thing down here; 'twas a disturbing and unsettling thought, even though it meant that I did not need to be quite as cautious as before.

I did not know which way might take me out of the Foundation's headquarters, so I prayed to Vilina of the Old Gods for guidance. I did not know if the Old Gods could even hear me on Xeeo, as they were said to live on Dela's moon, but I had to ask for her guidance anyway, as she was the goddess of travel and hence could grant me guidance in these matters.

Whether it was mine own feelings or an answer from Vilina, I eventually decided to go to the right. I reasoned that if it turned out to be a dead end, I could just as easily turn around and head back the way I came, could I not? (Of course, if it turned out to be the way to my death, then I would not be able to do much.)

So down that way I went. Although I was certain that there were no other living beings down here but myself, I nonetheless looked over my shoulder every now and then to assure myself that I was by no means being followed. I saw not a hint of anyone following me, not even when the lights flickered, but I still felt as unsafe as if I had walked into a den of vampires. That feeling made me pray even harder to the Old Gods for help and confidence, though not for safety, because there was no safety to be found down here.

The first corpse I came upon was a male human, clearly a native of Xeeo, if his metal lower jaw was a clue. He lay on his back, his eyes wide open in shock, a gruesome sight even in this dark place. His skin might normally have been as pale as the snow; now, however, it was charcoal black, likely as a result of the explosion, though his hands appeared to have been cleanly cut off, like a butcher had removed them.

'Twas his expression that most terrified me, for he looked as though he had died viewing the most horrific crime imaginable. That his eyebrows had been burned clean off only made his expression that much more frightening.

As terrifying and frightening as this man appeared, I could not help but peer at his feet, for I hoped he had some shoes I might be able to borrow. He looked to be about the same size as I, after all, so even if his shoes were some of those strange Xeeonite shoes that were more for fashion and comfort than work and wear, I might possibly be able to wear them anyway.

But to my limitless disappointment, the soles of this man's shoes had been turned to ash, revealing the blackened skin of the underside of his feet. Whilst I could still have taken his shoes off, 'twould have done nothing for me, as wearing those brogues would have been as good as walking without any shoes at all.

I knew not who this man was, nor what he may have believed or what religion he may have practiced. Knowing these Xeeonites, he likely saw no use for any sort of religion, yet it did not feel right to me to simply leave him behind. I could not give him much in the way of a burial, as the floor was metal and I had no shovel with which to dig.

Thus, I prayed another prayer to the Old Gods, asking them to guide the soul of this poor man into the next life. I knew not what happened to Xeeonites when they died, but perhaps they went to the same place as we Delanians. Or perhaps Xeeo had its own afterlife for its people.

I ceased thinking about such metaphysical speculation right away, however, when I heard the sound of claws scratching against metal. What an awful sound; it made me shudder with revulsion just listening to it.

But I could not tell where it was coming from or who was making it. Nay, the sound seemed to be coming from the walls themselves, though perhaps it came from one of the other rooms instead. I was hesitant to move forward any further, however, because my chunk of plaster did not feel adequate to deal with whatever was making that noise, even though I knew not what it was.

The sound faded away soon enough, but I doubted that that would be the last I would hear of it. Part of me wanted to leave it alone, but another part of me wanted to go and find out what it was. Perhaps it was not some sinister creature hiding in the shadows, ready to take me down as soon as I dropped mine guard; maybe it was an innocent person, dying or in pain, who needed my help.

Yet what time did I have to waste helping others? Mine largest priority was to find a way out of here and return to Dela, where I could report back to duty. Granted, I also still needed to find my sister, but knowing now what I do about her, I would come back some other day to save her instead. Perhaps on that other day I would even be strong enough to defeat Assassin.

I took a step forward, but stopped again. What if this person—assuming 'twas a person, though it could have been a machine or perhaps a beast of some sort, though this did not seem like the kind of place where animals would be kept—could show me the way out of here? And perhaps also tell me what happened?

Indeed, that seemed logical enough. This headquarters of the Foundation seemed as deep and complex as the tunnels beneath the foundations of Castle Una, based on the many doors I saw in the hallway in which I stood. In my mind's eye, I could see myself wandering through here forever before, perhaps, stumbling upon a smoke-filled room and then choking to death.

Therefore, I decided to search for this individual, whoever it was. It may have even been a sign from the Old Gods, the help I asked for, though I had no way to know for certain and would not until later. Perhaps they even had some shoes for me to wear or borrow; it was certainly worth the risk, in my humble opinion.

Hence, I listened as closely as I could, until I heard the claws scraping against the metal again. 'Twas slightly covered by the sounds of electricity sparking in the flickering lights, but mine ears were good enough to locate the sound some ten feet from where I stood, behind a door on the right side of the hallway. Holding my plaster chunk close to my chest, I stepped toward the door as carefully and silently as I could, ready to defend myself if necessary.

Like the rest of the Foundation's headquarters, this door had no doorknob nor handle. Likely it slid open, but I did not understand how those types of doors worked. Never had any reason to, for I spent most of mine time in Dela and had only ever traveled to Xeeo perhaps three times prior to my recent arrival.

I stood in front of the door and waved at it. Much to my surprise, the door tried to slide, but it made a strange groaning noise that made me worry that it would explode in my face. I held up mine plaster just to be safe, but after more groaning and sparking, the door ceased trying to open. Perhaps it was jammed, but I did not know how to un-jam it, if that was the ccase.

I scowled. How dare this door act this way. Did it not want me to enter? Yes, I knew this door was likely not animate, but I was still frustrated by it nonetheless, for I felt like the key to my escape from this place was hidden behind there and I had no way to get it.

Then another flicker of the lights above aided me in noticing that the door had opened slightly. 'Twas only an inch, perhaps less, but it looked like I could pry it open with my fingers, if I but tried.

Placing my plaster on the floor, I walked up the door and stuck mine fingers in the gap between the door and its frame, whilst also finding footing for my bare feet on the smooth floor 'neath me. Exerting all of my strength, I pulled the door to the right, in the direction it appeared to slide when it worked normally. It was a difficult effort, a feat worthy of the great Jameles himself, as the door did not appear to want to budge from its place.

Still, with some effort, I managed to push it open enough that I could slip through easily, and it stayed open, too, even if I was not holding it open. I snatched up my plaster chunk from the floor, though it crumbled slightly around the edges when I did so, and then stepped through the gap I had managed to widen between the door and the frame.

How dark this room was! Whereas the hallway outside had at least the flickering florescent lights, this room had no light in it at all, save for the little light that cut through the gap that I had created between the door and its frame.

What these occasional flickers of light showed was what appeared to be some sort of equipment room. On the walls were deactivated energy knives, some kind of Xeeonite gun I could not identify, and lockers with uniforms, though the sliver of light did not give me enough time to peer at them in any detail.

I groped along the nearby wall for a switch, for one thing I did understand about Xeeonite technology was that they had switches to activate the lights in their rooms. Yet mine fingers could find no such switch to flip, which made me wonder if the switch had been blown off by the explosion or if this room had for some reason not been designed with one. Mine feet did not feel anything, either, though that was good, because I did not wish to stumble or step on anything harmful or dangerous, for mine feet were my only mode of transportation, without which I would have been truly helpless.

In any case, I did not see or hear anyone in here, which made me think I must have been mistaken when I assumed that the sound of the claws scraping against metal must have come from this room. Perhaps they came from another room, or maybe I had heard something else entirely.

Least, that is what I believed until two claws wrapped 'round my neck and squeezed. Alarmed, I slammed the blackened plaster over my shoulder onto the head of whatever had grabbed me, causing it to squawk in pain and let go.

I staggered forward, rubbing mine neck, and turned around just in time to see a strange, birdlike creature crouching near one of the lockers. 'Twas visible only for a moment, when the light flickering from the hallway showed it; then it was gone, drowned by the darkness.

Yet I knew that the creature was no trick of the light. I reached behind me and grabbed one of the energy knives from the wall. Whilst I did not like to use Xeeonite technology or weapons, when mine survival was at risk, I was willing to do anything that would increase my chances of living.

And having confiscated these energy knives from more than one criminal over mine career, I knew to press the tab on the handle to activate it. When I did, an energy blade, made of pure skyras, flashed into existence, giving me a view of the birdlike creature again, which had not moved from where it had crouched before.

The light of the energy knife gave me some light, though it was not much more than the glow of a candle. Still, it was better than nothing, and unlike a candle, I could use this to defend mine self in case this creature tried to attack me again.

Looking at the birdlike creature, I was not entirely sure at first what it was. 'Twas humanoid, as I, but it had wings and feathers, feathers as golden as the sun on a summer day in the Fertile Lands, though they seemed grimy, as if the creature had been rolling about in the dirt. Its feathers were ruffled, too, and it stank horribly, like smoke and bird excrement, making me cover mine nose to save my sense of smell from its horrible assault. I was disappointed to see that it had no shoes on its clawed feet, though that did not stop me from hoping that it might have a pair hidden away nearby anyway.

The creature's eyes were green, but they did not seem to be its natural color; perhaps it had had them changed, as I had heard it was a common trend in certain Xeeonite subcultures. Then again, this creature's eye colors could just as easily have been its natural color; my knowledge of Xeeonite species was lackluster at best.

All I knew for certain was that I needed to keep my distance from this thing, at least until I was certain of what it actually was. Right now, I knew only that it was likely the source of those claws scraping against metal, for it had claws on its hands and talons on its feet.

"What be ye?" I asked, making sure to hold the energy knife in a way that let this beast know I would attack if I felt threatened. "Can ye speak Delanian? More importantly, do ye have a pair of shoes I could wear?"

The creature stood up to its full height, which was not much taller than I, and seemed not like it would speak at first. Perhaps it couldn't speak at all; indeed, I suspected as much, for it did not look capable of speaking any tongue I knew of.

But then it rasped, in a low voice, "I can speak many languages, Delanian, but I prefer to speak in Xeeonish. It is more practical than Delan or any other tongue out there. As for the shoes, no, I don't. And there aren't any in these lockers, either, so don't try looking in them."

The lack of shoes made me greatly sorrowful; however, I did not show it. Instead, I brandished my weapon at the creature, for I still did not know if I could trust it, and demanded, with as much authority as I could muster, "What is your name? And just what are you, exactly?"

"I'm a Checrom," said the creature, gesturing at its wings. "We're a species of birdlike people that live on Xeeo, far to the west of Xeeon. And of course, I am also a member of the Foundation, which you have probably guessed already."

"I noticed you still haven't told me your name, creature," I said. I narrowed my eyes. "For that matter, I find it hard to believe that a member of the Foundation would be hiding out here, rather than exploring the hideout to search for any of your surviving companions."

The Checrom shuddered and glanced at the door. "I would have done that, but I've never been particularly brave and I'm not much of a fighter. I didn't want to be killed. I thought I would be safer in here, especially with all of these weapons."

The Checrom gestured at the weapons hanging on the walls, of which I could now see that there was a far greater variety of weapons than I had first believed. Still, 'twas too dark for me to tell for sure how many and what kind of weapons there were; in any case, that was unimportant at the moment. For now, I had to focus on the current situation, as I still was not sure I could trust this Checrom.

Then the Checrom's aquiline eyes darted back toward mine face. "Are you the Knight that was saved from Assassin earlier? You look like him. I remember Janrex dragging your bloody body into HQ. Thought you were already dead, but I suppose I should have had more faith in our doctors and surgeons."

"Indeed I am that Knight," I said. "But why did you attack me when I first entered here?"

"I thought you were an enemy coming to kill me," said the Checrom with a shrug. "It was too dark for me to tell who you were for sure. That's the main reason you smashed that plaster on my head, right?"

"Correct," I said. "And I apologize for that. This place is dark and unknown and I could take no chances."

"Understandable," said the Checrom. He grimaced and rubbed his head. "That plaster still hurt, though. It hurt more than I thought it would."

"Just be thankful that I do not have mine sword," I said. "Otherwise, I would have split your skull open and exposed your brains to the world."

"Right," said the Checrom. "Well, what is your name? You didn't mention it."

"Call me Apakerec," I said, gesturing at myself. "'Tis the name I use when addressing non-humans."

The Checrom blinked, as if he did not understand what I said. "Why do you have two names like that? Why not just use one name for everyone?"

"'Tis a common custom that all Delanians of every species adhere to," I replied. "Ye need not know my human name anyway. Now, do ye know what happened here? What caused the explosion?"

The Checrom rubbed the top of his head, sending bits of blackened plaster falling from its feathers. "I don't know all of the details, because I wasn't there when it happened, but an explosion happened in the Energy Center, where HQ's power is generated. We thought it was an accident at first, but then some of the other Foundation members reported seeing strange, lizard-like creatures crawling out from the wreckage, killing anything that got too close. Including, unfortunately, several of my fellow Federation members."

"How odd," I remarked. I gestured with mine energy knife at the jammed, partially-open sliding door. "Did the explosion cause all of this damage?"

"I think so," said the Checrom. "When the Energy Center blew up, it sent powerful electrical charges through HQ's wiring system. That's probably what caused the power to become as erratic and unstable as it is now."

"How many people survived?" I asked. "Do ye know?"

"I don't," said the Checrom, shaking his head. "I hid in here because I wanted to avoid those lizard-like creatures, which I saw kill one of my friends. There might be more, or we might be the only people in this place who are still alive."

"There may be some grim truth to your words, I fear," I said. I nodded at the hallway. "Outside, I saw several corpses, perhaps your fellow Foundation members. They appeared to have been killed by the explosion, as though they had been burned by a dragon's fire."

"Burned by a dragon's fire?" the Checrom said. He sounded curious. "Odd. I didn't think the explosion caused *that* much damage. Are you sure it was the explosion?"

"What else could it have been?" I asked. "Unless, of course, ye are suggesting that these lizard creatures can breathe fire."

"Who knows?" said the Checrom with a shrug. "Anyway, did you see any of those creatures or at least hear them? It's been so quiet out there that I thought they might have gone, but I didn't look because I was afraid they were waiting for me to come out."

"No, I did not," I said, shaking mine head. "I did not even know they existed until ye told me about them. If they are as bad as ye say they are, then I am thankful to have avoided them."

The Checrom put his claws on his face like he was afraid. "You're lucky, but now I'm worried for the rest of my Foundation members. Those creatures were strong, much stronger than us, and I haven't heard from anyone else except for you."

"Then what are we waiting for?" I said. I jerked mine thumb over my shoulder. "Grab whatever weapons ye want. We will find a way out of here and, if we find any of those lizards, we will kill them in cold blood, as they deserve for their crimes."

"I would rather stay here, where they haven't been able to find me," said the Checrom, crouching low to the floor and putting his claws over his head. "Right now, this has worked out pretty well for me."

"Coward," I said. "Do ye not want to avenge the deaths of your comrades and allies? Or are ye going to allow these fiends to escape without retribution or harm? Indeed, I ask, is this what ye Foundation members do, simply run and hide whenever there is trouble?"

"I-I'm not a fighter," the Checrom said, looking down at the floor, away from my face. "I'm supposed to be the janitor of the Foundation's HQ. That's why I didn't fight, because I'm not a fighter and I don't know how to fight."

The cowardly bird seemed to be telling the truth, but I said nonetheless, "Well, now ye have me. I shall help ye fight these monsters, if they are still lurking in the shadows like thieves. Still, grab ye a weapon; 'twould make me feel safer, knowing that ye can defend yourself if necessary."

The Checrom gulped, but then he stood up and snatched a laser gun off the wall. "All right. I don't want to hide in here forever, anyway. I want to find out if anyone survived the attack and just what happened here."

"As do I," I said. "By the way, do ye know what happened to the she-elf named Lanresia? She was the one who spoke to me earlier. Is she still alive? I did not see her corpse in the hallway."

"I don't know," said the Checrom with a shrug. "I remember seeing her going to fight the monsters, but I don't know what happened to her after that. Why? Did you like her?"

"Not particularly," I said, shaking my head. "She was a freak, with that talking snake machine attached to her waist. Still, she was the only face of the Foundation I knew, so I asked merely out of curiosity 'tis all."

"A freak?" the Checrom repeated that word as though it were the most awful curse a wizard could lay on another being. "That's not very nice. She needs that speaking snake of hers to communicate with the rest of us."

"That may well be true, but it is still an unnatural abomination, one I hope to the Old Gods to never wear myself," I said. "But this is irrelevant. If ye are ready to go, then we shall go, and speedily."

Chapter Five

Ah! How good it felt to have a weapon with which to defend myself. For a while there, I had felt as naked as if a thief had stolen all of my clothes and hid them where I could not find them. 'Twas a relief to have this blade, even if it was an ugly piece of Xeeonite tech that felt awkward and strange in mine hand. I would have taken a sword, but the Checrom—who said his name was Resita, an odd name, to be sure, and different from other Xeeonite names I had heard—had said that there were no swords of any sort held in the Foundation's cache.

What a roaring disappointment that was! I had hoped to be armed with a sword, but now I had to rely on this pitiful energy knife. Again, I was pleased to have a weapon at all, even though this blade may not have been much. Resita offered me one of those infernal laser guns, but I refused, as I did not know how to use them and had no interest in learning how.

Once we were both ready, I stepped carefully through the gap between the door and the frame and looked both ways. The occasional flickering of the lights showed nothing, save more corpses. I saw no sign of those lizard-like monsters that Resita claimed had attacked this place, but perhaps they had moved to the upper floors.

As Resita followed me out of the room, I said, "How many floors does this place have? One? Two?"

"Eleven," said Resita.

I started. "Ye mean ten and one? And they extend underground?"

"Yes," said Resita, nodding. He pointed at some strange markings on the wall opposite us. "This is Floor Number Five. Unless there are a bunch of obstacles between here and Floor Number One, where the Command Center is, we shouldn't have any trouble getting out of here."

"I hope ye are right, because I wish to leave this place as quickly as a rabbit leaves its burrow," I said. I shuddered. "Look at all of this death. 'Tis like the battlefields of Saljamor, where death greets you at every turn."

"I don't know what the battlefields of Saljamor are," said Resita, shaking his head. "But I do know—"

He stopped speaking when he noticed the corpses on the ground. He made a strange choking sound, which I at first did not understand, 'til I realized he was shocked at the sight of so many of his deceased friends. His eyes in particular were focused on the dead human I had noticed before, the one with the burnt skin and the missing hands.

"'Tis indeed a grim sight," I said. I patted him on the shoulder. "But we cannot simply stand here and do nothing. Lead the way out of here, or at least tell me in which direction we must go."

"To the right," said Resita, turning his face away from the

corpses of his allies, nodding in the direction which he had indicated. "We'll reach an elevator that will take us to the next floor. We'll be passing by the Command Center on our way out, so we can stop there to see if anyone is still alive."

"How will this 'Command Center' of which ye speak show us that?" I said, tilting mine head to the side.

"There's a map of the entire HQ in there," Resita explained. "Assuming it's still functional, it should be able to show us the location of every Foundation member who was in here when the attacks started, assuming no one has left the place since then. We can also send a distress message to the other members who are out in the field, and to the Delanian branch."

"Ye mean to say that not all of ye Foundation people are in here?" I said, gesturing at the dark hallway in which we stood. "And what is this 'Delanian branch' ye speak of?"

"No one told you?" said Resita. He gestured at the hallway. "The Foundation has two branches; one here on Xeeo, another on Dela. We don't communicate often due to the difficulty in communicating between the two worlds, and I've never been there, but I've seen footage of it and met some of the agents who work there."

"Why does your organization have two branches?" I asked. "I thought ye were working to stop Xacron-Ah's plans."

Resita blinked when I mentioned that name. "Who?"

"The current Mayor of Xeeon," I said, frowning. "Lanresia told me that ye Foundation people are keeping an eye on him. He is planning something sinister for Xeeo, yes?"

"Oh," said Resita, realization dawning in his voice. "Him. Well, yeah, he's one threat, but ... well, I don't think I should be telling you about anything else. It's not really relevant and I don't have permission to blab about all our secrets to you anyway."

Did seem exceedingly relevant to me. After all, I still did not know as much about the Foundation as I would have liked. They had reassured me that they fought on the side of light, but what if this was all a lie and they were indeed trying to do something sinister? After all, Lanresia had not told me about the Delanian branch, which made me wonder what other major secrets these Foundation agents were hiding from me. 'Twould not be the first time that I was fooled by someone pretending to be mine ally, that was for certain.

I could tell, however, that Resita, at least, was an honest fellow, though it was not easy to do so, as his lack of human facial features made deciphering his feelings nigh impossible. I resolved to keep a careful eye on him until I could be certain that he was a friend and not a foe.

Before we went anywhere, however, I first asked, "But why should we head to the first floor? Why not check every floor between here and Floor Number One for any survivors who may be able to tell us more about what had happened?"

"Because I don't think there are any survivors," said Resita. "If there were, they'd have made an effort to contact us by now. No, I think everyone is either dead or has left. Which means it's probably just us and the monsters now."

"What luck," I said in the most sardonic voice I could muster. "But I will not argue the point. I have no great love for this place and would like to get out of here as soon as possible, for the quicker I leave, the quicker I can be reunited with mine sister."

So we began walking down the hallway, to the right, but

carefully. Though the flickering florescent lights above did not show any threats, the sheer silence of this place made me instinctively wary. I half-expected a vengeful spirit to come flying out of the shadows, wailing a terrible song, ready to gouge out our eyes and crush them betwixt it's teeth.

We found more corpses the further we walked. Resita identified them all: Jonark, Cadax, Ijir, Foxah, and others. He did not tell me much about them (for I was not interested enough to ask), except to identify their occupation within the Foundation every now and then (Jonark was a technician, for example), but even I could tell that their deaths must have affected him greatly. We did not dally too long on any of the deceased; we had to keep going, because the only way not to end up like them was to do what we were already doing. That, and none of the corpses had any shoes I could wear, which only added to my frustration, as though the Old Gods were intentionally keeping mine feet bare like some kind of cruel and unusual form of punishment.

As luck would have it, we did not run into any of those lizard creatures, though we did find several scratch marks on the floor and walls that indicated that some kind of monster must have been through here. There was also the stink of slime, which Resita told me was most likely left behind by those beasts. 'Twas a terrible smell that almost made me wish I could not smell anymore, especially when it mixed with the slightly smoky stink that already permeated the hallway.

We arrived at the end of the hallway, in front of the strange contraption that Resita called the 'elevator.' I had heard of these strange lifts before, which were said to be even more convenient than stairs, but this was the first time I had seen one in person.

Or would have been, if the accursed door would have opened. Like with the door to the weapon cache, this one was also jammed shut; only, unlike the previous door, this one did not have even once inch of a gap between the door and the frame for me or Resita to use to force it open.

Resita attempted to open it by pressing one of the dozens of buttons on the wall next to it, but as soon as he pressed the 'up' arrow, the elevator made a loud, groaning noise that reminded me of the shriek of a dying monster. 'Twas enough to make me back up and pull Resita with me, though after only a few seconds the machine went silent.

"Great," said Resita, throwing up his feathery hands. "The elevator is broken. I should have expected this. I just hope no one was on it when it broke."

"What terrible luck has befallen us," I said. "Tell me, Resita, is there any other way we could get to the higher floors? I do not wish to be stuck down here forever, where I could die of hunger and thirst or be choked to death by smoke."

"Yeah, there's a set of emergency stairs we could use," said Resita, gesturing at a door not far from where we stood. "I would have mentioned those before, but I figured the lizards might be hiding inside them, so they wouldn't be safe for us to use. But if the elevator really is broken ... well, it seems that we don't have much of a choice now, do we?"

"No, we do not," I said. I held up my energy knife, which blazed to life. "But fear ye not, my comrade. We shall fight any monsters that attempt to stop us on our way up. To the death, if necessary."

There was no mistaking the look of terror on Resita's birdlike face now. I had almost forgotten that Resita had not been trained in combat, unlike myself, but 'twas not a problem, as I would be leading the way and therefore would be the first to run into any creatures lurking in the stairs. Whilst I had never fought any of these lizard creatures he spoke of, I doubted they would be much of a threat to my combat prowess, for I had been trained in the way of the Knights of Se-Dela, and the Knights of Se-Dela were hardly weaklings.

The emergency stairs which Resita described were located only a few feet from the elevator's door. The door to the stairs had already been knocked off its hinges by something, likely by one of the monsters, based on the deep, long claw marks we found on its metallic surface. That almost made Resita faint, but I told him we would be safe so long as we kept our wits about ourselves and did not allow ourselves to be taken by surprise. Still he tried to faint, so I slapped him instead, which appeared to wake him better than any reassurances on mine part (though based on the way he rubbed his face, he clearly was not happy about how I hit him).

Upon entering the stairwell, a powerful stench, like rotten eggs mixed with melting rubber, assaulted mine nostrils, making me cover my nose to protect it. So too did Resita cover his face, though I could tell by the watering of his eyes that that gesture did little to aid him.

And by the Old Gods' three hundred names, what a narrow and dark stairwell this was! The hallway outside at least had the occasional flickering of light to allow us to see the path before us, but 'twas as pitch black as a vampire's heart in here, with a sticky, humid air that reminded me of the tropical jungles of the Trinity Isles. Where this humidity came from, I knew not, although I guessed this, too, was from the lizard creatures.

Looking up, I could not see anything, save for a handful of pinpricks of light that appeared to be the windows on the doors of the next several floors. But they were too small to show us anything of the upper levels. Indeed, for all I knew, the stairs had been completely destroyed by the lizards, which would undoubtedly make our escape from this place that much more difficult.

"Maybe we should rethink this," said Resita, his voice slightly muffled behind his feathery hands. "We don't know what's up there. We could try to repair the elevator instead. I mean, I've never actually repaired an elevator before, but I think I know—"

"Nay!" I responded, my voice echoing in the narrow stairwell. "We go up and into the darkness, whatever lies ahead. Unless ye would like to spend the rest of your short days inhaling the stink of your deceased friends, that is."

Resita held up his hands. "Fine, fine. But let's be quick. I don't like the darkness at all."

"Neither do I," I replied. "Yet I will not allow it to conquer me. I shall lead the way."

It was thus that I began to ascend the staircase, which felt like concrete under my bare feet. 'Twas still too dark; I heard the clicking of Resita's claws on the steps behind me as we climbed higher and higher into the shadows.

We had to ascend carefully, for though the stairwell seemed empty 'side from us, that did not mean that there were no lizard creatures hiding above us, perhaps lying in wait. Granted, I knew virtually nothing about the habits and practices of these beasts, but if they were smart at all, they would do just that.

As we climbed, I could not help but think about mine sister, Kiriah. Somehow, I knew she was connected to all of this. I did not know if she was currently aware that I was trying to find her, but I knew she had to miss me as much as I missed her.

After all, Kiriah and I had been the closest of siblings prior to her sudden disappearance. How I remembered our youthful days, when we would explore the deepest and darkest corners of our family's mansion! Even as a young child, she had been radiant, with her yellow blonde hair and her pale skin. I well remembered how she had always told me that she wanted to be a princess when she grew up, though 'twas an impossibility, for King Waran-Una had no children and we were not wealthy enough for that dream to ever be anything more than the whimsical desire of a child.

Yes, we had become somewhat distant when we grew up, but that was simply the normal passage of time, which erodes all things eventually. Even so, our bond had been strong, strong enough that her sudden disappearance had left a lasting scar on my mind that was unlikely to ever go away completely until I found her again.

It was the thought of reuniting with her that spurred me on toward greater heights. In this case, quite literally, for Resita and I had to keep ascending higher and higher on these stairs to reach the first floor, and, eventually, freedom.

One other thing that crossed mine mind was my fellow Knights. I still did not know for certain how much time had passed since I had been cast into sleep by that she-elf Lanresia; however, I could guess that it had been more than a few hours, which meant that Sir Lockfried was most likely expecting me to report for duty any minute now. That I had not, was as obvious as the sun was round, which no doubt meant that Sir Lockfried had noticed mine absence by now. In all likelihood, he would send someone—perhaps even my friend and closest ally, Sir Alart—to mine home to find out the reason behind my delay.

Though even then, I could not count on Sir Alart coming to my rescue. I had left no note or clue indicating where I might have gone, after all, as I had not expected to be gone from Dela for more than a day. Even if they found out I had gone to Xeeon, that meant nothing, because I was no longer there.

Thus, aside from Resita and mine faith in the Old Gods of my ancestors, I was truly on my own here. I could rely only on myself to get out of this mess, a very sobering thought indeed.

At least the stairwell that we ascended was empty of enemies so far. The strong stink of rotten eggs and melting rubber still afflicted my nostrils, and my feet felt cold against the concrete steps, but it seemed as though the creatures that had come this way had long since disappeared, though it would take the faith of a fool to believe that they had left entirely.

And believe me, despite not being a highly educated man, I was no fool.

Yet for a while there, I almost believed that we would reach the first floor without any issues or troubles. I believed that, until we reached the door to the second floor. I turned to walk up the next set of stairs, but then mine foot went through a hole where the next step should have been and I nearly fell in.

Thankfully, Resita's claws grabbed the collar of mine shirt before I could fall into the hole. 'Twas an abrupt grab, which hurt my neck, but it was better than falling in headfirst, which likely would not have ended well for me.

Resita dragged me back from the edge and then let go of my collar. Readjusting the collar of mine shirt, I said, "Thank ye for saving me, Resita. I thought I was going to meet mine end there."

"No problem," said Resita's voice behind me. "If you had fallen, you would have cracked your head open, which would have been very messy and would have left me to fend for myself in this place."

"Indeed," I said. "But why are these stairs missing the next steps? On Dela, no staircase is missing even one small step. Is this an example of the failures of Xeeonite engineering?"

"This has nothing to do with Xeeonite engineering," said Resita in annoyance. "I don't know for sure what happened, but I can guess that either the lizards destroyed the next few steps on these stairs or maybe the shaking from the explosion knocked them off."

"How peculiar," I said, stroking mine chin in thought. "How come we did not run into these missing steps on our way up? They should have fallen either way, should they have not?"

"Didn't you feel those little bits of concrete on the steps?" said Resita. "I did. I didn't think much of them at first, because I thought maybe it was just a few bits that had been knocked off the underside of the higher steps, but now I am starting to think that those were the remains of the next few steps. The only one that isn't missing is this one right here."

I could not tell which he spoke of, but I did hear his feathery fingers run along a concrete surface nearby. I reached out with mine hands and felt what was clearly a chunk of torn concrete. 'Twas so baffling a thing that I wondered just how strong those lizards must have been, to tear a chunk of concrete off the steps and rest it here like that.

But dwelling on that thought was not relevant or helpful to our current situation, so without turning to face Resita, I said, "How can ye tell there are a few steps missing? Seems like there was only one missing step to I."

"Because, like all Checrom, I have limited night vision," said Resita. "I can only really see the general outline of things in the dark, but it's enough for me to tell that there are at least three steps missing, maybe four or five at most."

"I can jump four or five steps easy," I said. "Then ye can follow, or perhaps wait here until I can find help."

I bent my knees, readying myself to jump through the air like a leaping tiger, when one of Resita's claws fell on my shoulders. Ordinarily, such a move, in such a black place, would have made me grab and hurl the attacker over my shoulder to defend mine life, but as I knew it was Resita, I refrained from doing so.

"Are you insane?" said Resita, sounding far too much like mine mother for my tastes. "You can't make that jump. Maybe if we had some light in here to help you see, you might stand a chance of not falling to your death. But with this darkness, you'd have to be the biggest idiot in the world to try it."

I stood back up to mine full height, shrugging off his claw as I looked over my shoulder at the bird-like humanoid. The light from the tiny window on the door to Floor Number Two showed me only part of his face, enough so that I could see how incredulously he was staring at me.

"Then what do ye suggest we do, bird?" I said. "Go back down to the fifth floor and die among the dead?"

"No," said Resita, shaking his head, causing a few feathers to fall out of it as he did so. "Instead, I think we should go into Floor Number Two. There's another set of stairs on that side that should take us up to Floor Number One."

This revelation utterly floored me. I was so taken aback by it that I almost stumbled backwards into the hole where the steps had once been, but I caught myself in the nick of time, though I was still shaken by Resita's words nonetheless.

Resita must have noticed my reaction, because he said, "Um, why did you do that?"

"Because I had never known about those other stairs before," I said. "Why did ye never mention them until now?"

"Because there was no reason to," said Resita. "If these damn stairs hadn't been completely trashed, then we could have gone up to Floor Number One easily. As it is, we'll have to cut across Floor Number Two to get to the stairs on the other side."

"What luck!" I said. I spread my arms. "Brother Resita, we shall hug to celebrate this brilliant stroke of luck, which must have been granted to us by Walnak himself!"

Resita, however, held up his hands defensively, as though I was about to assault him instead of embrace him. "There's no need for any of that. I mean, we can't celebrate just yet; after all, there's a good chance that those lizard creatures are in the second floor, unless they've already left this place."

"Even so, we shall fight them as though they were nothing, for we have righteousness on our side," I said, forming a fist with mine right hand. "The Old Gods themselves are protecting us, of this I have no doubt."

"I don't know who or what the 'Old Gods' are, nor do I want

90

to," said Resita, who now sounded as nervous as a tiny bird that knew that a hungry cat was nearby. "Let's just keep moving. If that door is locked—"

"Then I shall knock it down like the Tower of Malnuth!" I cried, shoving Resita aside as I walked over to the door to the second floor.

But as it turned out, when I tried to push the door open, it flew open without any trouble. Its hinges creaked loudly as it did so, an unnecessarily loud noise in this quiet place. Did make me cringe, but I still held my hand on my energy knife in case any monsters lay awaiting within, ready to take advantage of our momentary surprise.

Yet when I looked through the open doorway, I saw no sign of any of those lizard-like creatures at all. 'Twas nothing more than a long, empty hallway, similar to the hallway back on the fifth floor, though this place lacked the corpses of the lower floor.

"It appears that our worries were unfounded, my dearest Resita," I said, looking back over my shoulder at my bird-like friend, who stared at me as if I had acted like an idiot. "There is not one sign of any lizard-like creature; to wit, there is—"

Mine words of reassurance were interrupted by the screech of some kind of beast, a screech I had never heard before in my life. This sound was followed by something slamming onto the floor and coming at me at frightening speed.

I whirled around and saw a giant, humanoid lizard-like creature running at me, its claws bared. It moved almost too fast for me to see it in any detail; hence, I decided to act instead of observe.

I drew mine energy knife out of mine sheath in one smooth

motion. I clicked the tab on the handle and a blazing red energy blade popped out of it, hot and burning to the skin, but that mattered little to me, for I assumed that this heat would be enough to wound the accursed beast mortally.

But despite the speed at which I drew and activated mine weapon, the lizard-like humanoid was upon me faster than mine eyes could follow. I saw only one of its claws, sharp and jagged like a knife, coming at me like the talons of an eagle, but I responded by slashing at its arm.

How the monster roared in agony when my knife cut through its flesh like butter! It staggered backward in shock, perhaps too overwhelmed by the pain, as its lower arm fell to the floor with a clatter. 'Twas a gruesome sight indeed, seeing the yellow blood leak out of the stump that had been its arm, not helped in the slightest by the awful stench of cow excrement that followed. It almost made me gag, but I had no time for such luxuries.

Instead, I advanced, swinging my knife at the foul creature. The creature swiped at me with its good claw, but it was an ineffectual strike, for the pain in its cut-off arm must have been affecting its rationality, for it retreated just as quickly as it had come at me.

What a foolish creature, thinking it could escape me! I leaped forward, bringing mine energy knife sailing through the air down onto the creature's head, but it dodged far more swiftly than a beast of its size should have been able to.

Hence, when I landed on the floor, my knife cut into the tiled floor. Not only that, but mine feet—as bare as ever—found no secure footing, causing me to slip and stagger for any sort of balance I could find.

The creature screeched again, making me to think that it was about to assault me once more now that my guard was down. But I was mistaken, for the creature merely retreated further down the hallway, but as it did so, other beasts just like it emerged from the doorways on the other side. It hid behind its comrades, though I could still see the yellow blood oozing out of its arm onto the floor at their feet.

There were now at least a dozen of these monsters, though there could have easily been more. I managed to find mine footing again, but rather than charge forward, I walked backwards. Whilst I was no coward, I was no idiot, either. There were too many of these beasts for me to handle on my own, especially with my puny energy knife as mine only weapon.

The lizard monsters had no such qualms about attacking me, however, because they began to advance on me with the eyes of predators going in for the kill. I felt like prey, although I chose not to dwell on those feelings in order not to feel helpless.

"Uh, Apakerec?" said Resita behind me as I rapidly backed up. "What are you—"

I backed up through the doorway and pulled the door shut as hard as I could. Methinks I bent the door when I slammed it shut, but it mattered not, because I had far more important things to worry about than a slightly bent door.

"Quickly, bird," I snapped at Resita. "Aid me in finding something that we can use to barricade this door! Before the lizards break it open!"

"What?" said Resita. "I thought you were going to come up with some brilliant plan to defeat those monsters."

"Brother Resita, I am no tactical genius," I said. "Yes, I am a

Knight of Se-Dela, but all that means is that I have sworn mine life to protecting the innocent and following the Laws of Waran-Una. Now hurry, find what you can unless ye wish to spend the rest of your life in the belly of a lizard!"

That seemed to do the trick, because Resita ceased talking and began searching for anything he could find. 'Twas hard to tell for certain, however, because of the darkness of the stairwell, but I heard him rummaging around me anyway, and I decided to join him. Two heads were better than one, as I always believed, so what better thing for me to do than help him find a way to barricade the door?

And lo! I remembered the concrete chunk from earlier, the torn step. It was almost too dark for me to see it, but I knew it still had to be there and I knew where to look for it.

"Resita!" I cried as I felt for the broken step, ignoring the screeches of the lizards, which were now too close for mine comfort. "Help me move this broken step in front of the door! It shall be a fine barricade indeed if we work together to move it!"

I heard the clicking and clacking of Resita's claws along the floor as he scurried to aid me. The two of us grabbed the broken step and began pulling and pushing it toward the door, but it was as heavy as ten thousand mountains and was like trying to move a sunken elvish warship.

Still, we put our whole strength into moving this broken step. I internally called upon the Old Gods to grant us the strength to move it, but I could not feel my bones fill with their power. Were the Old Gods ignoring my pleas? If so, then we were well and truly doomed.

But I did not say that aloud, because I knew better than to jinx us. I simply continued to push and shove as hard as I could, putting every last ounce of my strength into this action. 'Twas hard to tell if Resita was working as hard as I, but I assumed that he did, because I heard him huffing and puffing like he too was putting all of his strength into moving this step.

Praise be to the Old Gods! We managed to budge the broken step just a little, but it was enough, for it gave us the momentum we needed to push it all the way in front of the door. Just as we did so, the lizards in the second floor crashed against the door, yelling and screeching as they did so, but neither I nor Resita stayed along enough to listen to their growls, because we turned and ran down the steps back to the lower floors.

Neither of us discussed what the next step of our plan would be, because there was no time to discuss much of anything. We just had to keep running down the stairs, perhaps all the way down to the eleventh floor itself. 'Twas not much of a plan, but there was little else we could do in this situation.

But just as we reached the landing of the third floor, the door to the fourth floor—which was directly underneath us—burst outwards. Light poured out of the doorway, followed by monsters, more of those damn lizard-like beasts, their hissing and screeching echoing loudly off the narrow walls of the stairwell.

What awful luck had befallen us! Above, I could hear the lizard-like beasts tearing through the door and broken step; below, I saw, by the light from the door they had burst through, more of the beasts already making their way up to us.

"Quick!" Resita said, grabbing my arm and dragging me toward the third floor door. "Through here!"

I did not argue with that. We burst through the third floor door together and hastily shut it closed. I found a metal pipe on the floor nearby and stuck it through the door's handle, making a makeshift lock, though I doubted it would last long once the beasts reached this door.

I looked over my shoulder at the third floor hallway. Did look like the other two floors I had been on, but without any lizard-like beasts to chase and kill us. Nay, it was empty, with only half of the lights on, whilst the other half flickered. 'Twas indeed an eerie sight to behold.

Even eerier were the corpses of Foundation members on the floor, though there were fewer than there had been back on the fifth floor. Not only that, but one of the corpses was the body of one of the lizard beasts, which told me that these creatures could indeed be killed, though it hardly mattered when neither I nor Resita were in any position to kill these beasts ourselves.

But neither of us had much time in which to think about this. We just ran down the hallway as fast as we could, Resita's claws clacking against the tile, mine own feet slapping against them loudly. The floor was much colder here than it had been elsewhere, but I did not complain about it because I had no time to complain.

"Resita! Where are we going?" I asked as we tore through the hall. "Is there a secret escape route in here that will allow us to avoid the lizards and escape with our lives?"

"Of course not!" Resita snapped, glancing over his shoulder at me as if I was being dull. "Don't be silly. This isn't the a telescreen play where the protagonists always stumble upon the escape route that they need when they need it. We're just going to have to hide in one of these rooms and hope the monsters don't find us."

I skidded to a halt when I heard him say that. Resita also came to a stop, but whereas I drew mine energy knife again, Resita did not even touch his gun. He just turned to look at me, disbelief etched into his bird-like features.

"Apakerec, what are you doing?" said Resita. He jerked a feathery thumb over his shoulder. "Weren't you listening to a word I said? Or are you Delanians that dumb?"

"Neither, my friend," I said, shaking my head. "I simply do not wish to run and hide from our enemies. 'Tis neither honorable nor practical, for I am certain that these creatures could find and kill us no matter how well we hid ourselves. And as a Knight of Se-Dela, I would rather go down fighting than hiding."

"Are you suggesting that we fight the damn monsters?" said Resita. He clucked. "That has to be the stupidest thing I have ever heard you say. I thought you were at least smart enough to realize that this is not a fight we can win."

"So says the scared chicken," I said. I turned around, holding my energy knife before me again. "Ye can run and hide, if ye wish. But I, I will stand and fight, even if it is to the death."

As I said that, I caught a glimpse of the lizard creatures' green skin through the tiny window in the door at the end of the hall. Then I heard pounding noises on the other side of the door, likely from the attacks from the monsters, although I was pleased to see that mine metal pipe was holding it firm. How much longer that would last, however, even I couldn't say for certain.

"Uh uh," said Resita behind me, his annoyance giving way to panic. "No way. You're coming with me, big guy. No way am I going to hide alone. Not when I'm about as good at fighting as you are at speaking normally."

I glanced over my shoulder at Resita irritably. "Do not insult the High Tongue of my ancestors, bird. Though I am not surprised; ye Xeeonites tend to be very jealous of the beauty of our languages."

"Jealous? You're delusional," said Resita. Then his shoulders slumped. "But fine. Do what you want. I'm going to find the perfect hiding place, but when those monsters kill you, don't come whining to me about it."

I was about to comment about how silly that idea was—after all, if the monsters killed me, I would not be able to coming whining to anyone—but then Resita was off, running down the hallway far faster than I had seen him run before. I watched as he pulled open a door closer to the end of the hall and vanished inside, slamming the door shut behind him as he did so.

Do not get me wrong; I was still angry at Resita leaving me behind to deal with these monsters myself. Despite my words of bravery earlier, I was terribly afraid of these beasts. I had seen the bodies of the other Foundation members, how cold and stiff they were, and I could not help but imagine myself looking like them once the lizard beasts were done with me. 'Twas hardly an encouraging thought, for certain.

Yet the only other alternative was to run and hide, but I doubted that would do us much good. As I said, those lizards would likely find us no matter where we hid; therefore, I was going to be a true Knight of Se-Dela and go down fighting.

True, if I died here, then that would end all of my chances of reuniting with Kiriah. But I knew I was going to die either way, so I was going to die the way I wanted to, on mine own terms, not on the terms of these foul reptilian beasts. Perhaps I would be reunited with Kiriah in the next life, after she dies.

Whilst I thought these thoughts, the door at the end of the hallway kept groaning under the repeated blows from the lizards on the other side. That metal pipe must have been mightier than it first appeared, for it continued to hold even under the constant pummeling from the lizards. The tiny window on the door shattered, sending glass falling onto the floor with a crash. One of the lizard creatures stuck its arm through the new opening, waving it about wildly as if it thought I was near enough for it to strike.

I held mine energy knife before me, feeling its heat radiating from the blade. I positioned myself to fight, but the floor was still too smooth under my unshod feet for me to have any guarantee of finding the footing I needed for victory. Likely I would go down quickly, unless a miracle of the Old Gods occurred and saved me from the end I was destined for.

I thus prayed to the Old Gods for that miracle, but at the same time, the door crashed down onto the floor and the lizard beasts poured in, two dozen in all by my count. They came as fast and swift as an invading army, holding their claws before them as though they wielded powerful swords instead.

This was it. There truly was no way that I could defeat them all. I merely tried to look as threatening as I could, but already I could feel my bones turning to jelly. What were these creatures? Just where had they come from? And what was their ultimate objective?

I had no answers to any of those questions, but I thought little about them. Instead, I charged at the creatures, yelling the battle cry of the Knights of Se-Dela, swinging mine energy knife before me wildly as I did so.

"For Se-Dela!" I cried. "For the Old Gods!"

The stench of the lizard creatures was almost overwhelming now, but I did not allow it to keep me from running at them as fast as I could. The lizards roared and screeched and the closer I got, the more detail I saw on their ugly, leathery faces and thin, twisting bodies. The combination of their stink and their ugliness was by itself almost enough to defeat me, though I persevered nonetheless.

Before we could collide, something small and shiny went sailing over mine head. It landed with a clatter on the floor between the lizards and I, and then rolled forward quickly, heading toward the incoming lizard creatures as though drawn toward them by some mystical power.

I skidded to a halt and watched, with great uncertainty and trepidation, as the object—which I could now see was a metal sphere of some sort, though I could not tell for sure what kind of sphere it was—rolled toward mine enemies. The lizard creatures stumbled over each other in an attempt to stop, but it was no use because the tiny sphere rolled in amongst them before they could come to a halt.

I did wonder what it would do before I heard Resita behind me shout, "Get these goggles on, quick!"

Before I could ask him what he meant, a pair of thick, heavy rubber goggles were pulled over mine eyes. The sudden appearance of these goggles took me by surprise, not helped by their surprising tightness, which made me feel as though mine skull was being crushed between the straps. And how dark did the goggles make mine vision! The hallway did look like midnight now, which made me wonder for a moment if Resita had cast some sort of spell on me to make my vision pitch-black.

Then one of Resita's claws gripped my hand, almost cutting into mine flesh, as he dragged me away from the lizard creatures, which were now hopping around the sphere and examining it as if it was some kind of amazing object they had never seen before. Did make me question their intelligence, for they seemed to have forgotten all about me now.

"Come on!" Resita said. I looked and saw that he wore goggles similar to mine, large, round, and darkened. "Before the bomb goes off!"

Despite Resita's rather thin body, he managed to drag me along behind him nonetheless. Though that was less due to his strength and more due to my own surprise, for I still did not know what was going on here.

However, I quickly regained mine senses and, shaking mine head, I said, "Hold on, fowl! What are ye doing? What did ye mean when ye said—"

Mine words were cut off when a loud popping noise—like a massive bag of popped corn going off—exploded in mine ears, followed by the shocked cries and screeches of the lizard creatures.

Then it was followed, not even one second later, by a massive burst of light that blinded me, a light which made even me cry out, even though it did not hurt. Yet I did not stop or slow down Resita; indeed, I actually picked up speed without urging, for the sudden light and sounds had startled me greatly, causing mine heart rate to increase beyond measure, for I did not wish to be consumed or harmed by the light.

Chapter Six

Thus, Resita and I dashed down the hallway, stumbling blindly through the light, whilst the lizard creatures roared and cried in agony and anger. 'Twas the most horrible sound I had ever heard from another living creature, for it sounded like they were being melted to death, or perhaps burning underneath a lamp hotter than the sun. Methinks I smelled their burning flesh, which was like roasted chicken, though it could just as easily have been mine flesh being broiled in the heat of the bomb.

I wanted to ask Resita what had happened, but we were both running as fast as we could and I had no breath with which to utter even one word. I merely ran, ran and ran and ran, until Resita shouted, "We're almost there!"

There? Where was there? I could see naught in the bright light, which I now realized was not as bright as it could have been thanks to the goggles covering mine eyes. I had thought there was nothing down this way, Resita must have found some alternative escape route for us.

Without warning, Resita turned to the right, causing me to

nearly trip over myself as I turned to follow. Then I felt his claw let go of mine arm and heard him shout, "Jump forward, Apakerec!"

Whilst I still had no idea what was going on here, I obeyed his command anyway. I leaped forward, like I was diving into a pool, but rather than hit the floor as I thought, I found myself sliding down a chute that was shockingly dark after the brightness of the hallway.

Gah! How dark was this chute! How my stomach twisted and turned as we went down, down, down! The stench in this chute was like rat excrement and slime and icky slime clung to my body as I slid down after Resita. A muddy, slimy goop entered my mouth when I opened it to shout, causing me to hack and cough as we fell faster and faster down the chute.

Soon, I could no longer hear the frightened cries and growls of the lizard creatures. All that mine ears did hear was the rushing of the wind as Resita and I slid, plus the hideous squelching of goop under my sliding body.

Then a light appeared up ahead, though between mine darkened goggles and the slime that stuck to them, I almost did not recognize it at first. But soon it became obvious that that was to be our destination, though where this chute emptied out to, I knew not.

And then we shot out through the light into what felt like a disgusting swamp. Resita went out first, but I followed soon after, and crashed into him, sending us both tumbling through the stink and slime in a confused heap. How awful it was, tumbling like this! For mine hair and clothes became sticky with the goop and slime, and I could feel Resita's feathers getting all over me like parasites!

But then we slammed into something solid and hard, which not only stopped our progress (thank the Old Gods!) but also separated us. How, exactly, it did that, I did not understand, because the collision was so sudden, like a bee's sudden sting.

Yet the fact now was that I lay in the slop on my back, my whole body aching from the crash. The goggles had slipped on my face; my left eye saw a much darker world than mine right, though the right one was still adjusting to the sudden change in lighting.

"Ooooh," said Resita, who based on his moaning sounded as if he had broken every bone in his body. "You know, I don't think I will ever do that again."

I lifted mine head to get a better look at Resita. He lay flat on his back, just as I, though his legs were up in the air, as if he had fallen from the sky. His yellow feathers were now covered in a muck and goop that made mine stomach crawl, even though I was in no right mind to understand what that coating on him even was.

"What … did ye do … exactly?" I said. I spat out some of that foul tasting muck from mine mouth, banishing it like the toxin it was. "I do not understand what happened to us."

"Well, it was supposed to be … simple," said Resita, who sounded as if his vocal chords had been ripped from his throat. "That bomb I set off? It's what we Xeeonites call a blind bomb. As the name suggests, it blinds people by creating a ridiculously bright light. Some models make loud sounds, too, but most of them just do the light."

Panting, I said, "Ah, I see. 'Twas like a miniature sun had exploded in the middle of the room. How did we not go permanently blind?"

"The goggles," said Resita. He gestured with one chipped claw at his face and then at mine. "Why else do you think I put those goggles over your eyes? If I hadn't done that, both of us would have gone completely blind. It's one of the side effects of the blind bomb."

"What a gruesome thought," I said with a shudder. "But why did ye come back for me? I thought ye were going to hide and hope that the monsters did not find ye."

"That *was* the original plan," Resita admitted, his chest heaving up and down. "But I just couldn't stand the idea of letting you die. I mean, we don't know each other very well, but if you had died, I would have felt responsible for it."

"Ye speak kind words, Resita, but ye need not worry about I," I said. "'Twould not have been your responsibility if I had died, for I had made that choice on my own and would have been the one to live with the consequences."

"Technically, you would have *died* with the consequences of that decision," Resita remarked. "Anyway, that's not the whole reason I saved you. It's because I discovered another way out that didn't force us to fight two dozen of those monsters to escape."

"Indeed?" I said. "And what was that?"

Resita raised one feathery, muck-covered arm slowly and waved it around. "This is it."

For the first time since we had crashed into here, I looked around at mine surroundings. I normally did this as soon as I entered a new and unfamiliar area; however, my initial entrance had disoriented all of mine senses, though by now they had recovered and I could see where we were.

REUNIFICATION

Four tall, solid concrete walls surrounded us, like we had fallen into a large box. The walls were coated with more of that disgusting muck, layers so thick I would not even have known that the walls underneath were concrete if I had not observed the tops of the walls, which were not covered with the muck.

On each wall was a gaping chute, like the mouth of a dragon, from which the stinky, awful muck came. Not much was leaking out of these chutes, but I could tell that all of the collective gunk and slime down here had come from those chutes, for there was no other place all of this could have come from.

I sat up, raising my arms, from which the excrement and goop dripped. It was the most disgusting feeling in the two worlds, even worse than the time Sir Alart and I had gotten stuck in the swamps of the Lower Panhandle. How long this stink would last, I did not know, but I could foresee many months of hard scrubbing and bathing before I came close to being half as clean as I was before.

"What pit of disgusting grime is this?" I said, looking at Resita, who, like I, was also sitting up. "'Tis like a pigpen, except pigpens are infinitely cleaner than this."

"That's because this is ..." Resita looked like he was searching hard for the right words. "This is basically where we Foundation members toss all of our garbage and other, uh, unwanted things when we're done with them. A sort of garbage/sewer system hybrid, if you will."

Some blue candy wrapper, with Xeeonish words written on it, floated by me. A half-eaten chunk of meat stuck between two coarse-looking buns also stood out of the muck, making my stomach churn.

"Why in the names of the Old Gods would ye do this?" I asked. I felt hot vomit rise in my throat before I pushed it down. "This is horrifying. 'Tis like being condemned to an eternity in a baby's diaper."

"Hey, I hate this just as much as you do," said Resita, shaking his arms, though that appeared to do little to make him cleaner. "But it was either this or we get torn to shreds by those lizard creatures. I'd rather drink a gallon of sewer water than get ripped apart by those monsters."

"Speak for yourself, bird," I said, scowling and wrinkling my nose, which burned as hotly as if it had been set aflame. "At least if those lizards had gotten us, we would have gone down fighting. This is simply disgraceful. If Sir Alart or the rest of my fellow Knights knew of my current predicament—"

"Then don't tell them about it once we get out of here," said Resita. "But honestly, I can't believe this. Are you really saying you would have preferred to *die* than to get a little icky? If all of you Knights are like this, then I'm shocked you guys are still around."

"We Knights are not suicidal, if that is what ye are implying," I said. I peeled off some kind of fruit skin from my shirt and tossed it aside. "We simply understand that in some instances, it is much better to die than to suffer this kind of embarrassment. Though I wouldn't expect ye to understand; clearly, ye know nothing about the depths and dimensions of honor or the words of the Knight's Code."

"Guess I don't," said Resita, rolling his eyes. "Anyway, I think we're safe here. Those lizards back there are probably all blind as bats now, and even if they do figure out where we went, they

108

won't be able to follow us. None of them can fit in those chutes."

"That is good to know indeed," I said as I scraped off some of the thick muck on my arms. "Though if I may ask, why were these chutes designed to be large enough for us to slip through? Do ye Foundation people regularly slide down these chutes?"

"Ha, ha," said Resita. "Very funny. But no, I don't know for sure why these chutes are so big. I think it's supposed to make sure that the pipes don't get clogged with junk. Whatever the reason, I'd say it worked out quite well for us, wouldn't you say?"

"If by 'well' ye mean 'made us dirtier than the filthiest pirate on the Red Sea,' then yes, it did work very well for us," I said. I began to stand up to mine full height. "Anyway, I do not wish to stay in this place any longer. The stink is as awful as a thousand poisons and my tolerance for it is rapidly waning."

Resita, too, rose to his feet, though he did not look much the better for it, for his feathers were all messy and his clothes were covered in that gunk. "Yes, I agree. The sooner we get out of here, the sooner we can find a working shower. Or better yet, a full-body disinfectant system."

"A what?" I said.

"A full-body disinfectant system," Resita repeated. He looked at me with concern, like I was one of the slower folks who lived at the asylums back on Dela. "They're like showers, except that they use lasers to kill one hundred percent of germs on your body. Don't you have them on Dela?"

"Nay," I said, shaking mine head. "We allow the cool, clean and imminently natural water to cleanse us when we become dirty. Some wizards and witches will use magical spells, but I know of none that use lasers in the way ye describe."

"Well, that explains why you Delanians are always so dirty," Resita said with a huff. "You use outdated and inefficient ways to clean yourselves. But maybe one of these days, someone will figure out a way to convince your people to bath better."

"Only peasants are dirty," I said. I gestured at myself. "We Knights of Se-Dela are held to only the strictest of cleanly standards, for we serve King Waran-Una, who does not tolerate dirt in his presence. Every night, we scrub thoroughly until we are cleaner than the air of the Fertile Lands."

"Soap and water isn't as effective as lasers," Resita argued. Then he shook his head, causing a couple more feathers to fall out. "Never mind. We need to find a way out of here. After that, then we can find the field agents, maybe reunite with the Delanian branch, and ... I don't know what to do after that."

I raised an eyebrow. "What do ye mean, ye don't know what to do after that? Don't ye Foundation people have a plan in case of this sort of emergency?"

"If there *was* one, no one ever told me about it, since I was the janitor," Resita grumbled, shaking his hands to get the gunk off them.

"I wonder if Xacron-Ah is behind this," I said. I reached up to stroke my chin, but stopped because mine hand was still covered in this muck, so I lowered it back to my side. "Is this the sort of thing someone of his character would do?"

"Maybe? I don't know," said Resita, shrugging. "I've never met the man. Nor have I ever been given any orders to look into his past. From what I do know of him, though, I don't see how he could possibly be behind this, unless he just happens to have an army of lizard humanoids for the express purpose of killing his enemies."

"Perhaps he does," I said. "Though I will admit that I know of no such species like that on Dela. Perhaps there is such a people in the Underside, but I do not know for sure."

"We can worry about this later," said Resita. He coughed like he was dying of a terrible disease. "As I said, we need to find a way out of here. I've studied the blueprints of HQ, so I know that there is a drainage pipe around here somewhere. It should take us out of the city and into the Dead Lands."

I grimaced. "The Dead Lands? Is that where Xeeon's waste is dumped?"

"Yep," said Resita, nodding. "There's nothing out there, so it's not a big environmental issue or anything."

"But I have heard rumors of decadent mechanical monstrosities living out there," I said. "Such as the Destroyer, for example."

"We don't have to worry about that right now," said Resita in a dismissive voice. "Anyway, the drainage pipe will probably dump us in the middle of nowhere. But that's not a problem, because once we escape, it shouldn't be hard for us to contact the field agents or the Delanian branch and regroup."

"I shall defer to your expertise, for ye, as a Xeeonite, are far more knowledgeable about your world and your city than I am," I said. I looked around the four concrete walls around us. "Now, where is the exit?"

"It should be around here somewhere," said Resita as he began walking through the muck, his claws making squashing sounds as he did so. "It's covered under all of this crap. This place isn't very big, though, so it shouldn't take us very long to find it."

I did not wish to scurry about this place like a rat, but the only other alternative was to stay in this vile place and let the stink slowly suffocate me. I prayed to the Old Gods for strength and then began slogging through the excrement and garbage at my feet, feeling it get betwixt my toes. This must have been my punishment from the Old Gods for something wrong I had done recently; it had to be because I had mocked Sir Alart's mechanical eye behind his back that one time. This seemed like disproportionate retribution to me, but then I remembered the story of the Old Gods and the burning house and I decided that I had gotten off light (though I still made a note to apologize to Sir Alart the moment I got out of this vile pit).

"What may we be looking for, friend?" I said as I sloshed through the garbage. "I do not know what this exit would look or feel like."

"We're looking for a hatch," Resita said without looking at me, for his beady bird eyes were focused on the garbage at our feet. "The way this system is set up, there should be a hatch that opens occasionally when the dump gets full enough. It then transports the garbage and crap to a landfill in the Dead Lands, though it's not a landfill connected with the city, so we don't have to worry about Xacron-Ah or any of our other enemies meeting us on the other end."

Mine stomach churned at the thought of sliding down yet another pipe with this awful mixture coating its interior. 'Twas as appealing as rolling in the mud with a pig, though pigpens were far cleaner than this filth.

Then I felt a handle of some sort beneath the slop. It felt like a ring, round and metal, but even so, I could tell that it was likely the handle of the hatch that Resita had mentioned. What great luck, I thought, though I did not bend down to grab it, for that would have meant bringing mine face closer to the stinky mess covering my feet.

"Resita!" I called out, waving at him from where I stood. "I believe I have found the hatch of which ye spoke! 'Tis right here."

Resita made his way over to me with much sloshing and squelching, until he was right next to me. I kicked at the handle to indicate where it was before he could ask.

"That was fast," said Resita, though he did not sound at all disappointed with the speed at which I found it. "Well, what are we waiting for? Let's open it."

"We can just open it ourselves?" I said in disbelief. "I thought that ye Xeeonites had set it to open itself, perhaps through some technological sorcery of yours."

"Technological sorcery?" said Resita, repeating the phrase as if it were a foreign term. "What is—never mind. Anyway, ordinarily it is supposed to open on its own. But that doesn't mean it can't be opened manually as well. Why else do you think it has a hatch with a handle on it?"

I folded my arms over my chest and stepped back. "Well, I am certain ye can do it on your own, Resita. I will simply stand back and watch as ye do it and then follow once the drain is open."

"Me?" said Resita. He looked as mortified as if I had suggested that he climb Mount Karna without any ropes. "But I'm just a weak little janitor. That hatch is very heavy and, because you're a big brave Knight of Se-Dela, you could probably lift it far easier than me."

"How do ye know how heavy that hatch is if ye have never

113

opened it before?" I demanded. I pointed sharply at the muck around our feet. "'Tis no time for us to be arguing, anyway. The stink in here is starting to suffocate me, so we should not waste precious time arguing about who should open it and who shouldn't."

"I agree," said Resita. He stepped back and gestured at the spot where the hatch was. "You first, my friend. And no arguing; as you yourself said, we have no time for that kind of nonsense."

I gritted mine teeth. Xeeonites were always annoying to me, because they did this sort of trickery and deception whenever they thought they could get away with it. They may have been a technologically advanced people, but sometimes they were as sly as the cleverest thief. Such as now, with Resita catching me in mine own words like a trapper frog caught in its own trap.

Grudgingly, I nodded and said, "Very well, then. I shall do it, and I shall do it in such a way that not even the Old Gods will forget it."

So I stepped forward again and then bent over, reaching down toward the muck with my hands. Yet I hesitated when the tips of mine fingers were not more than an inch from the surface of the goop, as I did not wish to get myself any dirtier than I already was.

But 'twas only for a moment that I hesitated. In the next instant, I plunged my hands beneath the surface of the excrement and garbage and searched for the handle. Praise be to the Old Gods, for I found the handle after only a little searching and wrapped mine fingers around it easily.

Thus, I was fooled into believing that opening this hatch might not be as difficult a task as I once feared. I pulled hard, but the hatch did not budge. I pulled and heaved, putting all of mine strength into it, but the hatch still refused to budge, as if it were heavier than Castle Una itself.

But perhaps I could have opened it, if I had had any sort of footing. For the floor underneath the goop was slimy and slippery under mine bare feet, though there was naught I could do to improve that situation much.

After a few minutes of struggle, I let go and stood up. Mine back ached from having been bent over for as long as I had been, and my hands smelled as awful as if I had stuck them into a pile of cow manure. I looked at Resita, who still had his feathery arms over his chest, appearing more like a slave master disappointed by his slave's work than a friend.

"What?" said Resita, spreading his arms when he saw me looking at him. "Can't open it?"

"The hatch is quite heavy," I said, gesturing at the surface of the muck where the hatch was under. "I cannot find any footing in this place, nor can I get a good grip on it. Notwithstanding the muck itself, which I fear is adding too much weight onto it."

Resita sighed in exasperation. "Oh for the love of … never mind. Why don't we work together and see if we can lift it by combining our strength?"

"What is the heaviest thing ye have ever lifted?" I asked.

Resita looked at me as if I had asked him what color a square was. "What?"

"Ye heard me," I said, jerking mine thumb at my chest. "What is the heaviest thing ye have ever lifted?"

Resita folded his arms again and put a thoughtful look on his bird-like features, a look of contemplation on par with the look of a Sage considering the future. "Uh, I think that would be the collapsible work desk I bought for my home when I was a freelance reporter for the *Xeeon Daily*. Why?"

I had no idea what a 'collapsible desk' was, but it did not sound very heavy to me. Still, I asked, "How much did it weigh?"

"Probably a little more than ten pounds, though I don't remember because that was years ago and I sold it after I quit my job at the paper," said Resita. "Again, why?"

"A ten pound desk is hardly what I would call heavy," I said with a snort. "I doubt ye will be of much help in opening this hatch."

"So you just want to live in this stink pit for the rest of your livelong days?" said Resita. "Just because I'm not a bodybuilder like you?"

"I did not say that," I said, shaking mine head. "I was simply acknowledging the truth of the matter, which is that ye are clearly not a very strong individual."

"That's still not an excuse for not allowing me to help," said Resita. He flexed his feathered fingers. "Let's at least try before you write me off as a weak little bird."

I sighed a deep sigh, a profound sigh, for I knew what was destined to happen next. "Very well. Let us not dilly-dally, for I grow immensely sickened of this place by the second."

Thus, the two of us bent over and grabbed the handle with both of our hands. 'Twas somewhat difficult, no doubt due to the fact that the handle was not very large, but we managed to get our hands around it nonetheless. Resita's feathered fingers brushed against mine, which combined with the muck that we stood in, made me wish to lift this hatch as fast as we could.

"All right," said Resita. "On the count of three, we'll both pull up. Got it?"

"Understood," I said, though I tried to say it without opening my mouth widely, for I did not want to inhale the stink that rose from the filth we stood in.

"All right," said Resita, who looked as though he too was trying to avoid the stink just like me. "One … two … three!"

As soon as that word left his mouth, the two of us pulled up together. Again, I put all of mine strength into this effort, pulling as hard as I could, drawing on every ounce of strength I had in mine body. Based on the groans from Resita, I could tell that he also was using all of his strength to lift this hatch, which made me feel far less alone in this struggle than I thought I would.

We pulled and pulled and pulled, but the hatch did not budge no matter how hard we pulled. Mine feet began to slip, and I heard Resita's clawed toes scraping against the floor 'neath us, which told me that he, too, was beginning to slip. And still the damn hatch did not moved; 'twas as though it was glued to the floor.

My fingers began to ache, but I still did not let go. I redoubled my grip and repositioned my feet, though whether that would do any good I did not know. It was much harder to do than before, largely because of Resita's presence, for he stood quite close to me, giving me little room in which to maneuver and reposition myself. Still, I could tell that Resita was not going to give up, which made me think that what he lacked in physical strength, he made up for in mental strength and courage.

Even so, I was starting to lose hope. The burning desire to escape that had lit me up like an oven was slowly dying down as

117

it became clearer and clearer that we could not escape. I did not know whether Resita shared these feelings, but whether he did or did not, all I knew was that I must continue, for if I did not, then the filth would claim us forever.

Then, without warning, the hatch began to rise. My spirits rose with it, even though at first I was not certain if the hatch was indeed rising.

All of my doubts were swept away down the drain, however, with the filth, because I heard a sucking sound underneath the hatch. I felt the filth being sucked past my feet into the hatch, which Resita and I were still in the process of lifting.

Then a loud popping noise, like unplugging a drain, echoed off the concrete walls and the hatch flew open. Resita and I let go of it at the same time, while even more garbage and filth flowed past our feet like disgusting water in a river of sludge. Resita cried out—or perhaps chirped, for that's what it sounded like—in happiness at our success, while I praised the Old Gods, who must have granted me and Resita the extra strength we needed to open the hatch.

Indeed, I likely would have begun to sing a hymn of the Old Gods right there and then, if I had not noticed the exact size and width of the hatch. My stomach churned again, but this time, it was less due to the sludge and filth around us and more due to the sudden realization that had just dawned on me like the early morning light.

But I did not dare speak this realization aloud, at least not until the last of the filth and garbage had been sucked into the drain, which revealed one problem that neither of us had anticipated:

REUNIFICATION

The drain was too narrow for either of us to fit in.

Chapter Seven

The beautiful happiness that had filled my body was almost instantly replaced by sheer rage at our failure. I looked down at the narrow drain, unable to think clearly, wondering if this was all some cruel joke that the Old Gods were playing on us.

The entire waste chamber was empty of the filth and garbage now, save for a few spare empty food bags and some puddles here and there. Nonetheless, that stench—that awful, demonic stench that reminded me of a thousand tons of cow excrement piled on top of each other—remained, entering my nostrils and clouding mine thoughts.

I was so angry that I barely even paid attention to Resita. He had ceased chirping in delight; instead, he made choking sounds until he threw up onto the floor. Seeing him throw up—which he had no doubt been holding in—almost made me do the same, but I did not want to lose even that false South Delanian tea I had had earlier, so I held it in.

When Resita ceased hurling, he looked up, breathing hard, and wiped bits of barf off his beak. I saw no reason for that, as his arms were hardly much cleaner than his mouth, but I kept mine silence.

"God ... *damn it*," Resita hissed, his voice much hoarser now. "I forgot. While the other drains are big enough for people of our size to slide through, this drain *isn't*."

"How could ye have forgotten that?" I said, without any sympathy in mine voice. "Doth seem like a mighty large thing for ye to forget."

"Because it's been years since I last looked at the blueprints for this place," Resita snapped. "And the sludge hid it, so obviously I couldn't see it and figure out its actual size."

"I take it ye did not have a backup plan of any sort?" I asked, putting my hands on mine hips.

Resita's arms fell to his sides and he sat down on the slimy concrete floor, apparently not bothered by the puddle of sludge he sat in or his barf on the floor before him. "No, I don't."

Anger coursed through my veins as hotly as my own blood, but I tried to keep a calm head, for I knew that anger, when not righteous, could lead to darkness.

"What about the other drains?" I said, gesturing at the ones on the walls all around us. "Could we not climb back up one of them and escape this 'HQ,' as ye call it, that way?"

"Nope," said Resita, shaking his head, without looking away from the narrow drain that we had thought would be our smelly savior. "They have no ladders or footholds of any kind. Their surfaces are too slimy for us to gain any footing. Those drains were designed to get *rid* of things, not allow things to crawl *out* of them."

I rubbed my forehead, for my head was starting to hurt as I

considered all of the possibilities before us. Granted, there were very few that came to mind, but I believed that both of us were overlooking something, an escape route that was not obvious. I wished only that I could know what it was.

Then Resita looked up at me. His bird-like eyes were shining with hope, which made little sense to I, because I saw no hope in this situation whatsoever.

"Say, you're from Dela, right?" said Resita.

"Yes," I said, nodding. "Though I thought we had established that by now, my friend."

"I know that," said Resita, waving off mine sarcasm. "I just wanted to be sure. So does that mean you can use magic? I've heard that the Knights of Se-Dela can channel skyras energy, which is basically the same as magic on Dela, right?"

I sighed. These Xeeonites had such strange ideas about our 'magic,' as they called it. Granted, we Delanians also referred to it as such, but I did not much like the term, for it made the works of our Sages and wizards and witches sound trivial and childish, even though they were far from that.

I said none of that, however, as I was in no mood or condition to argue with this bird. Instead, I said, "No, I cannot use magic. Not every Delanian is a wizard, witch, or a wise Sage. Indeed, most Delanians cannot use magic; I mean to say, everyone could learn how to use it, but most do not."

"But that doesn't make any sense," Resita said, tilting his head to the side. "I remember reading an article on the Knights of Se-Dela about a month back. It said that you guys use skyras to cast magical spells and enhance your weapons."

I rubbed my forehead again. 'Twas hard for me to think

clearly down here, for the stink of the filth and garbage filled mine nostrils deeply, while Resita's silly questions and assumptions about us Knights of Se-Dela only added to the headache that was coming on.

Thus, I said, "That article was not entirely accurate. You see, we Knights of Se-Dela wear metalligick armor. Skyras energy is contained in and flows through the armor. Whilst we Knights can use the energy stored inside the armor to enhance our weapons and do things such as increase the temperature of our bodies, without our armor, we are utterly powerless."

"You mean, since you don't have your armor on right now, you can't use skyras magic at all?" said Resita. The hope was draining from his voice as quickly as the sludge had disappeared down that foul drain in the center of the chamber. "Not even a little?"

"I could not even light a candle with skyras, for I never bothered to learn the ways of magic," I admitted. "But even if I had mine armor, I am uncertain how useful it would be in this situation, as our metalligick armor was not designed to aid us in these kinds of situations."

"Damn it," said Resita, punching the concrete floor upon which he sat. "Here I was hoping that you would be able to use some of your magic to get us out of here."

"If I could, I would, without hesitation," I said. "But I cannot. It thus appears that we must rely on the grace of the Old Gods to save us."

With nothing else to do, I sat down on the floor next to Resita. 'Twas a disgusting thing, for the floor was covered in the filth and sludge from earlier, but I was getting tired of standing and wished to rest, at least for a while. There was little else I could do here besides that.

Resita was no longer looking at me. He was staring at the drain, as if it had once been his best friend, only to betray him when he least expected it. At least, I assumed that that was what he was thinking; 'twas hard to tell, for his bird-like features were still not very easy for me to read.

"The grace of the Old Gods," Resita suddenly repeated, in a mocking tone. "What the hell are the Old Gods, anyway? I've never heard of them before."

It took all of mine willpower not to grab Resita by the throat and throttle him like the chicken he was. Sadly, this was not something I had little practice dealing with, for the Old Gods were not very well respected even on Dela, when they were remembered at all, of course.

I rested my hands in my lap. "Not very surprising. Few people, even on Dela, know of the Old Gods ... and of those few, even fewer of them respect those deities."

"Why?" said Resita. "Were the Old Gods bad?"

"Nay," I said, shaking my head. "They were good, better than King Waran-Una at any rate. They once ruled all of Dela eons ago, having laid the foundations for that world at the beginning of time. Peace was associated with their reign, until Waran-Una came and ended all of that."

"But I thought Waran-Una always ruled Dela," said Resita. "That's what I was always told and what I've always believed."

"That does not make it any truer than it is," I replied. "For you see, King Waran-Una came from somewhere else. I do not know where, exactly, but I do know that he did not always live on Dela.

And when he did come to Dela, he clashed with the Old Gods over its leadership."

"Let me guess," said Resita, "he won, right?"

"Yes," said I with a sigh. "He defeated the Old Gods in combat and then banished them to the moon, where all of them sleep to this day."

Resita scratched the back of his head in puzzlement. "I don't understand. It sounds to me like you don't really like Waran-Una. If so, why do you work for him as a Knight of Se-Dela?"

"Because not all of us Delanians have rejected worship of the Old Gods," I said. "Waran-Una has banned worship of them in Se-Dela, as have the leaders of other Delanian countries, but that has not stopped a minority of us Delanians from continuing the worship practices of our ancestors in secret."

"You still didn't explain why you work for Waran-Una," Resita pointed out.

I put a hand over mine heart. "I work for him because I was offered knowledge of mine sister's whereabouts if I would become a Knight. And whilst I have never had much respect for the Knights of Se-Dela, I did not want to lose the best opportunity I had to find and reunite with my sister."

"So you did it for your sister, basically," said Resita. "You mean you aren't afraid that your Old Gods are angry at you for serving the being who defeated them?"

My hands balled into fists, but I kept mine anger from bubbling up. "Nay. My father told me stories about how understanding the Old Gods are of our particular circumstances; besides, my true allegiance is not with Waran-Una anyway. Should it ever become necessary, I will break away from the

Knights and never look back."

"Pragmatism, then," Resita said. "You do what you need to do in order to survive."

"I loathe that term, for it makes me sound like an unprincipled thief who would do anything to ensure his own survival," I said, "whereas that is not me at all. While I am no fan of the Knights of Se-Dela, I do recognize the good they do in the world, which appeals to my innate sense of justice."

"Yeah, yeah, whatever," said Resita. His head sank lower onto his chest. "I don't even know why we're talking about this. It's not like any of this stuff will help us get out of here."

"Perhaps not," I said. "But what else shall we do? For there is clearly no other way for us to escape this place. Talking takes the mind off our unpleasant situation."

"True, but sometimes it's necessary to focus on our 'unpleasant' situation, as you call it, if we're going to survive," said Resita. He gulped and gagged. "And the smell … it's the worst smell I've ever had the displeasure of smelling."

"Agreed," I said. I looked around the chamber again. "But there must be *some* way we can escape. After all, don't ye Foundation people have to come down here occasionally to ensure that nothing needs to be repaired or replaced?"

"We have robots for that," said Resita. "Very small ones, too, with cameras so they can take pictures and video. Then we send other robots down to fix any problems, such as cracks in the chutes or any chunks of crap clogging up the drain or whatever."

"Of course," I said, not hiding the disgust in mine voice. "Ye Xeeonites never do anything yourselves. All ye ever do is rely upon your automatons and your machines. Your hands are as soft as pudding."

"Is that supposed to be an insult?" said Resita with a snort. "And here I thought you Delanians were the people that the great poet Granga came from. Guess not all of you Delanians can be as creative with your words as he was, now can you?"

I sighed. "Let us not argue. I tire of it. It does nothing except make us more frustrated and angry."

"Then what do you suggest we do?" said Resita, throwing his hands into the air. "Simply sit here and hope that these 'Old Gods' you speak of wake up long enough to actually help us?"

"Nay," I said, shaking mine head. "The Old Gods could help us, but they can be capricious and choosy in how they distribute their aid. Therefore, we are on our own right now, which means we must rely on our own smarts to escape this bleak situation."

"That would be a bit more encouraging to me if you had any smarts to begin with," Resita said in a tone as sharp as a knife. "Remember how you tried to fight those monsters earlier? With only an energy knife?"

"'Twas better than fleeing like a frightened chick," I replied. "Or must I remind you just who it was that suggested we escape into this garbage pit in the first place?"

Resita folded his arms over his chest and looked away. "Why don't we change the subject to something more constructive? Like finding an escape route?"

"Oh, so now ye want to speak kindly and respectfully," I said. "How convenient."

Resita stood up and walked away, still without looking at me. "Shut up. I'm going to see if I can find a way out of here on my own. You can just sit there if you want."

"Or are you just trying to avoid facing your own hypocrisy, my friend?" I said. "Because that is what I sense from ye, which is typical of ye Xeeonites, for I have never heard a Xeeonite apologize for his failings before."

As I expected, Resita did not respond to that. Nor did I expect him to, much, for the current situation left me not wanting peace but conflict. Perhaps 'twas the stink of the concrete pit in which we were trapped, making me surly and unsociable, or perhaps it was just Resita's own bothersome attitude. In either case, I found I was more than happy for him to leave me alone for the moment.

I sat, therefore, with mine arms around my legs and my chin resting on my knees. I paid little attention to Resita's attempts to search for a route through which we could escape. Click, click, click went his clawed feet against the concrete floor, though I did not look over my shoulder to see him, for there was no need.

How awful a situation I found myself in. I had been in some narrow situations before—such as the time I was arrested by the Knights of Se-Dela when they attacked a Red Ring Smugglers' hideout—but never one quite as hopeless as this. After all, that arrest had led to me being offered a position in the Knights of Se-Dela, where I had some freedom in where I could go and what I could do.

Here, however, I could go nowhere and do nothing. The air was impossible to breathe due to the sheer stink that permeated every inch of this chamber. In my mind's eye, I saw myself slowly dying from the lack of fresh air and my corpse being buried by more of that excrement and garbage that had been thrown down here by the Foundation's members (even though I doubted this place would ever be used again, considering how those lizard creatures had apparently thoroughly rid this place of all Foundation agents).

I shuddered at the thought. Yet I knew not what I could do to avoid that fate, for it seemed as inevitable as the rising and setting of the sun each day. The Old Gods did not seem likely to save us, even though they were the only ones who could, at this point.

Indeed, perhaps we were not meant to survive at all. My father had always told me that, when a person is born, the Old Gods decide on that person's fate as soon as they leave the womb. Perhaps this was my fate all along: to die in this narrow, stinky pit of despair with a bird man who hated me. 'Twas certainly a harsh fate, but none of the Oracles ever said that every fate was to be sweet and light.

What made all of this even worse was that I knew I would never see my sister, Kiriah, again. She would not even know what happened to me. Perhaps a whisper in the wind might tell her that I came to Xeeon looking for her, only to vanish into nothing, but that seemed as likely as a dwarf becoming a master swimmer.

Just as I was about to give up all hope and simply lie there and wait for death to claim me, Resita suddenly chirped and said, "Apakerec, I found something."

I jumped to my feet and turned around without even thinking about it. "What did ye find, bird? The way out of here?"

Resita stood in front of the wall behind me, which looked as solid and thick as any barrier. But then I noticed that one of his hands had pushed in what looked like a portion of the wall into a niche that had not been there before.

"What is that?" I asked, walking over to Resita to get a better look at his discovery. "A secret button?"

"Looks like it," said Resita, his green eyes locked on the panel he pushed into the wall. "I didn't even know this existed. The blueprints never showed any secret passageway—"

Resita's words were interrupted by the sound of thick and heavy concrete scraping across the floor. The wall before us moved inward, then slid to the side, revealing a secret passage that was as dark as the moon on a shadowy night. 'Twas impossible to see beyond it; however, I did not sense any villainy or maliciousness waiting in the dark, so perhaps it was safe to enter.

"Walnak's luck is with us after all," I said in amazement. "Resita, I thank ye for finding this. I had thought we would never get out of here alive."

"But it doesn't make any sense," said Resita, who did not sound even half as joyous as I. He scratched the top of his head. "As I was saying, the blueprints for HQ do not show any sort of secret passageway down here at all. There's no reason for this."

"Perhaps it was added at a later date by someone else?" I inquired. "For I know that many old buildings have additions on them that were not part of the original design, which may be the case here."

"No way," said Resita, shaking his head. "I saw the blueprints. There is no room for a secret passageway down here, even for a very small one that you'd have to crawl through, much less one big enough for both of us to walk through upright. I have no idea where this could possibly lead."

"Maybe the original architect purposefully chose to omit this passageway from the blueprints, so no one could find it," I said, stroking my chin in interest. "'Tis a practice I have heard the wind whisper of, though I do not know for certain how common it is among Xeeonite architects."

"Possibly," said Resita. "But why would the original architect omit this passageway from the blueprints? What was he trying to hide?"

"How am I supposed to know?" I said with a shrug. "I barely understand the minds of Delanian architects; the minds of Xeeonite architects are a puzzle I do not wish to put together."

"Once we get out of here, I am going to find those blueprints and look at them again," said Resita. "Assuming, of course, that those lizard monsters didn't completely trash all of our computers, though I know we have several backup servers that hold that same information off-site."

"A goodly decision, I dare say," I said, nodding. "But enough talking. Let us enter this passageway and see where it leads us; at the very least, I doubt it will take us anywhere much worse than this gods-forsaken place."

And thus, we plunged into the darkness, though with our weapons out, in case we discovered something wicked lurking within.

Chapter Eight

Praise be to the Old Gods! This passageway—while hardly as fresh smelling as a field of strawberry flowers—did not smell nearly as raw and smelly as the disposal pit we had been in. It smelled old, however, as if it had not been exposed to fresh air in decades, but the air was much more breathable and not nearly as lethal as the stink—not air, for that was an insult to actual air—back in that pit. Of course, our own stink filled up the hall, but it was not quite as bad as the earlier chamber had been.

Yet, while this air was indeed far more breathable, the passageway itself was even narrower than that place. Not only that, but metal pipes ran along the walls and ceiling, pipes which appeared as though they had not been used in years. 'Twas hard to tell their exact age, however, because there was so little light to see by, and mine energy knife did not glow quite so much to let me see.

Though it mattered little to me how old this place was or who had built it. To I, this place was merely a possible path to freedom, perhaps even a path to my sister, who was still somewhere in Xeeon. Granted, once I left, I would probably need to return to Dela first and report back to Sir Lockfried, but I was already planning another trip back to Xeeon, even though I did not yet know when that trip would be.

Resita, on the other hand, was running his sticky, stinky fingers along the pipes, as if by feeling them they might reveal their secrets. He behaved much like a little child who is told that the Gift Man is not really real but was unsure whether to believe that or not, which somewhat concerned me, as I did not want him to be unaware of our environment in case this place turned out to be more dangerous than it appeared.

"This place ..." Resita sounded mystified. "I don't understand."

"What is there to understand?" I asked, annoyed by his confusion. "'Tis a mysterious passageway, true, but as it will likely lead us to freedom, I care not to uncover its secrets. Nor do I believe in questioning the luck of Walnak, not when it is so freely given like this."

"You don't find this strange at all?" said Resita. "I can't even tell what this place was supposed to be used for. It looks like a maintenance tunnel to me, but why is it abandoned and how come no one in the Foundation ever told me about it?"

"Perhaps no one ever knew about it," I said. "After all, if ye did not know of this place's existence, then I consider it likely that your allies did not, either."

"I guess so, but it just seems strange that no one discovered this before us," said Resita. "It's not like we don't explore HQ. We have security cameras and robots constantly combing the place at all times. Not to mention we handle any and all repairs ourselves;

while it would be nice to hire someone, that would compromise our secrecy, so we never do."

"I find it a pointless mystery to ponder right now," I said. "After all, how likely are we to run into someone who might know what this tunnel was originally built for? 'Tis better for us to keep walking until we find the end, which will hopefully be an exit that will take us outside of this infernal hole in the ground once and for all."

"I know, I know," said Resita, nodding. "But still, I don't like it. Walking into an unknown place like this … it doesn't feel right. Especially since I didn't even know this place existed until just now."

"If there are indeed any vile villains lurking in the dark, we shall be able to take care of them valiantly," I said, holding up mine energy knife. "They will not stand a chance against our righteous, combined might."

"Speak for yourself," said Resita. He patted the laser gun at his side. "I barely even know how to operate these damn things."

"Ye can learn, and quickly, I imagine," I said, "for urgency is often the mother of learning. 'Tis how I learned to communicate with mine elvish brothers in arms, though I admit to not being very fluent in Elvish Delan."

Resita did not answer that; perhaps he did not believe me. Or perhaps he was simply too distracted by this place and the questions it aroused in his mind to listen to what I said.

Either way, I kept mine eyes and ears as wide open as possible. I still did not sense any danger here, but I knew that sometimes danger could—and often did—appear when ye least expected it. I was determined not to be taken by surprise, especially when I was so certain that freedom was close at hand.

The tunnel turned to the left slightly, then inclined upwards. When it inclined, we were forced to walk up a small stairway, which felt rough and dirty under my bare feet, though considering I had just spent the last ten minutes standing in only the Old Gods knew what, it did not bother me much.

Of course, the stairs ended after only a few steps, at which point the tunnel leveled out again. Only this time, the ceiling was much lower, which was clearly an intentional part of the design. It was not low enough for me to scrape mine head against; however, it was low enough that I began to worry that we would be crushed under tons of rock, or whatever was above the ceiling, as I noticed cracks in the ceiling that made me nervous.

There was not much light in this place at all; indeed, the only light that we had was the glow of mine energy knife. The purple glow did not extend deeply into the shadows or show us much, however. Hence, 'twas like walking into the darkness, without any idea of what might lie ahead, only that it was likely dangerous.

We heard scurryings in the shadows, but it was impossible to tell what was making those noises. It might have been rats, or perhaps spiders, but we could not see them. I did consider asking Resita if he might know what they were, but every time I looked at the bird, I saw that he was clearly busily thinking about the strangeness of this place, and so I did not interrupt him. Instead, I focused on the path we traveled upon, in case any threats were lurking ahead, waiting to kill us when we least expected it.

But the longer we walked, the less likely it seemed to me that anything but rodents did make their home down here. No enemies or monsters came out of the dark; nothing to indicate that anyone besides ourselves had ever been down here. Indeed, I began to believe that this place perhaps had been designed by the Old Gods as a way to let us escape, so maybe I had not angered them after all.

Though I kept that particular opinion to mine self; Resita would likely ridicule me if I shared it aloud. After all, he clearly did not believe that the Old Gods existed, which was a shame, but not unexpected, considering how skeptical the Xeeonites were of religion and spirituality in general.

We kept walking until we reached what appeared to be a dead end. There was no way to keep walking here; nothing but a solid concrete wall in our way, like a mountain range separating two countries. Resita and I searched its surface, hoping to find another panel that would open to a secret passageway, but alas, we found no panels for us to push, nor any clues that might have hinted towards this wall being anything other than a simple wall.

"Great," said Resita, throwing his arms up. "Stuck again. Looks like I got my hopes up for nothing."

I said nothing, because I was busy feeling along the other walls for anything that might help us to escape. I doubted severely that this was a true dead end, because it made no sense for someone to go to the trouble of creating this tunnel only to make it impossible to leave. Therefore, there had to be another way out, even if it was not immediately obvious.

Then mine fingers wrapped around what felt like the bottoms rungs of a ladder. 'Twas too dark to tell for certain, of course, but that was what it felt like, so I grabbed the ladder as tightly as I could and pulled.

The ladder came down with a *clang* that echoed in the tunnel

The clanging made Resita cover his ears with his hands, though it was not very loud to me. Perhaps Resita's ears were simply more sensitive than mine.

"How did you find that?" Resita asked, lowering his hands now that the sound was no more loud.

"I felt for it, of course," I said. "Now, let us climb this ladder and see where it goes. It will probably take us to freedom; but if not, then at least to some place better than where we already are."

"You go first," said Resita, gesturing at the ladder. "If there's some kind of threat or enemy up there, you will be able to fight it better than me."

"Indeed I will," I said. "Once I scout what's ahead and confirm that it is safe to proceed, I shall call ye up after me."

"All right," said Resita. "Hope you catch a good updraft."

I stared at him in puzzlement. "What?"

"Oh," said Resita. "I forgot. You're not a Checrom, so obviously you wouldn't know. Well, that phrase is basically like saying 'good luck.'"

"Ah," I said, turning off my energy knife and putting it in the pocket of my pants. "Well, thank ye for the luck. I hope that I do indeed catch a good updraft, then, as well as continue to have the luck of Walnak upon me."

Thus, I began climbing the old ladder, which did feel strong enough to hold my weight. It creaked slightly under my weight, but it did not feel like it would break or drop; hence, I climbed upwards without fear.

It did not take me long to reach the top, where I discovered some kind of hatch—much bigger than the drain in the waste chamber—closed above mine head. I at first feared that the hatch might be locked, but when I pressed one hand against it, it lifted slightly, which renewed my courage once more.

But I did not push it up completely. I lifted the hatch carefully, for I did not know what lay on the other side. There might have been an enemy, perhaps one of Xacron-Ah's minions, watching this hatch, waiting to attack anyone or anything that came out of it. Perhaps even more of those lizard creatures, a thought which made me shudder.

Hence, I pushed it gradually, inch by inch. As I did so, tiny rays of light sneaked through the gap, an encouraging sight, for it meant that this hatch did indeed lead us outside. Praise be to the Old Gods!

'Twas not the light that most excited me, however, but the air. A clean air, better than the stink that had clung to mine skin like a parasite, entered my lungs. It was not as pure as Delanian air—the Xeeonites were polluters of the highest order, after all—but it was superior in every way to the air of the tunnel below, and then some.

Indeed, for a moment I almost allowed myself to be swept away by the air's cleanness, for it felt like it had been eons since I had last tasted pure air. But then I remembered mine mission and put aside my feelings of joy in order to focus on my current objective.

By now, I had lifted the hatch enough for me to see the outside environment. I peered through the crack, eager to see where this hatch led. I hoped it would be somewhere near Xeeon, because then I would be close enough not only to contact my fellow Knights, but also possibly run into Kiriah again. Maybe I would even see Xacron-Ah and teach him a lesson for attempting to murder a proud Knight of Se-Dela.

Sadly, however, what I saw was not the concrete pavements and massive skyscrapers of that city, but barren, rocky desert. I lifted the hatch a little higher in order to see my surroundings better.

Yes, I had indeed emerged in some kind of desert. I saw reddish sand, like it had been painted thus by an artist, and boulders of a similar hue wherever I looked. In the early morning sky above—for that was what the time seemed to be, based on the position of the sun, though I was no expert on Xeeonite time, so I did not know for certain—a dozen bat-like creatures soared in a circle, perhaps honing in on some poor creature that had been unlucky enough to end up out here.

With a grunt, I pushed the hatch all the way open. It fell backwards onto the sand with a *clang*, but I did not pay much attention to that, for I was now looking at mine environment even more closely than before.

What I discovered was that I had not ended up in a desert, not exactly. It appeared I had emerged onto what appeared to be a canyon of some sort, though knowing nothing about Xeeonite geography, I could not tell exactly where we were. Harsh, jagged scars ran along the reddish rock walls of the canyon, while some kind of whitish snake slithered only feet from the hatch (though thankfully it did not notice me; it was about six feet long, from what I could tell, and its fangs must have been three inches long).

No matter what direction I looked in, I did not see any sign of civilization. No skyscrapers, no loud, noisy hover vehicles, no roads, no law enforcement robots, no big telescreens of any sort, and most certainly no businesses or restaurants for me to patronize. Did appear that we were in the very middle of nowhere, a thought which hardly comforted me.

"Hey, Apakerec!" Resita's voice called from below. "What do you see? Where are we?"

I looked down into the dark hatch and yelled, "I know not where we have emerged, my friend! Does look like some kind of canyon, but which canyon, I do not—"

"Canyon?" repeated Resita's voice, rudely interrupting me before I could finish mine sentence. "What do the canyon walls look like?"

"They appear as if a giant knife had been run through them by a god," I reported, though not kindly, as I was still bothered by his rude tone. "Why? Do ye know this place?"

"Apakerec, get back down here *now*," Resita's voice boomed from below, so loud that I almost lost mine footing. "Quickly, before he gets you."

"He?" I repeated in annoyance. "Just who is this 'he' ye speak of? I see no 'he' around here, nor even a 'her' for that matter."

"I'll explain when you get back down," said Resita, whose voice now sounded as concerned as a mother hen's cluck for her chicks. "I know it probably doesn't look like he's there right now, but I promise you that if you stick around long enough, he'll—"

"Stop speaking in riddles, you cur," I shouted back, not bothering to be polite about it. "Until ye explain to me exactly what ye are so concerned about getting me, I will not go back down into that infernal, hateful—"

I ceased speaking when I heard something large crunching across the sand nearby. I nearly turned mine head to look, but then two thick metal fingers clamped around my head and lifted me out of the open hatch before I could so much as scream.

I kicked and punched, but my hands and feet only flailed about uselessly in the air. I heard Resita crying out my name in the hatch, but then a metallic tentacle slammed the hatch shut, immediately cutting off Resita's cries.

"There, there," said a deep, mechanical voice behind me, a voice so cold that it made me freeze in terror. "You don't need your little friend, not when you have me."

The fingers rotated, turning me around until I was facing the speaker of the voice. I knew not what to expect, but whatever expectations I may have had in my mind, they were utterly shattered by what I saw in front of me.

'Twas a robot; that much was certain, for its entire form was covered in unnatural metal skin. But it was not a clean, well-kept robot, like the kind I had seen back in Xeeon. Sand crusted its metal plating, and where sand did not reign, there was instead rust. The machine appeared to have been out in the wilderness for its whole life, as if no one had taken care of it.

Yet that was the least disturbing thing about its appearance. It had twin green eyes—optics, I believe the term was, though I knew little about proper robot terminology—perched atop a head that was almost entirely sharp, jagged teeth that looked like actual teeth. Its arms were thick and long, though instead of having a left hand, it had a tentacle, that same tentacle that I had seen close the hatch.

This thing was far taller than any robot I had seen. Whereas most Xeeonite robots were roughly as tall as a full-grown human, this thing had to be at least twice as tall as I, if not taller. 'Twas so tall that I feared that I would suffer great pain if it decided to drop me onto the sand below.

Perhaps most disturbing and disquieting of all was the intelligence in its eyes, intelligence I had never witnessed in the eyes of any machine before. 'Twas not the cold artificiality of a robot, but the thinking natural warmth of a living being. How that made any sense, I knew not, but I was too terrified to even think about it.

"What's this, what's this, what's this," said the machine, grinding, mechanical noises punctuating its words. "A human, I see, but not a mere human, oh no. A Delanian human. Hmm, I have not seen many of your kind around here before, but it doesn't matter. I wonder how close you Delanian humans are, biologically-speaking, to Xeeonite humans? It would be interesting to find out."

Its question did seem nonsensical to I, but I did not answer it. Instead, I drew mine energy knife from my hilt, activated the blade, which roared to life, and slashed at the machine's hand.

The energy knife slashed through the machine's metal wrist like a knife through butter. More mechanical noises followed, and then its grip on my head loosened and I fell to the sand below.

I landed on my feet and rolled forward betwixt and underneath the mechanical monstrosity's legs. Jumping to mine feet, I turned around just as the machine whirled around to face me, its tentacle whirling through the air like the sling of a child. Its arm, the one I had injured, sparked where mine knife had cut into it, but that did not seem to slow it down at all.

"That hurt," said the machine, though its voice hardly sounded bothered by that. "Why did you hurt me? What did I do to you?"

"Threaten to dissect me like a frog," I replied, walking

backwards out of its reach, "which I am clearly not."

"Why should I not dissect you?" asked the machine, this time sounding quite genuine in its question. "How else am I supposed to learn if you are similar to the Xeeonite humans that hate me so?"

"I know not the answer to that question, clicker," I said, "except perhaps that ye would do better to find a book on the subject, with pictures, than to do it yourself."

The machine's eyes started blinking rapidly, a sign I did not understand, and then it growled. "Then I will rip you apart piece by piece, you stupid organic!"

Its tentacle launched toward me with the speed of a rattlesnake. In alarm, I dodged the attack, jumping to the side out of its path, but then the tentacle twisted in midair and slapped me across the face.

Whilst the tentacle did not appear very strong or heavy, when it slammed into me, it was like being hit by a bag of bricks. The blow sent me staggering across the sand and I tripped over mine own bare feet, landing on my side onto the sand. Pain exploded in my side, which I realized was due to the hard rock I had fallen on, which explained the pain.

My head spun like the sun around Dela, but I had little time to focus on that, because I heard the machine coming at me. Shaking mine head, I looked up in time to see the machine almost upon me, swinging its tentacle over its head while growling terrible mechanical grunts that reminded me of a malfunctioning Diamusk vehicle engine.

I jumped back to my feet, despite mine aching and spinning head, and ran the other way. 'Twas no way I could defeat this villain on my own; after all, it was clearly no ordinary machine and I lacked my metalligick armor and sword to fight it with. It had bloodlust, and it would not be satisfied until it had torn me to shreds.

But mine attempt at fleeing was no use. I heard its tentacle whipping through the air behind me and then felt it wrapped around mine ankles, causing me to trip and fall face-first into the sand.

Some of that sand got into mine mouth, making me hack and cough, but I had no time to get it all out, for I was soon lifted off my feet until I was above the machine's open maw. Looking down, I saw, just beyond its front teeth, what appeared to be a series of saws, blades, and pistons in its mouth that looked more than enough to tear me apart.

I slashed at the tentacle with mine knife, but the energy blade did not so much as scratch the tentacle's surface. That perhaps was for the best, for if I had indeed succeeded in making the tentacle let me go, I would have fallen directly into the machine's mouth, where I surely would have died for certain.

Then again, it did not matter much whether I wounded it or not, for either way I would end up in its bowels. I knew not what the stomach of a clicker looked like, but I did not wish to find out.

Unfortunately, as I looked down into the gaping maw of the machine, I knew I had no chance at survival now. For its spinning saws, sharp teeth, and clashing, clanging blades came closer and closer to my face. And though I should have screamed, I did not, for I was too overcome by terror to do so.

Then, without warning, the machine's tentacle swayed, making me sway with it. Not only that, but the machine cried out, as if in pain, and threw me away.

My whole world spun several times before I landed hard on the sand several feet away. Thankfully, this time I did not fall on any rocks; however, the impact of the fall was indeed enough to knock me almost silly. Mine back and head ached, making me wish that I could just lie here and rest until I was better.

But alas, I had no time to do that, for that monstrous machine was still active. Therefore, I gathered all of my strength and willpower and sat up, rubbing my aching head as I did so.

I heard the machine roar again and looked over mine shoulder. The terrible clicker that had been about to devour me was now on its knees, its back sparking as if 'twas about to explode. I did not understand why that was until I heard a familiar voice call out, "Apakerec!"

I looked in the direction that that voice had came from. Resita was running toward me, his laser gun clasped between his talons, the hatch open behind him. I had almost forgotten about mine bird friend while I dealt with that machine; nonetheless, I was happy to see him just the same.

"Resita?" I asked as I got up to my feet, dusting off my clothes as I did so (though they still stunk as horribly as ever). "What are ye doing here? Are ye responsible for injuring that machine?"

"You mean the Destroyer?" said Resita, coming to a halt a few feet from me. He raised his laser gun as if it was the most important item in the world. "Yes. I used my laser gun here to shoot it. My aim isn't all that great, but I think I must have hit something vital, based on the way the Destroyer is acting."

"Indeed, ye did," I said, mine eyes wandering over to the

groaning machine, which sounded like 'twas dying, though I knew robots could not. "Shall we finish it?"

"No," said Resita, shaking his head fast. "I mean, I would like to, of course, but I don't think we can. That thing has survived way worse than a shot from a laser gun and we really don't have the kind of weaponry necessary to even think of killing it."

"Then let us flee," I said, "before it recovers."

Of course, I knew not which direction in which to run, for the canyon was as unfamiliar to me as Xeeon's winding streets. Resita did not seem any better informed, yet the Checrom janitor took off to the east, toward one of the canyon's exits. Not wanting to be stuck with this 'Destroyer,' as Resita had called it, I dashed after him, though I did mine best to keep an eye on the rocks in the sand to avoid cutting my feet open on any that peeked out.

Even as we ran, however, I could hear the Destroyer yelling at us to stop. 'Twas too bad for it, for neither of us even slowed down when it called for us; in fact, I believe we ran faster than ever, as though its words had had the exact opposite effect than it had intended for them to have on us.

Still, I looked over mine shoulder anyway, though it was just in time to see the Destroyer's legs vanish beneath the sand. Where it went, I did not know, but that mystery would be for later. For now, we had to run and find safety, if indeed such a thing existed in this desert.

Chapter Nine

Although I was more certain than ever at this point that the Destroyer would pop out of the sand and slay us before we got within one inch of the valley's exit, the machine did not appear anywhere near us. Indeed, I almost fancied that it had simply vanished into the sand, never to return, although I knew that that was a silly thought for certain.

Resita and I climbed up the sloping valley exit, which 'twas a difficult feat, for the hot sand burned my feet and was unstable to walk upon. Nor was this trek made any easier by the rocks that sprouted out of the sand here and there, sharp, jagged little things that reminded me more of knives than stone. I stepped on more than a few on our way up, which sent sharp pains through my feet, but I was in such a hurry to get out of that valley that I did not mind it too much.

Eventually, Resita and I emerged from the valley into what appeared to be a vast, rocky wasteland for as far as the eye could see. And indeed, mine eye could see far, for my eyesight was clear and allowed me to see rock spires, boulders, and grottos and cave openings wherever I looked.

Again, neither of us knew with any certainty where we should go, but Resita continued running to the east and I followed. I noticed that Resita was heading toward what appeared to be a cavernous hole in the ground, though I did not know for certain what lay in that hole. It was likely better than that Destroyer from before, but I did slow down when I saw where we were going, for I still did not know what lay hidden within there, perhaps waiting to kill us.

Resita entered the hole first. I followed soon enough, for I did not hear him cry out in pain, which led me to assume that that place was indeed much safer than it appeared. At least, I thought that until a large, brown snake slithered out as soon as Resita entered, causing me to jump, but the snake merely slithered past me without a second look, as if it saw barefoot, stinky humans every day.

Once the snake was gone, I then entered the hole, which was much smaller than it first appeared. The ceiling was low overhead, forcing me to squat and bend over, and the cave smelled like blood and dead animals, perhaps the remains of whatever that snake had been eating earlier.

Nonetheless, I discovered that there was indeed room for both of us. A trail of Resita's feathers—which must have fallen off him in his attempt to escape the Destroyer—showed me that Resita sat near the back, forcing me to sit closer to the entrance, but 'twas fine by me, for it afforded me a goodly view of the outside so that if some beast or machine tried to sneak up on us, I would indeed see it.

Panting, I rubbed the bottom of my feet, for they burned from the hot sand and hurt from the sharp rocks I had stepped on. I had drawn no blood, thank the Old Gods, but that did not mean that mine feet were in perfect condition.

"That … was … close," said Resita, shuddering as he drew his legs up to his chest. "If I hadn't gotten that lucky shot in, both of us would have died for sure. And hey, maybe we still will anyway, since I doubt it will be very hard for the Destroyer to track us down."

"You have much to explain, my birdie friend," I said, wincing at the pain I felt in my feet. I nodded my head at the entrance to our cave. "Was *that* the Destroyer of legend I have heard so much about?"

"Unfortunately, yes," said Resita. "We Xeeonians, though, don't think of it as a legend so much as a natural disaster."

"What be natural about a machine that looks exceedingly *un*natural?" I asked. I glanced outside, but saw no sign of that mechanical monstrosity.

"It's a metaphor," said Resita. "See, the Destroyer—which was originally called 'Helper' by its creators and only got its current nickname later—was an attempt by Annulus Robotics, Inc. to create a brand new type of robot that could be used by militaries in both Xeeo and Dela to aid soldiers in war."

I frowned. "How so?"

"Well, say some soldiers are penned underneath a crashed vehicle or were caught under the debris of a destroyed building," Resita said. "The Destroyer was supposed to go in and get them out safely. It was given a brand new artificial intelligence chip called the Module that would make it smarter even than the J series of robots."

"If it is supposed to be so smart, then why did it try to kill us?" I asked. "Do we resemble enemy soldiers to it?"

"And there is the problem," said Resita with a sigh. "On its first day of testing about six years ago, something went wrong with the Destroyer's circuitry. It was supposed to be controlled via a remote, but it somehow broke free of its creators' control, killed the people who were testing it, and then ran into the Dead Lands, where it has lived for the past half decade killing anyone or anything that it comes across."

"What a peculiar story," I said as I ceased rubbing mine feet, for they no longer hurt quite as much as before. "How come ye Xeeonites have done nothing to stop it?"

"The Xeeonian government has tried to stop it several times over the years," said Resita, who sounded offended by mine words. "It's just that Destroyer is, well, smarter than even most organic beings. They've worked with Annulus Robotics to figure out how to exploit its weaknesses, but every attempt to take it down has utterly failed. That's part of the reason why the government has made it illegal for anyone to enter the Dead Lands; they don't want the Destroyer to kill any innocents."

"What a savage creature," I said. I looked out the hole again, but still saw no sign of it or any other threat to our safety. "You mean to say that it has been wandering out in the Dead Lands for six years, yet it has never broken down? I thought all machines broke down if no one took good care of them."

"That's another problem," Resita said, nodding. "The Destroyer is technically a prototype of the final product, which means that it's made out of inferior materials, but the fact is that it has shown no sign at all of falling apart or breaking down. Now it might just be taking really good care of itself, but where it could possibly get the parts to repair itself, no one knows."

"How come ye did not mention this to me before?" I said, placing the bottom of my feet gently on the stone ground under us. "'Tis seems like important information to me."

"I didn't think we'd ever run into the Destroyer," said Resita with a shrug. "That's why. Besides, the Destroyer usually stays away from Xeeon and other cities along the Dead Lands border, so it's not much of a threat even when you're not in HQ."

"Then why is the Destroyer considered such a terrible threat?" I asked. "Ye don't sound much happy about the fact that it leaves most cities alone."

"Note that I said 'usually,'" said Resita, putting strong emphasis on that word, like a wizard speaking an incantation. "Sometimes, it does attack people completely unprovoked. Nothing major. Usually it will sneak across the border and destroy some vehicles or buildings before the law enforcers arrive and drive it off. We don't know why it does that. My personal theory is that it's because it thinks of the Dead Lands as its territory and it doesn't want any of us intruding on it, but that's just my speculation."

"Are we, then, in the Dead Lands?" I asked. Sweat began to moisten my brow due to the heat from the outside.

"Yes," said Resita. "I thought you had figured that out already."

"But this makes no sense," I said. I gestured outside. "I thought your headquarters were located underneath Xeeon. How, then, did we end up out here?"

"As I said, Xeeon is located on the edge of the Dead Lands," said Resita. He lifted his wrist, but then lowered it and sighed. "I forgot. I lost my wrist-mounted holographic projector back in the chaos of the initial explosion, so I can't show you what I'm talking about. But anyway, the Foundation's waste system opens up into the Dead Lands, which is how we got out here."

"I see," I said, stroking mine chin. "How far are we from Xeeon? Do ye know?"

"No, I don't," said Resita, shaking his head. "I doubt we're that far away, as I don't think that that secret passageway was that long, but it's not like we can just stroll up to Xeeon's border, either. But again, I don't know."

"Doth ye have any way of knowing?" I asked. "Do ye have some kind of locator device, perhaps implanted under your skin, that could point us to the way back to civilization?"

"Wish I did," said Resita, looking down at his clawed feet. "But I don't. I'm not like most people on Xeeo. I don't have a whole lot of robotic implants or mechanical add-ons, so I usually have to make do with exterior devices."

"How curious," I said. "I thought all Xeeonites had marred their natural bodies with your abominable technology. Indeed, I even thought it must have been the law of your world that mandated it."

"There aren't any laws that say you have to have robotic implants if you don't want any," said Resita. He sounded as though that were the silliest thing anyone could say. "It's just that most people do because it makes life easier for them. I'm what you'd call an untouched, though that's the kindest term to describe someone like me."

"I take it that your kind are not very common among the

Xeeonite general population?" I asked, shifting my legs so that they would not fall asleep from lack of movement on my part.

"The untouched are a very tiny percentage of the planet's population," said Resita. He began to trace a circle on the floor with one of his feathery fingers. "Especially among my people. Studies say that most Checrom have at least a dozen implants, though that's on the conservative side. My older brother, for example, replaced his old beak with a new metal one that he says is stronger, but I don't know."

"I find these implants and 'add-ons,' as ye call them, disgusting and unnatural," I said with a shudder. "Back on Dela, we do not mess with our bodies like that. Most Delanians die with the body that they are born with. Even many wizards and witches do not alter their bodies for any purpose, save for a few."

Resita looked up at me, an annoyed look on his face. "Hey, just because I'm an untouched, doesn't mean I think implants and add-ons are useless or immoral or whatever you Delanians call it. I just happen to think I don't need any. That's all."

I bit my lower lip. Seemed that I had misunderstood his words. I had thought that Resita might be as against implants as I was; however, it was obvious that he was not. Though when I thought about it, I found no surprise, for Resita had shown no real animosity towards this common Xeeonite practice aside from his own personal preferences.

Nonetheless, I did not apologize. I simply said, "Well, it sounds to me as if ye must face much pressure from your friends for your decision."

"I do," Resita admitted. "Or did, anyway, before those lizard creatures killed off the other Foundation members. My older brother used to randomly subscribe me to magazines like *Implants Weekly* and *Add-ons Monthly* just to trick me into wanting to get some, but they've still never tempted me much."

"Why do ye not want them?" I asked. "After all, is it not a custom on Xeeo for all people to use mechanical implants on their bodies?"

"I just don't want anyone messing with my body," said Resita with a shudder. "You usually need to go to a trained mechanic or surgeon, depending on what it is you need done, to get the implants put in correctly. Then you have to do routine maintenace to make sure that they don't fall apart or break or glitch in some way. Basically, it's just too much work."

"It certainly sounds like it," I said, nodding. I looked out the cavern entrance again, just to be certain that the Destroyer was nowhere nearby, and I was glad to see that he was not. "Well, what should our next course of action be, Resita? I ask ye because ye know the Dead Lands better than I."

"We should find out how far away we are from Xeeon, and what direction that city is in," Resita said, gesturing toward the cave mouth. "Then we head in that direction until we reach the city."

I frowned. "And what do we do if the Destroyer attacks us?"

Resita looked down at his feet. "Hope he doesn't."

I waited, thinking that perhaps this was a strange Xeeonite joke I did not understand, but Resita's expression remained serious and he did not amend his suggestion with a laugh. Did disturb me for a moment before I remembered that neither of us stood much of a chance against the Destroyer in the first place; therefore, Resita spoke only the truth, as grim as that truth was.

"But first," said Resita, as he leaned back against the cave wall and yawned, "we sleep. After everything we've been through, I am just about ready to fall down and call it a night. How do you feel?"

I was about to say that I felt like I could stay up all day, but then a sudden drowsiness fell over me like a curtain, and I yawned. "Aye, I am also tired and sleepy. Perhaps I will take a nap as well."

"All right," said Resita. He glanced out the cavern mouth. "I just hope that the Destroyer doesn't get us while we sleep."

"There is not much we can do about it, should that monster attempt to kill us while we rest," I said. "Therefore, it would be best for us not to worry deeply about it, for worry is the killer of sleep."

"You're right," said Resita, nodding. He put his feathered hands behind his head and closed his eyes and in a moment, was fast asleep, his chest heaving up and down with every snore from his beak.

As for me, I lay down on my side as best as I could, for I did not think I could sleep sitting up. I folded my hands under my head as a pillow, and not a very comfortable one, either, but better than the hard ground or the rocks in the desert at any rate.

Before I drifted off into dream land, however, I prayed to the Old Gods once more for protection while we slept. It seemed unlikely that the Old Gods heard any of my prayers, for they had no power in Xeeo, but I did it anyway, for prayer had been a regular part of my before bed routine ever since I was a little boy.

Yet though I prayed for safety and protection, I kept mine energy knife near my hands, so that I could instantly grab it, if necessary.

I must have been far more tired than I thought, for when I awoke, the sun in the sky outside of the cave mouth had crossed much of the heavens, which meant it must have been the afternoon, though I knew not for certain whether that was so, for mine internal clock was still not quite adjusted to Xeeon Standard Time yet.

But, praise be to the Old Gods, I was still alive. I saw no sign of the Destroyer anywhere, which made me relieved. I wondered if perhaps the Old Gods had indeed protected us ... or if, perhaps, the Destroyer had simply decided that we were not worth killing.

In any case, my legs felt cramped, for I had pulled them up to my chest while I slept to give Resita more room in which to rest. 'Twas not much of a problem, however, because I knew I would get the cramps out of them soon enough, once we both got up and started our journey back to Xeeon, wherever that city was.

My stomach rumbled, causing me to grab it. I had forgotten that it had been at least a day—perhaps longer—since I had had a decent meal. The only thing I could remember having since arriving in Xeeo was that cup of that so-called 'genuine' South Delanian tea I had drunk at that cafe in Xeeon. The thought of that disgusting concoction made my stomach twist; nonetheless, the hunger within me was as real as the cramped-ness in my legs.

And my mouth was as dry as the Dead Lands themselves. Thus, I needed water as well, but I did not know if there was any water or food around here. Of course, I did not need water purely to quench my thirst; my mouth burned with the stink of the waste from the Foundation's HQ, a stink that could only be cleaned out by the purest of water.

Thinking of that stink made me aware of the awful smell my own body gave off. 'Twas not as strong as it had been before; however, I could still smell the rat excrement and slime from before. That gave me yet another reason to find water, though I wondered if there was pure enough water in Xeeo that could wash away this filth or if I would smell this awful for the rest of my life.

But now 'twas not the time to be lying on the floor of this place, thinking about mine problems. Now was the time to rise, rise to my feet I say, and set forth out into the Dead Lands and hopefully to civilization itself.

Hence, I stretched my legs and yawned widely. 'Twould take me a minute or two to get all of the kinks out of my legs, but that was no matter, for I had plenty of time in which to do it.

As I stretched my legs, I looked over at where Resita had been resting earlier. I intended to see if he was awake, but to my shock, I saw not one sign of my feathery friend anywhere. Well, that was not entirely true, for I did spot a few of his sludge-covered feathers on the ground, but aside from that, there was no other clue as to his whereabouts.

Worried, I sat up without thinking about the cramps in my legs and looked around the tiny cave. 'Twas pcrhaps a useless gesture, for the cave was not very deep or large, but I searched for him anyway just to be certain.

"Resita?" I said, though I did not raise mine voice very high. "Resita? Are ye there? Resita, where are ye?"

No answer came from anywhere at that moment. There was a slight breeze blowing outside, but that only made me feel lonelier than ever. Clearly, then, Resita had gone missing, but whether he had been kidnapped or not, I could not say.

My first instinct was to get up and begin searching the area for Resita. He was my only ally in this strange and hostile world, after all. I did not feel safe traveling the Dead Lands without his guidance, even though he himself was not a very strong or powerful fighter. After all, I knew even less about the Dead Lands than he. I had no idea how to navigate it or find out how far I was from Xeeon.

But I did not get up right away. For I remembered, in my training as a Knight of Se-Dela, a lesson that Sir Lockfried had taught me when I first joined the Order a year past. It was a lesson I had not thought on in a while, but remember it I did, for it now seemed relevant to my current situation.

Sir Lockfried had taught me once what I had to do when I found myself alone in the middle of the wilderness like this and my only ally had gone missing. He had said that I should first examine what clues or evidence that had been left behind before I acted rashly, for if I did not, then I was in danger of running into more danger than I was able to deal with. 'Twas not bad advice, though not advice I had ever thought would be relevant to any situation I found myself in.

So I crawled across the floor toward Resita's feathers, even though they were as awful-smelling and hideous as a dead skunk. Though that matter little to me; after all, I did not smell much better and my clothes—which had since dried out after being out of that waste dump for so many hours—stuck to mine skin in a way that was exceedingly uncomfortable, though I tried to ignore it for now.

Then I noticed a trail of Resita's feathers that led from the spot where he had been resting out toward the cavern's exit. Then, a little outside the cave, I saw the trail of feathers turn to the right and vanish from my view.

Odd. It appeared as though Resita had simply walked away, for I did not see any signs of a struggle. Perhaps there was nothing nefarious about this situation; perhaps Resita had simply gone out to relieve himself, or perhaps he was searching for any sign of the Destroyer or trying to determine how far we were from Xeeon.

Yet why would he leave a trail of feathers behind him like that, if indeed nothing nefarious had happened to him? There was something about this situation that left me deeply unsettled, for I knew that Resita would have told me if he was going anywhere. After all, the Dead Lands were too dangerous for someone to go wandering about on their own without telling their own ally of where they went.

Therefore, I had to assume that Resita must have been captured by something, though by what, I did not know. Nor did I know why this thing had apparently left me alone; maybe it was some creature that liked to prey on Checrom and had no taste for humans.

I thought it queer how I had not heard Resita's struggle against whatever had taken him. This cave was small, and it seemed unlikely to me that Resita had gone without a fight. He may have been a scrawny chick, incapable of doing much harm to anyone, but I could tell he had a fighting spirit that would not allow anything, even a terrible monster from the Dead Lands, to take him out without a lot of pecking and scratching.

Whatever had taken my friend, then, must have gotten him while he slept. Or somehow made him walk out of the place silently. In any event, Resita was undoubtedly in trouble, which made it my job to rescue him.

I did a quick search of the cave for his laser gun, but I did not find it anywhere. That meant that Resita likely still had it on his being, though I doubted he could use it against whatever had taken him. Otherwise, I likely would have heard it been used by now, for most Xeeonite weapons were not very silent.

So, after making sure that my energy knife still worked, I crawled toward the cavern entrance. I followed the trail of feathers that Resita had clearly left behind, though I did not follow it quickly, for I did not want to be ambushed by any creatures that might have been waiting for me outside.

As it transpired, however, my caution was unfounded, for when I crawled out of the cave and stood up to my full height, I did not see any living being for as far as mine eye could see. I saw rock and sand, jagged cuts in the earth that were most likely caves like mine, rock pillars here and there, and much else besides, but no life.

I now understood why the Xeeonites referred to this part of their world as the Dead Lands. For it truly was a land of death; there was not even a scrub of vegetation to be seen anywhere. That worried me, for if there truly was no life here, then that meant there was no water, which meant my parched throat would only get drier and drier as time went on.

And the heat! Oh, by the Old Gods' thirty names, the heat! It had not seemed quite so hot earlier, when Resita and I had escaped the Destroyer, but now, the heat was nigh unbearable. It was oppressive, beating down on me as a butcher prepares his meat. The heat seemed to make my stink worse, for now I could smell it as freshly as ever, and it made me gag, which with my dried mouth was a horrible sensation.

My feet burned when they stepped out of the shade, forcing me to return them to the coolness of the shade quickly. I still had no shoes I could wear to help me cross the burning land; however, I could not simply stand here, either, for Resita needed my help, in addition to the heat of the sun being too hot for me to ignore.

Hence, I would simply have to bear it, like a true Knight of Se-Dela. That would not be very fun, perhaps, but when I considered that mine only two options were essentially to stand here and die or search for Resita and possibly live, I decided that the second option made more sense.

Besides, it wasn't as if I would be wandering around the Dead Lands with no sense of direction. The trail of Resita's feathers would guide me, for I could now see that it went all the way toward some nearby hills. It appeared to go beyond those hills, though to where I did not know; therefore, I decided to go check.

So I gathered my courage and resolve and walked out on the hot earth and in the burning sun. 'Twas difficult, for without any water to drink, my parched mouth became even harder to ignore than before, and of course, mine feet kept burning on the hot ground.

Nonetheless, I did not yield to my pain. I followed the trail of feathers without trouble, though I had to avoid the rocks on the ground, for they were still sharp enough to cut me if I was not careful. That slowed mine progress somewhat, but not significantly, for I did not know how much time I had left in which to save Resita.

As I had observed before, the feather trail led to a group of hills several dozen feet from my cave. I did not recall seeing those hills yesterday; however, that was likely due to the fact that we had been in a hurry to escape the Destroyer, and therefore had had almost no time in which to observe our surroundings in detail.

These hills did not look like Delanian hills to I, however. They rose like the humps of omas, with sharp, tall rocks rising out of them. 'Twas an odd sight, for the hills appeared to have been tall rocks covered with dirt, though whether that was the case or not, I could not tell.

Aside from Resita's sludge-covered, stinky feathers, I saw no sign of anything that might have lurked in those hills. I did not hear anything, either, though when I thought about it, I realized that I did not hear any sounds in the Dead Lands, period, aside from the sounds of my footsteps against the sand and my own breathing.

And it was not a good silence, either, but a dead one, like the kind of silence ye find in a graveyard. 'Twould have made me shudder under normal circumstances, and indeed, I did feel a slight shiver run up mine spine, but I tried not to focus too deeply on it, for I did not want to allow my nerves to overwhelm my critical thinking skills.

Besides, slowing down would mean that my feet would have to rest on the hot sand a little while longer. That thought alone propelled me forward quickly, or as quickly as I could without stepping on any of the sharp rocks poking out of the ground, anyway.

Nonetheless, I drew my energy knife, putting my thumb on

the tab, ready to use it as soon as any hostile creature showed itself. Though if it turned out that the Destroyer was behind this—as unlikely as it seemed, for this did not seem like something that it would do—then it mattered very little what I did or did not have on me.

Still, my knife brought me safety and comfort. Not the same kind of safety as my Knight's sword, but safety and comfort nonetheless.

Soon, I reached the hills, which were as bunched together as items packed tightly in a shipping crate. Or so it felt, for there was not much room for me to navigate among them, and due to their height, I could not see as much as I would have liked, which left me open for an attack from whatever lurked within these hills.

Yet I did not think I would get attacked, even though I was in the perfect position to be assaulted without anyone else knowing. The hills were silent, devoid of the sounds of any creatures, but more than that, Resita's trail of feathers did not show any signs of a struggle having caused them, which made me suspicious of my previous theory that Resita had been taken away against his will.

But that was silly. Why would Resita willingly leave me alone? Whilst the two of us were not the best or closest or loyalest of friends, out here in the Dead Lands, we needed each other. We could not afford to go our separate ways, for if our chances of survival out here together were slim, then we were guaranteed to die if we separated.

'Twas a puzzling mystery, to be sure, one that left me more troubled than anything. Had Resita left me to die? It seemed a cruel thing to do, if indeed he had done it, but who ever said that the members of the Foundation were kind or loyal? Perhaps they were all secretly backstabbing traitors who abandoned their friends when the going got tough.

I wiped the sweat off my brow as I stepped over a rock in my path, mine eyes still fixated on the feathers before me. The heat must have been getting to me; why else would I be thinking such negative, unfounded thoughts about Resita? After all, they were nothing more than the basest speculation. There was likely a better reason for Resita's disappearance, some other explanation that would make sense of these strange happenings. I merely had to find out what it was.

The trail of feathers took me deeper and deeper into the hills of the Dead Lands, hills I had not even known existed until ten minutes ago. I had seen images of the Dead Lands before, heard descriptions of it, but none of the images I had seen nor descriptions I had heard of it had ever even hinted at the existence of these hills, causing me to wonder why that was. Perhaps there was still much about the Dead Lands that even the Xeeonites did not know.

It was hard to think deeply about this, however, because the heat continued to beat upon me heavily. My throat was as dry as the desert and my feet burned against the sand. How I wished for nothing more than a simple pair of shoes; not anything expensive or fancy. Just something I could wear to give comfort to my poor feet. And a cup of ice cold water as well, which was far more important than a pair of shoes, for certain.

Mine thoughts were interrupted when I heard a sound that I had not heard before. Before I even registered what this sound was, I stopped, for I was too amazed by the mere fact that I heard something other than mine own footsteps and breath to think much about what I heard. But I got over that quickly enough and listened closely so that I would better understand what it was.

The sound that played among the hills now was like a song, but not just any song. Nay, it was a low, mournful tune, played with what I could only assume were electric instruments, for I did not recognize the sounds from anywhere else. It reminded me of the music I had heard in the city parade earlier; whereas that had been loud and joyous, this was as sad as if someone of great importance had just died recently.

Indeed, 'twas so sad that I began to feel depressed as well, though I quickly dismissed the feelings as nothing more than distractions, for I still did not know for certain what was making that song or if it was in some way connected to Resita's disappearance.

From what I could tell, the song came from the hills to my right, which also happened to be the direction that Resita's feathers went in. But I did not hear Resita anywhere; all I heard was the mournful 'music,' if indeed ye could call that electric noise such.

I slowly advanced in that direction, thumbing the tab on my energy knife, ready to attack whatever was playing that music. I had no way of knowing for certain if the player of that music was a villain or not; however, considering this was the Dead Lands, I doubted the musician, whoever it was, was in any way kindly.

Then I peeked out from around one of the mounds and saw a scene I had not expected to see out here in this vast wasteland of death.

Resita sat cross-legged on the ground, his feathery hands on his knees, his back to me, listening to a strange-looking machine I had never seen before in my life. It was shaped like a box, square and squat, but it also had a couple of appendages arising from it, appendages that resembled speakers, from which the music seemed to be sounding.

Mine first thought was that this was some kind of robot, but that made no sense to me. For one, it resembled no robot I had ever heard of or seen, though perhaps that said little, for I was indeed not an expert in robots. Sir Alart would know, as he was much more interested in robots than I was, but Sir Alart was currently back on Dela, too far away from here for me to ask him even one question about this odd machine before me.

Perhaps it was an automaton. I had heard of such creatures, which were said to be somewhere between humans and the highest of artificial intelligences, such as the J series robots. Sir Alart had once told me about how many robots were in fact automatons, essentially very simple robots that were not quite as smart as many of the more advanced kind. Could that be what this thing was?

I did not know for certain. Whatever this thing was, I did not understand what it was doing out here or why Resita was apparently entranced by it. The way he looked at the machine reminded me of the way that men looked when put under the sway of enchantresses; indeed, I had a feeling that I could run up behind Resita and scream loud enough to be heard from Xeeon, and I would not disturb him from his trance even slightly.

I did not see what was so hypnotizing about this music. 'Twas like garbage in my ears, this 'music' was, and I was overcome with a righteous desire to smash that machine into pieces. Perhaps there was a less violent way of dealing with the music produced by that machine, but in this blasted landscape, I would take no chances, especially if this machine turned out to be a villain of some sort.

While its mournful, electronic noise blared from its speakers, I pressed the tab on the energy knife, causing the blade to flare to life. I did not know anything about this machine or how it worked; however, I did not need to know how it was put together in order to destroy it.

So I stepped out from behind the mound and, without waiting for even one moment, dashed at the machine, raising my energy knife as I did so. Resita did not appear to hear me coming, for he did not turn to look at me, but that was fine by me, for he would know soon enough what I was about to do.

The closer I got to the strange machine, the louder its music blared, but I did not stop or slow down. As soon as I was upon it, I slashed my knife at its speakers, its hot energy cutting through the appendages as easily as if they were made out of butter.

And how did they fly! And with what colorful sparks! The speakers flew off over my head, while the sparks from the sliced appendages shot out gold and yellow and red. One of the appendages shocked me in the arm, causing me to jump back, but 'twas only for a moment. The appendage fell to the sand, still sparking, but that was not the end of the spectacle.

For as soon as my knife had cut through the appendages, the music ceased playing abruptly, like a raven swallowed by a lion. But it was replaced, not by silence, but by loud sparking and hissing noises from within the strange machine. It sounded as if there was some overly large beast trapped within the machine trying to claw its way toward freedom, which made me retreat backwards in fear.

As I did so, I heard Resita groaning behind me and I looked over mine shoulder. Resita was shaking his head, rubbing his hands against his forehead, perhaps finally free of whatever terrible spell that that machine had cast upon him. That did fill my heart with joy and gladness, but that joy and gladness was interrupted by the sudden abrupt sounds still spluttering from the machine.

I still had no idea what was about to happen, but even I could tell that I must have done far more damage to the machine than I thought, for it was now vibrating as violently as if the Old Gods had caused a massive tremor to shake all of Xeeo. Something told me something deadly was about to occur and that I needed to get not only mine self, but also Resita, out of this place before it was too late.

So I turned and ran, grabbing Resita as I passed him. He smelled like sewage and waste left out in the sun, but he managed to get to his feet fast enough when I grabbed him and pulled him along. He still seemed confused, however, which made me wonder just what that thing had done to Resita to leave him like this.

But I spared no time wondering about that. I simply ran around the mound, dragging Resita along behind me, and as soon as we were behind it, a massive *boom*—like a thunderstorm on a dark stormy night—rattled my jaw and stung my ears.

The explosion 'twas so powerful that I fell down onto my hands and knees, pulling Resita with me. I covered my head, as did Resita, for I feared that the explosion would send all manner of debris flying our way, including mechanical parts that could impale our bodies.

And indeed, something black and smoking and metallic flew over the mound and landed on the ground directly in front of mine face. Though it was a small thing, not much bigger than my energy knife, it radiated enough heat to make me back up enough to avoid burning my face, though I dared not back up too much, for I could still hear the sounds of the exploding machine and I feared moving around might put me in the path of its flying parts.

But my fears turned out to be unnecessary, for in a short time the machine ceased exploding and no more bits and pieces of its fell from the sky. Keeping my hands over my head, however, I looked up carefully, just to be certain that we were all right, but it did turn out to be an unnecessary precaution, for the sky was as clear and warm as ever.

Hence, I took mine hands off my head and looked over my shoulder to ensure that Resita was all right. Though he had not yet removed his hands from his head, he did not look injured or hurt in any way. And for that, I was thankful, for I had worried that he might get injured by the machine's flying debris.

Nonetheless, I had to be certain, so I asked, "Resita, how do ye feel? Are ye all right?"

My throat and mouth were still quite dry, so my voice did not sound quite as strong as it normally did. Still, I managed to speak as clearly as I could given the circumstances, though whether he could even hear me at all 'twas doubtful, for that explosion had been loud and might have taken out his hearing for all I knew.

But then Resita looked up at me and nodded. "Yeah, Apakerec, I'm fine. It's just that my head hurts, like someone had taken a club and smacked it against my skull."

"Praise be to the Old Gods that we both made it out of that situation alive," I said with a sigh. I wiped the sweat off my brow and sat up, dusting off my chest as I did so. "That was indeed a dangerous situation we found ourselves in back there. I had not expected the machine to explode so violently, however."

Resita, too, was sitting up, a confused look on his bird-like features. I noticed now that he was missing far more feathers than he normally was, which made him look skinnier and weaker than ever. He appeared much like the abused chickens I had once seen back in my hometown when I was a child, which made me feel even sorrier for him than I normally did.

"But tell me," I said, turning so that I was facing him squarely. "Just what was that thing? Why did it play music? And how come ye were entranced by it? Is this some form of witchcraft that I must be aware of?"

Resita simply shook his head, however, as if I had just said the dumbest thing in the universe. "No. This wasn't witchcraft, but science."

"Science?" I repeated. "That still does not explain what that was, however. It bares no resemblance to any 'science' that I know of."

"No surprise there," said Resita, dusting off his body, for the sand had gotten all over his feathers when I had pulled him to the ground. "That kind of machine isn't exactly well-known among most Xeeonites, either, or at least anymore. Only reason I recognized it is because my father used to have one, so I got to know all about it because he'd always ramble on about it to me when he would—when I was a kid."

I caught Resita's stumble, even though he appeared to think

that I had not, if the way he looked at me was any clue. Nonetheless, I chose not to pursue the point any further, because I was not interested in what he meant to say. 'Twas too hot and tired to care about something that was not directly related to our dire situation.

"Then tell me," I said, feeling somewhat annoyed as I gestured at the mound, though I was really gesturing at the spot on the other side where the machine had been, "what that machine was."

"An old '94-B Player," said Resita. He frowned. "Oh, right. I forgot. You don't know much about Xeeonite music machines, do you?"

"I recall having seen some such machines when I came to Xeeon to see mine sister," I said. "And I have heard stories about them from my fellow Knights who have visited your world. But on Dela, we do not have any need of such atrocious machines, for we have musicians of all stripes who play our music for us when we need to."

"Right," said Resita. "Well, this particular machine is an older model. The '94-B was quite popular in its day. It was the most popular music machine in all of Xeeo for the longest time until Annulus Robotics came out with the Mechanical Musician model late last year, but it's still popular among the older crowd like my father."

"I see," I said. I glanced over my shoulder at the smoking bit of metal that had fallen in front of my face. "Then what was this machine doing all the way out here? And how did it hypnotize ye? Did these "94-B Players,' as ye call them, have the effect of hypnotizing whoever listened to them?"

"No," said Resita, shaking his head. "At least, I don't think so. My father says they have the best sound quality ever, but that doesn't mean they can actually hypnotize you. Not without special equipment, anyway."

"Then explain your story to me," I said, putting my hands in my lap. "When I awoke this morning, I discovered that ye were missing from our cave. I followed this trail of feathers—" and here I gestured at the feathers left behind by Resita, "—all the way up to here, but I do not know what happened before all of that."

Resita stretched his arms, though he looked a little ashamed, as if he was embarrassed by his actions. "I ... well, I got up before you because I wanted to scout the area quickly to find out where we were in relation to Xeeon. I planned to come back and wake you up as soon as I figured out where we were, but then I heard that music."

"The music played by the machine," I said. "The mournful electronic."

"That," said Resita. He shuddered. "It was just the most hypnotic tone I had ever heard in my life. It reminded me of my childhood for some reason, so I went and followed the noise until I found it here."

"Then it hypnotized ye," I said. "Correct?"

"Right," said Resita. "I don't know what happened. One minute, I was following the sound, and the next, I was sitting in front of it and it was exploding and you were pulling me away from it."

"How come I did not hear it until I got close?" I asked. "Furthermore, why was I not hypnotized like ye? Am I mentally stronger than ye?"

"I think it's because the music was designed to hypnotize Checrom like myself," said Resita, pointing at himself. "The tone, the way the music shifted and moved, all of it pointed toward a song that had been designed specifically to hypnotize my people. I'm surprised you could hear it at all. I thought for sure only I could hear it."

"What a strange device," I remarked. "But that does not explain what this machine was doing out here, nor why it was playing such music in the first place."

Resita rubbed his forehead, causing a few more feathers to fall off onto the sand under him. "Well, I have heard rumors that sometimes people drop off their old unwanted or broken devices out here in the Dead Lands. It's technically illegal—you're supposed to either recycle you broken or unwanted things or put it in with the rest of your trash—but it's a common enough occurrence that I wouldn't be surprised if that was where that '94-B Player came from."

"I find that highly convenient," I said, scratching my chin. "Though even if that is true, I do not understand why that machine exploded when I cut off its speakers."

"Well, that's because, as good as those old machines might have been in their day, it was discovered sometime after production that quite a few of the units were defective and prone to exploding if damaged," said Resita. "Most likely, whoever used to own that '94-B Player had tossed it out here when he found out that it was defective. Probably didn't want it exploding in his face."

"That is plausible enough, I suppose," I said as I rose to my feet, dusting off my clothes as I did so, "but this still fills my soul with dread and unease. I had thought that the only dangerous machine we would run into out here would be the Destroyer, yet ye say that there are more unwanted or broken machines here."

"Most likely," said Resita, nodding. "But don't worry. As long as we're careful—more careful than we already are—we should be fine."

"I hope so," I said. "Anyway, did ye find anything during your scouting of the area? Food and water, perhaps? Or maybe a good pair of shoes?"

Much to my disappointment, Resita shook his head. He then stood up, though as he did so, even more feathers fell from his body. I felt sorry about his appearance, for he now looked as ugly as a newborn chick, but I did not see anything I could do about it.

"No," said Resita with a sigh, dusting dirt off the front of his clothes. "I didn't find much of anything thanks to that music machine. I still have no idea how far we are from Xeeon."

"Damn it," I said, slamming mine fist against the mound. "I was hoping that something good might come out of this, but it appears that my hopes were dashed against the rocks."

"It's not an issue," said Resita. "We can still find our way back to Xeeon. We just need to be smart."

"Smart?" I said. "How so? We do not have a map of the Dead Lands, nor do we have any of that tracking tech that ye Xeeonites are so fond of using to find your way around. Do ye suggest we simply wander in circles until we find civilization?"

"Nope," said Resita. He looked around the mounds around us. "We need to find out which way is north. Xeeon is supposed to be north of the Dead Lands and the Foundation HQ; therefore, if we can find out which way is north, then we can also find out which way to go."

"'Tis that simple?" I said, putting my hands on my waist. "Why did ye not mention this to me before?"

"Because between the stress of everything that's happened within the last day or so, I really haven't been thinking as clearly as I normally do," Resita replied. "That's why."

"Well, then finding north ought to be easy," I said. I pointed up at the hot sun in the sky. "We need but only follow the trail of the sun. If the sun is heading west, then it will be easy to find which way north is. After all, the sun sets in the west."

"The sun doesn't set in the west," said Resita. He pointed to the right. "The sun sets in the east."

"What a peculiar statement," I said. "But a wrong one. The sun does indeed set in the west. I should know, for I have spent many days of my life watching the sun set in that direction."

"Wait," said Resita. "Do you mean that the sun sets west in Dela? Because that might be true there. Here, though, I know for a fact that the sun sets in the east."

"Yet another irregularity betwixt our worlds," I said, brushing my hair off my forehead. "How confusing this all gets sometimes. It makes me wonder how those who frequently travel betwixt our worlds ever keep anything straight."

"Who said that they did?" said Resita. "But anyway, your idea is still sound, even if the direction is wrong. It should be simple to find out what direction that the sun is going to—"

He ceased speaking so abruptly that at first I was certain that I must not have heard the rest of his sentence. Perhaps my ears had temporarily failed me or maybe I was not listening as closely as I ought to have; either way, 'twas my fault.

But something told me that I had not misheard anything he said. He looked as though he were listening to something, but what, I did not know. And I was afraid to ask, because I had a feeling that whatever he heard was not good.

"Do you hear that?" Resita asked, his voice so low I had to strain to hear him.

"Hear what?" I asked. I kept my own voice low, as something in his voice made me want to match his tone, though I don't think I spoke as low as he.

"Just listen," said Resita. "You might not be able to hear it right away, because … there it is."

And indeed, as soon as he said that, I heard it. It sounded like a couple of large men were walking nearby, though I could not see them no matter which direction I looked in. Their footsteps sounded close; based on what I could hear, it sounded as though they were making their way through the mounds around us.

Whether they were friends or foes I did not know. Nonetheless, I redoubled my grip on my energy knife and listened closely to their every movement. One of them had heavy footsteps, as if he was obese, while the other's was light and quick, like a fox.

"Oh, goddammit," said a voice on the other side of the mound, sounding so close that I almost jumped. "Look, Lauz, this must be what caused that explosion we heard."

"Aw," said another voice, this one dim and gruff, like a brute, and which must have belonged to this 'Lauz,' whoever he was. "And it was a '94-B Player, from what I can tell. My grandpa always used to play his whenever I was a kid. Good music machine."

"Who cares if it was a good music machine or not?" said the other voice irritably. "The real question is, why did it explode? I don't see any bombs around here."

"I heard those old machines were kind of defective," said Lauz. "Like, they were prone to blowing up randomly. My grandpa's machine blew up in his face once, but he got better and then went out and bought a new one after that. And *that* one blew up in his face, too, but—"

"Lauz, did I say that I wanted to hear more about your stupid grandpa?" said the other voice in a tone as sharp as a knife. "No, of course I didn't. The boss told us to go out here and find out caused that explosion that tripped our security systems, just in case there's someone out here who might be a threat to our operations."

I exchanged puzzled looks with Resita, but neither of us spoke. We simply listened more closely to these mysterious speakers, whoever, they were, because we had no way of knowing if they were good or kind. I did not trust the sounds of their voices, but I knew better than to attack when we still knew so little about these men. That neither of us were in any real condition to fight was another reason to keep silent.

"Well, I don't see nothing that could be a problem," said Lauz, who I judged as being not very bright based on the tone of his voice. "Maybe one of those sand snakes accidentally blew it up. My grandpa always said that the government dumped a bunch of genetically-modified sand snakes out here after the Portal War ended, so maybe one of those caused it."

"Your grandpa was a conspiracy theorist," the other voice

177

snapped. "Anyway, I don't like this one bit. Even out here, machines don't just randomly explode for no reason. I think someone is out here; actually, I *know* someone is out here, and not just one person, but two someones."

I tensed. So did Resita, though again neither of us made any sounds. I hoped that the other man was merely boasting to his friend, but for all I knew he could be telling the truth. If he was, then I expected a fight.

"Really?" said Lauz, who sounded a little skeptical. "How do you know that?"

"See those footprints in the sand?" said the other voice. Though I could not see him and did not know what Lauz's friend looked like, I nonetheless imagined a shadowy figure gesturing at our footprints in the sand. "Granted, most of them were blown away by the explosion, but there are still a few that are clearly visible."

"Hey, you're right, Arn," said Lauz. He now sounded as impressed as a child shown a simple magic trick. "And look, there are some claw marks, too. Do you think that means there's a gigantic chicken walking around here, Arn? 'Cause those look like chicken claws to me."

As soon as Lauz ceased speaking, the sound of something heavy hitting into something thick broke through the air. It almost made me jump, while Resita just made a chirping sound in surprise before he caught himself. We waited to see if either of those two had heard him.

Then Arn said, "Gigantic chicken, Lauz? Really? Let me guess, did your grandpa tell you that there are giant chickens walking around the Dead Lands?"

"Well, my grandpa did say, uh, that the government was—"

Another whacking sound and Arn snapped, "Shut up, Lauz. Those are clearly not the marks of a giant chicken. Nah, those are Checrom marks."

"Aren't Checrom basically chicken people, Arn?" said Lauz, who did not sound quite as enthusiastic as before, perhaps because he had been hit twice already. "So what's the difference?"

"God, Lauz, how do you even dress yourself every day?" said Arn. "Anyway, what this proves is that there is a human and a Checrom running around here. I bet they blew up this '94-B, too."

"Why would they do that?" asked Lauz. "I don't get it."

"That's what we're going to try to figure out, idiot," said Arn. "But you know, I think it's probably that Delanian human, uh, what did the boss say his name was? Rii Whatever?"

"Uh, I think he said Rii Apakerec," said Lauz. "Or something. I dunno. I've never been really good with Delanian names."

'Twas my name that Lauz just mentioned! Technically, of course, he used my human name—Rii—and my non-human name, Apakerec. Still, I used both names, but I did not know either of these two. How, then, did they know mine name?

"And that Checrom from the Foundation," Arn continued. "I think the spy said his name was Resita or something? Anyway, their bodies were never recovered from the wreckage of HQ. And look, those human footprints don't even have shoes. I was told that that Rii guy didn't have any shoes, which can't be a coincidence."

Resita's beady eyes had grown to almost twice their size, and his thin frame visibly trembled. There was no mystery there. Based on what this Arn fellow said, it was quite clear that these two were associated with those lizard monsters that attacked the Foundation's HQ.

Which meant one thing was clear: If they found us, they would likely finish the job that their allies had started. And that was something I would never allow, for we had not survived this long simply to die at the hands of two common crooks, based on their manners of speech.

"But how did they get out of HQ and all the way out here?" said Lauz. "The Hunters had all of the exits and entrances blocked off. No way they could have escaped without us knowing."

"Doesn't matter how," said Arn. "What matters is that they survived. And the boss said that no one was supposed to survive that assault, especially that Rii guy."

Though they did not say so, I knew that their boss must be Xacron-Ah. After all, his Assassin had already tried to kill me once; 'twould not surprise me if it turned out that he had attacked the Foundation HQ for the sole purpose of killing me. He probably did not want me to find mine sister, which meant that I would have to work harder than ever to save her from him, if he was as dangerous as his 'Hunters,' if that was the proper name of those foul beasts from before.

"So how do we find 'em?" said Lauz. "'Cause I don't see them anywhere. They might be far away now, maybe."

"I doubt they got far," said Arn. "That explosion happened what, five minutes ago, maybe less? They couldn't have gotten far in that time. Shouldn't take us long to find them, even without our sensors."

I gestured for Resita to follow me. Whilst I did not know exactly how strong Arn and Lauz were, I did not want to fight them, for I was still too tired and thirsty and hungry to do much. Though when I looked down at the trail of feathers that Resita had left earlier, I wondered if running was even an option for us, for it would not be difficult, methought, for those two evildoers to follow us that way.

"But you know what?" said Arn. "My favorite screen show is on tonight and I frankly don't want to spend hours looking for a human and an oversized bird. Do your heat sensors work, Lauz?"

"Yes," said Lauz, who sounded quite proud of himself. "I clean them every day."

"Then use 'em to find those damn idiots, who are probably hiding in the mounds like rat," said Arn. "Then the fun can begin."

Before Resita or I could run, a strange humming sound emitted from the other side of the mound. 'Twas a queer noise, for it was high-pitched, but not like the humming of a singing bird; rather, it was strangely metallic and screechy. It was unlike anything I had ever heard, though that did not surprise me terribly, for many of Xeeo's sounds and noises were foreign to me.

Then, without warning, the sound cut off. Resita and I stood there, as still as the wind in the Dead Lands, waiting for whatever was going to happen, to happen. My cars still rang from the humming noise, but I had enough sense in my head left to turn to walk away from this mound.

But as soon as I did, Arn shouted triumphantly from behind the mound, "There they are! Get 'em!"

Then something sharp and small, like the sting of a bee, stung my neck. I reached for it immediately, feeling something metal and spiky, but 'twas no use, for my eyelids became heavier than Castle Una and I was soon lost in the darkness of unconsciousness before I even realized what had happened.

Chapter Ten

The darkness around me was thick and impenetrable. 'Twas not the darkness of midnight, which is a natural thing and easily dispelled by the light of day or the light conjured by a wizard or witch; nay, this was a complete darkness, one I could no more see through than I could see through a thick mountain or stone wall.

But it was not death. That much I knew. I was as alive as ever, for I could feel air going in and out of my lungs, and I still felt the sand betwixt my toes, sand which was likely from the Dead Lands.

Beyond that, however, not all of mine senses had returned yet. Though I did feel the temperature around me, which was an even and cool temp, though why that was, I did not know. I last remembered being out in the hot, dry sun of the Dead Lands, but now I was in a much cooler place, or so it seemed to me.

I did not like being in the dark, however, whether literally or figuratively. Hence, I began to force my eyes open; not only did I want to see where I was, but I also wished to find out if Resita was all right. For I vaguely recalled being in severe danger before being knocked out; and if Resita was dead, then I would indeed be angry at myself for allowing that to happen.

Did take me only a few seconds to fully open mine eyes, but when I did, I blinked several times, for mine vision was not quite clear. When my vision finally did clear, I looked around at my surroundings in order to better understand where I was.

I knew not where I lay. 'Twas a bed of some sort, soft and plush, the silk blankets nice against mine skin. It was infinitely superior to the heat of the outside; indeed, my skin no longer felt as rough as it used to. It was as if someone had rubbed a kind of lotion over my skin, though I did not know if that had happened or not.

And I no longer smelled the icky stink of sewer sludge and garbage. That alone made me feel better than I had in many hours, though the replacement smell was not much to speak of. It smelled like soap; not exactly mine favorite scent in the world, but far superior to the sewage stink that I had feared would never leave my body.

Near the foot of mine bed was a small stool, which I assumed was for visitors to sit on, though there was currently no one upon it. It had five tiny wheels supporting it and appeared to be height-adjustable, though did appear as if no one had sat on it in a while.

As for the rest of my surroundings, I noticed that I was in a fairly large, square room, my bed in one corner. On the opposite end of the room stood a wall of clear glass, through which I saw what appeared to be construction equipment—such as massive cranes—rising from the ground. I also saw what appeared to be piles of dirt on the perimeter of the area, though where those piles came from, I did not know. It appeared to me like I was in the middle of a Xeeonite construction site, though that made no sense, as I last remembered being in the middle of the Dead Lands, well away from civilization of any sort.

I sat up. That took less effort on my part than I thought; indeed, I felt quite well rested, like I had had a good nap. Eager to get up, walk around this place, and find out where I was, I noticed a door on the left side of the room that appeared to be the only way out.

Therefore, I decided to get up and walk to it. But when I tried to raise my legs, a powerful pain shot through them, almost enough to make me cry out. I managed to keep mine mouth closed, however, because I did not wish to scream.

Instead, I pulled the blanket off my legs to see what had caused the pain. I almost covered them back up when I did.

Mine legs were broken. That much was obvious. They were bent in awkward positions and whenever I tried to move them, pain unlike anything else I had ever felt in my life shot through them. I had never had broken legs before; however, I still did not scream, though I groaned involuntarily every time I felt the pain.

What happened to mine legs? I lay back down, doing my best to keep still, but 'twas difficult, for it seemed like every movement caused terrible pain in my legs. I knew of no way to fight the pain, which made me angry with a righteous fury, for now I could not get up and find out where I was.

Then I noticed a camera hanging above the doorway. It did resemble the security camera from the Foundation's HQ, except that it was smaller and less noticeable. Seeing that camera there reminded me of how I had felt when I first awoke inside the HQ, which was a feeling I did not wish to relive at all.

Nonetheless, I understood that if there was a camera there, then that meant there was someone on the other side watching me. If so, perhaps I could communicate with them and ask them to send someone to meet me; after all, I deserved to know where I was and what was going on, did I not?

So I shouted at the camera, "Camera! Tell your creators, whoever they are, that I, Rii of the Knights of Se-Dela, demand to speak with them! Or I will call the wrath of the Old Gods down upon ye and your family!"

That was no idle threat. I was in such a bad mood, not helped by my broken legs, that I was willing to ask the Old Gods to summon the Annihilator itself to destroy them. Granted, that was no guarantee that the Old Gods would listen, for the Annihilator was a weapon meant to be used only under dire circumstances. Still, it was the most deadly and serious threat I knew to make and I intended to make sure that these people, whoever they were, understood that I was not in a diplomatic mood.

As I expected, the camera did not respond. It simply continued to stare at me, likely recording my every movement, as if I had not spoken to it at all. 'Twas a frustrating thing, for I felt as though no one had heard my threats and demands at all. If so, then I might be stuck in here far longer than I would have liked.

But then the door to my room opened. I tried to sit up again to see who was going to enter, but the pain in my legs was still overwhelming, so I simply raised my head to see who had decided to enter.

A human woman stepped through the doorway. She had short blonde hair that was achingly familiar to me as a cherished memory; she wore a red body suit that looked more Xeeonite than Delanian, plus a dark cloak that shrouded much of her body; and she had a little communicator device wrapped around her wrist, though not being an expert on Xeeonite technology, I did not know what it was called.

But I did not need to know the name of that technology to recognize the woman. She was a woman who I had not seen in six years, at least up close and in person. I barely believed mine own eyes—indeed, for a moment, I thought I was merely seeing an illusion, as if the heat of the Dead Lands had permanently affected my view of the world.

The woman closed the door behind her and then turned to face me again. I still did not believe it was her until she smiled at me and said, "Long time, no see, big brother."

I could barely utter her name, for I was too shocked by her words to speak. Nonetheless, I did manage to say, "Sister Kiriah … is that ye?"

The woman laughed, and when she did, it sparked memories of the summers from our youth, when she would laugh at my jokes or mine antics. It was a more mature laugh, of course, as she was no longer a girl, but there was no mistaking it for the laugh of anyone else.

"Yes, big brother, it's your baby sister, Kiriah," said my sister, giggling a little as she said that. "You sound like you've seen a ghost."

I had forgotten all about the pain in my legs now. I simply stared at my sister, took in her whole form. Despite the many proofs that I had of her existence, a part of me still refused to believe that the woman standing in the same room as I was indeed my sister.

"Kiriah," I said, "I ... how ... I thought ... No. This can't be true. Ye must be an actress hired to fool me into believing that ye are my long-lost sister."

Kiriah rolled her eyes, the exact same way she always used to when we were younger. "Oh, please. Is that what you think I am now? An actress? You know there's not a single actress on Xeeo or Dela who could possibly imitate me."

She said that as she brushed some of her hair off her forehead. That was another quirk of my sister, but I still was unsure whether to believe that this woman was indeed her, despite the evidence before my eyes. With so much trickery and deception on this world, I was not in the mood to dash into the arms of a friend who might be a foe. Especially when I noticed how Kiriah spoke much more like a Xeeonite than a Delanian, which made me deeply wary of this woman and her claims to be my flesh-and-blood sister.

"Then give me proof," I said, folding my arms across my chest. "Tell me something that only Kiriah would know. If ye are indeed who ye say ye are, then that should be no obstacle for you."

Kiriah again rolled her eyes. "Just as pigheaded as ever, I see. Very well. Do you remember that night when we found Grandpa's old skyras rings in the attic and tried to use them? The ring I used made your eyebrows grow out like a shaggy dog's fur."

Despite my suspicions of her, I could not help but smile at the memory. "Ah, yes. I recall that quite well. Father was as angry as the Old Gods when he found out what ye did."

"And he was angry when he found out what you did to me,"

Kiriah added. "Remember, you shrank all of my clothes. Father didn't like that at all."

"I even remember the defense I used to excuse our actions," I said. "I blamed our older brother, Sura, for showing us how to get to the rings ... even though Sura had been visiting a friend at the exact time as our unfortunate little adventure."

"Then Father grounded us for three months because of that," Kiriah continued. "And had us apologize to Grandpa's grave, remember? Boy, was that weird."

I frowned. It was a common occurrence among us Delanian humans to go to the graves of the deceased and apologize to them whenever we offended them; not always, perhaps, but we at least did it when we remembered. Kiriah had never mentioned thinking it strange before now, which made me uneasy, even though I now no longer suspected of her being a fake.

"Well, I am glad to see ye again, mine sister," I said. I held out my arms. "Why do we not celebrate our reunion with an embrace? It has been too long since we last hugged like siblings."

But for some reason, Kiriah simply stayed where she was. Her arms remained folded behind her back and, unless mine eyes were playing tricks on me, it seemed as though she regarded me with distaste.

"Nah," she said, shaking her head, speaking in a tone that she clearly meant to be casual but which came across to me as dismissive. "I think the fact that we got to see each other again is good enough, don't you think?"

"But ..." I lowered my arms. "But it has been so long ..."

"Your legs are broken, anyway," Kiriah said, gesturing at my legs under mine blankets. "It's better that we don't make too much physical contact right now. I don't want to hurt you more than I already have."

I frowned. "Hurt me? Sister, what do ye mean by that? Ye have never hurt me; well, ye haven't hurt me in a long time, anyway. I remember ye used to hit me quite a bit when ye were a child, of course, but I thought ye had grown out of your immature violence when ye became a woman."

"That's where you're wrong," said Kiriah. She pushed a strand of hair out of her eyes. "Because I have hurt you more than I wanted to. But I can assure you that it was all necessary."

"Necessary?" I said. "Forgive me, sister, but I do not understand. Why would ye hurt me? I have never done anything to hurt ye. I have always protected ye. Remember during our school days, when I stood up to those bullies who made fun of your nose?"

"I remember," said Kiriah, nodding, though she did not sound happy about it. "And that's why I am so sorry about hurting you. If things had been different, I can assure you that I never even would have thought of harming you."

"Sister, ye speak like a mad woman," I said. I gestured at the stool near my bed. "Why don't ye sit down right here and talk with me? Ye can tell me all about what ye have been doing since ye disappeared all those years ago."

I could tell immediately that my sister did not wish to sit down and talk. That puzzled me greatly; after all, why would she not wish to speak with me? I had countless questions to ask her, and she no doubt had just as many to ask me, seeing as she had probably not been keeping up with me either. I could not wait to catch up with her and learn about where she had been and what she had been doing since her mysterious disappearance so long ago.

Nonetheless, she did walk up to me and sit down on the stool. It moved slightly when she sat on it, but she took control of it fairly quickly and put her hands in her lap.

"I know not where to start," I said. I gestured at my broken legs. "But perhaps first we can start with mine legs. They are broken and in desperate need of aid. Is there a doctor or healer nearby? If so, could you please find him and bring him here?"

Kiriah did not so much as stir from her spot when I made that request of her. She simply shrugged and said, "While there is a doctor in the place, he's not supposed to heal you. We broke your legs for a reason."

Mine eyes widened in horror. "Wait … 'we'? Are ye saying —"

"I ordered my men to break your legs," said Kiriah, nodding. She sounded apologetic, though not as apologetic as she should have. "I'm sorry, Rii, but it was the only way to ensure you wouldn't get in the way of my—our—plans."

I blinked several times. There was no way that Kiriah had just admitted to breaking mine legs, or ordering her men to do it, rather. That made no sense. Kiriah and I were siblings. We had been as close as any two siblings could be. My ears must have been broken or perhaps none of this was real; 'twas all some illusion cast by a mischievous wizard for reasons unknown to me (even though I was quite aware that very few wizards lived on Xeeo and even fewer knew how to cast illusions at all).

So I smiled, despite the pain in my broken legs making me want to grimace, and said, "Grand joke, sister. Of course ye didn't order your men to break my legs. Your sense of humor was always a bit odd, but—"

"This isn't a joke," said Kiriah. Her tone became harsher. "I am telling you the truth. I've deceived you for so long, but this is no deception. The truth of the matter is, I did order my men to harm you. Again, I apologize, but I hope you understand that it was necessary."

Now I knew that this was no trickery or deception. I had not wanted to accept it, but there was no more rejecting it now. I was forced to accept the reality of this situation, the grim reality that I had tried to ignore and reject in favor of my own lighter and kinder one.

"Based on your expression, I can tell you have a lot of questions about what is going on here," said Kiriah. "Questions I probably should have answered a long time ago, but I just didn't think you needed to know them."

"Of course I have a million questions to ask," I said. I shuddered when I felt the pain in my broken legs, but I did not let it distract me from my purpose. "I barely know where to even start. I could start by asking why ye broke my legs or where I am or what is even going on, though first of all I suppose I'd like to know where Resita is."

"That bird?" said Kiriah. She gestured at the floor. "He's in the dungeons, chained up and unable to escape. I considered killing him, but I decided that he probably knows where the other Foundation agents are, the ones who escaped the attack on their HQ, so I'm keeping him alive until I can decide on a way to get that information from his brain, plus anything else he might know."

I sighed a sigh of relief, for I was happy to know that Resita was still alive, even if he was currently imprisoned.

But my relief at Resita's survival vanished when I realized what else Kiriah had said about him. I looked at her in disbelief and asked, "But why would ye want to know where the other Foundation agents are? Are ye—"

"Behind that attack on their headquarters earlier?" Kiriah finished. "Yes. I ordered it done. I take full responsibility for it."

"But I thought Xacron-Ah was behind it," I said. "He's the villain who kidnapped ye and has forced ye to work for him, has he not?"

Kiriah chuckled harshly. "Xac? He doesn't have any power over me. He answers to me. If he tried to kidnap me, I'd have him dead and replaced within a week."

She said that with such coldness and quickness, it was as if she had already given that scenario a great deal of thought. That did not seem at all like my sister, who I remembered as being the kindest and sweetest girl I had ever known. I felt like I had stepped into some strange parallel world, where everything I knew was opposite.

"I do not understand," I said. "I thought ye were under Xacron-Ah's control, not the other way around."

"Don't feel bad, brother," said Kiriah. She reached out and patted me on the arm. "Very few people outside of our organization even know I exist, much less that I have any sort of connection with Xacron-Ah. See, Xacron-Ah works in the public, while I work behind the scenes and make sure that everything goes off without a hitch."

"Your organization?" I asked. "I did not know ye had an

organization. What is it called?"

Kiriah tapped her chin, like she was thinking about whether or not to tell me even that much. This was completely unlike the Kiriah I had known, the one who had always answered my questions without hesitation or fear. What changes had come over her, I wondered?

Then she said, "We don't really have a name, because names can be traced and used to incriminate people. But we have always called ourselves Reunification. It's an accurate descriptor of our goals as an organization."

"Reunification?" I said. "Why do ye call yourselves that? More importantly, how long has your organization existed? How did ye even find it?"

"Reunification is much older than me," said Kiriah. "I am just its newest leader and the one who will finally achieve the goals set into motion by its Founder so many eons ago."

Kiriah said this with a fervent enthusiasm that I had not seen in her in a while. She no longer looked at me. Her eyes were glazed over with excitement. She seemed smitten by the idea of achieving the Founder's goals, whatever they may be, as if it was her whole destiny to do that. It disturbed me because my sister was usually far more reserved than this, which made me wonder what kind of changes had come over my sister between the time of her disappearance and today.

"But I think I should start from the beginning," said Kiriah, looking at me again. "You're my brother, so I think you deserve to know what is going on here. Maybe you can even help, once you understand exactly what we're trying to do here. It's a noble goal, after all, and I would love it if the two of us could work side by side to accomplish it, just like when we built that makeshift fort as kids. Do you remember that?"

I nodded. "'Twas a mighty fort, for children of six and five, but I am not so sure about Reunification. But I shall reserve my judgment until ye tell me the whole story."

"All right," said Kiriah. She leaned back in her chair and took on a thoughtful expression, as if she was trying to figure out where to start. "I guess I should begin with my 'disappearance' six years ago."

"Yes," I said. "'Tis a good place to start, for I have always wondered how you disappeared on that fateful night. I had thought some vile cur had kidnapped ye, especially after I first saw those pictures of you sitting with Xacron-Ah."

"Well, first off, no one kidnapped me," said Kiriah. She snorted. "As if anyone *could*. If someone tried to kidnap me, I would have broken out by myself within a week. I left of my own free will."

"That is good to hear," I said. But then I frowned. "But why did ye not tell Sura and I? We were worried sick for your safety. We blamed each other for our failure to protect ye."

"I know," said Kiriah, "but I couldn't tell you where I was going. I was told that I had to leave without telling anyone, because no one is supposed to know about Reunification. And that is how it is supposed to be. Even I didn't know about Reunification until the day they contacted me with an offer."

"I see," I said. My hands balled into fists. "But Sura and I could have used any hint of where ye had gone. Even just the tiniest of clues assuring us of your safety would have saved us years of worry and strife."

"If I had told you about Reunification and why I left, they would have killed you," said Kiriah in a flat tone. "Any non-members who find out about us are always killed before they can get a chance to tell anyone else. And if any members of the organization tell non-members about it, they get killed, too. It's how Reunification has managed to stay hidden for so many years."

"That does not sound much like a noble organization to I," said I. "Sounds indeed closer to a group of miscreants that has something to hide."

"Our goal isn't evil or wicked," said Kiriah. She leaned forward again, with such passion in her eyes that I found it hard to look at them. "We just know that if anyone—whether on Dela or Xeeo—knew about our plan, they would try to stop us. We can't allow anyone to get in the way of the Mission."

"And just what is this 'Mission' ye speak of?" I asked. "Killing innocents who stumble upon your plans?"

"Those deaths are collateral damage," said Kiriah. She adjusted the collar of her cloak, which had moved out of position due to her movements. "If no one tried to stop us or get in our way, then we could do our plan without killing anyone. Unfortunately, many misguided people have made it their job to fight against us for no reason other than they don't understand what we're trying to do."

She did not sound very mournful or apologetic to me. Indeed, if I had not known Kiriah very well (though listening to her ramblings now, I questioned just how well I actually knew my dearest sister), I would have assumed that she was quite satisfied indeed with the fact that the organization had killed people, as if they deserved it for daring to stand in her way.

That thought did deeply unsettle me, making me no longer wish to be in the same room as my sister. In spite of all of the years of anticipation up to this moment, I found myself praying to the Old Gods to whisk me away to some faraway land. Even running into the Destroyer again would have been better than speaking with my seemingly remorseless sister.

"You see, Rii, Reunification has existed for eons, even before Dela and Xeeo became connected through the Portals that people use to travel regularly," said Kiriah. "Every so often, they need a new leader, someone they can trust to carry out the dictates of our Founder. Sometimes this person is from Xeeo; other times, from Dela. Nonetheless, they are always very careful about who they choose, because a leader can make or break an organization. I am the newest leader and have led Reunification for six years now."

"Why did they choose ye?" I asked. "Not that I doubt your leadership abilities, sister, but I do not understand why they chose ye in particular."

"Because it's my destiny," said Kiriah. She put her hand over her heart. "The Elders—the men and women who make up the actual leadership of Reunification—consulted our Founder, who picked me to lead the organization, because he saw what my destiny was."

"Your Founder?" I repeated. "But ye say that Reunification has existed even before the two worlds became linked through the Portals. How can the Founder still be alive, then? Or are ye referring to one of his descendents, perhaps?"

"Because our Founder is a great man, greater than any of us," said Kiriah. She sighed in great contentment. "He's immortal.

How he got that way, I don't know, but he's the same Founder who lived in the First Days, when he founded Reunification."

"What is his name?" I said.

"I don't know," said Kiriah. "No one is allowed to know his name. And I don't need to know it to serve him. I am perfectly content not knowing, because I trust him totally."

"That does not sound much like the Kiriah I knew," I said. "The Kiriah I knew did not trust anyone totally, particularly strange men who do not reveal their true names."

"You don't understand," said Kiriah, shaking her head. "I'm not the same Kiriah you used to know. I've changed. I've learned so much more about Dela and Xeeo than any of us could possibly imagine. If you only knew what I knew … why, then you wouldn't be so skeptical."

"Then tell me," I said. I gestured at my broken legs. "I have nothing better to do at the moment, after all, but listen."

"I can't tell you everything," said Kiriah. "Not yet. The Founder doesn't think you're trustworthy enough to be given that kind of information right now. Maybe later, after you've proven your worth, but for now, I can't tell you as much as I want to."

"Fine, then," I said. "Continue with your story. What happened after ye vanished from our home? Where did ye go?"

Kiriah glanced at the glass wall on the other end of the room, well away from us. "I can't tell you that, either. A lot happened between then and now, much of it knowledge that only Reunification members are allowed to know. I will tell you, however, that I went to Xeeon, where I began to work with Xacron-Ah, to finish the work that was started so many years ago by our Founder."

I bit my lower lip, though Kiriah did not seem to notice. The reason I bit mine lip was because I remembered how Lanresia, that she-elf who worked for the Foundation, had told me that they suspected that my sister and Xacron-Ah worked together. I had thought it a silly theory, one that had no basis in reality, but now Kiriah had just confirmed it and she was obviously not joking, as much as I may have wished that she was.

"So ye were indeed at the Parade in Xeeon, then?" I said. "That was ye?"

Kiriah nodded. "Normally, I don't get out much, because I'm not supposed to be seen in public. I decided to go out just that once, however, because I was getting bored and I've always loved parades. I didn't even know you were in Xeeon at the time. If I had, I wouldn't have gone out at all, because you're not even supposed to know that I'm alive."

"But why?" I said. "Is it because ye know that I would not agree with whatever this Founder fellow is up to?"

"Only a select few people are allowed to even know about the existence of Reunification," said Kiriah. "And you, unfortunately, were not chosen to know. Even Sura wasn't."

"I see," I said, stroking my chin. I cringed when the pain in my legs flared up again, though as before I tried to ignore it. "Then ... did ye send that Assassin machine to kill me?"

Kiriah did not meet mine eyes as she said, "Well, it was actually Xacron-Ah who ordered it to attack you. It wasn't even supposed to kill you. I was promised that it would just delay you until I could get back to my place in the city."

It may have been six years since I last spoke with Kiriah, but I could still tell that she was not telling me the whole truth about

Assassin. Aside from her refusal to look me in the eye, she still had the habit of tugging at the strands on the sleeves of her robes whenever she was lying. It was a habit she had had ever since childhood, and I was pleased to see that she still had it, for it meant that she had not changed quite as much as I thought she had.

"Xacron-Ah didn't send that robot after me," I said. "Did he?"

She stopped tugging her sleeves, perhaps understanding that I remembered her habit. Then she looked me in the eyes and said, without hesitation, "You're right. I sent it. And I told it to kill you."

Though I suspected as much, hearing her confession from her own lips shook me to the core of my being. "But why? Why would ye order your machine to kill your own brother? I thought ye loved me."

"I do," Kiriah admitted. "But I wanted you out of the picture because I didn't want to keep worrying that you would find me and get in the way of my plans. I knew that once you got even the tiniest whiff of my existence, you would stop at nothing to find me again."

"And ye thought that *killing* me would be the right way to keep me away from ye?" I said in indignation. "Killing your own brother because ye didn't want him to get in your way and ruin your precious 'plans'? You are a mother of crows."

"How else was I supposed to ensure that you wouldn't try to find me again?" said Kiriah. She pushed away from my bed, as if she was afraid that I would try to harm her. "Besides, you survived, didn't you? All thanks to those Foundation idiots."

In anger, I tried to sit up, but my broken legs stung with pain again, forcing me to lie back down. Nonetheless, I glared at her, so angry that I wished that the Old Gods would miraculously heal my legs so I could get up and leave this place forever, even though I doubted the Old Gods would do such a thing for me. Still, I liked to dwell on that thought anyway, as 'twas the only way to distract mine mind from the pain in my legs.

"Did ye intend for me to die in that assault on the Foundation's headquarters as well?" I demanded.

"Everyone there was supposed to die," said Kiriah, nodding. She stood up from the stool and turned away, perhaps because she was too ashamed to look me directly in the eye anymore. "The Foundation has been a thorn in Reunification's side for years. It wasn't until recently that we were able to deal them a lethal blow, and that is only thanks to the tracking device that Assassin planted on you before the Foundation agents whisked you away to their headquarters."

I felt my body quickly, but did not find any sort of tracking device on it. Still, I believed my sister, for I had heard about Xeeonite robots that could 'plant' tracking devices on their enemies. Sir Alart had once told me that these devices could be quite small indeed, too small for the human eye to see or for a human hand to feel.

I ceased feeling my body and said, "What were those monsters ye sent after us? I have never seen anything like them before. Granted, I am no expert on Xeeonite species, but even Resita said he did not know what they were, and he is a native of this world."

"That's because they aren't native to Xeo or Dela," said Kiriah, her back still to me. "Our Reunification scientists made them by splicing the genes of Grand Lizards—a type of Xeeonite lizard that you probably don't know anything about—with humans. Our scientists call them Lizard-men, though we also call them the Hunters. This is the first time we've used them in the field. And I must say, they were a complete success."

"Gene splicing?" I repeated. "What doth that mean?"

"You don't need to know that," said Kiriah, waving off my question as if it was irrelevant. "Just know that we are finally going to be moving ahead with the gene splicing program, now that we know that it works."

That sounded mightily ominous to I, but I decided to worry about it later. For now, I had to focus on other, more urgent things, though I made a mental note to ask Resita what 'gene splicing' was later, assuming I ever saw him again, of course.

"Is everyone at the Foundation dead?" I asked. "All of them?"

"According to the reports I've read, most of the Foundation members at their headquarters at the time were killed by the Lizard-men," said Kiriah. "Some, like you and Resita, managed to escape, but they'll be easy to find because Xacron-Ah has given orders to the J series robots to search for and arrest them like the criminals they are."

"What about the agents who were not in there during the attack?" I demanded. "Are they, too, on the run?"

"Probably," said Kiriah, "but I don't know for sure because we don't have any way of tracking them. Anyway, I'm not going to blab to you about all of our secrets, because you're still not a loyal member of Reunification like I am. Just know that it won't be long now before the Foundation ceases to be a threat to us or anyone else ever again."

She said those words with such cold contentment that I had to shiver. This woman who spoke so coldly and yet happily about the deaths of her enemies could not be my sister. The Kiriah I knew would never have been this happy or this cold about such evil. As a child, she would burst into tears every time she even accidentally stepped on an insect. To talk the way she did about these other living beings made me certain that I was in some strange dream where nothing made sense.

Nay, not a dream; but a nightmare.

Yet the pain in my legs hurt so badly that I could not honestly believe this was a dream. This was indeed real, every moment of it, from the color of Kiriah's blonde hair to my broken legs. 'Twas a heartbreaking realization, for certain.

"What next?" I asked. I did not hide the pain in my voice, for I wished for her to know the true extent of my pain. "Are ye going to kill me? I heard your two servants, Arn and Lauz I believe they were called, heavily implying they would like to do that to Resita and I."

"Arn and Lauz are just a couple of idiots," said Kiriah. "They know better than to kill my brother, and I had already given them orders to bring any surviving Foundation agents like Resita back to us anyway. I imagine they only implied that because they are brutes who want nothing more than to beat and kill their enemies."

"What charming fellows ye employ under your service, sister," I said, rolling mine eyes. "Indeed, I know of no other individuals more moral than your employees."

Kiriah did not respond to that. She folded her arms behind her back and still did not look at me. Her eyes seemed to be on the crane outside, which was now turning, as if someone were operating it (though knowing Xeeonite technology, it was likely a robot controlling itself). I also heard what might have been a large drill burrowing through the earth somewhere, though the sound was muffled and difficult to detect over the sounds of people shouting outside.

"I see ye are ignoring me," I said. "Very well. Are ye going to tell me where we are, at the very least? Or are ye going to tell me nothing?"

"We're in the Dead Lands," said Kiriah. She gestured at the crane outside. "It's a secret dig site, far enough away from the Xeeonite city states that it is extremely unlikely that anyone will accidentally stumble upon us. We have a bunch of digging and construction equipment designed to dig out the area and help us find what we are looking for."

"May I ask what ye are looking for?" I asked. "Or is that a secret ye aren't allowed to share with me also?"

"You don't need to know that," said Kiriah. "But I can tell you that it is an integral part of the ultimate goal of Reunification. Can you guess what that is?"

I shook my head. "Nay. You speak cryptically and have revealed nothing to me save that your organization is far too mysterious and strange for me to trust."

"Fine," said Kiriah. She turned around to face me again, though she was not smiling anymore. "The goal of Reunification is to unite Xeeo and Dela as one world again. That is what we have been working toward for years … and we are getting very close to achieving that goal, I must say."

"Ridiculous." I shook my head. "Xeeo and Dela have never

been one world. 'Tis a silly thing to say."

"Actually, at one point, they were," said Kiriah. "Our two worlds were indeed one world in the past. It was a long time ago, well before the peoples of both worlds began to keep historical records, but our Founder has confirmed it. The two worlds were once one … and soon, they will be one again, as they were meant to be."

"Where is your proof that Xeeo and Dela were once one?" I asked. "'Tis a hard to believe claim to make without any solid proof."

"The proof is all around us," said Kiriah. She gestured at the air. "The skyras energy that permeates both worlds is proof enough that our worlds were connected; after all, how is it that both worlds have an almost equal amount of skyras in them? Why are conditions for life similar enough on both worlds that travelers from Xeeo can go to Dela without dying and vice versa? It's because the two worlds were once one, that's why."

"Then how did they split?" I asked. "Explain that, sister. For surely, there must be some reason for the split, yes?"

"There is, but you don't need to know that," said Kiriah. "That's the kind of information we're not supposed to share with anyone. Not that it would do you any good to know it; after all, you are currently not in any situation to do anything about it."

"How will ye reunite Dela and Xeeo?" I said. "That seems a truly impossible task, one fit only for the Old Gods."

"We have people working on both Dela and Xeeo to bring about this change," said Kiriah. "You think Reunification is limited solely to Xeeo? Of course not. Our Delanian members are currently working to find what we are looking for even as we speak."

"I suspected as much," I said. "Where are these Delanian people ye speak of?"

"They're in the Winterlands, searching for Dela's version of what we are looking for here on Xeeo," said Kiriah. She then scowled. "At least they would be, if our operations there weren't currently being disrupted by a J bot that has been tracking down one of our agents. Kalcan says they have it under control, but I really am not happy about what is going on there at all."

I, on the other hand, was quite happy to hear that someone else was working against these villains. I did not know who this robot was, but I hoped to meet him someday. I still did not like machines very much, but if he was working to stop these people, then I decided I could make an exception for his sake.

"But that's irrelevant and temporary," said Kiriah. "Once that situation is under control, we can begin the process of bringing Dela and Xeeo back together. Then Reunification's mission will finally be complete, just as the Founder has been working toward for countless years."

"That does not sound very good to I," I said. "What if the reunification of our worlds causes much death and destruction? If the two worlds have been separated for so long, then I doubt their reunification will be easy or kind on the inhabitants of either world."

"It is a necessary step," said Kiriah. She put a hand over her heart. "The separation of Dela and Xeeo was an unnatural event, one that has done more to harm both worlds than anything else in history. There may be some pain and chaos in the initial reunification, but it won't matter in the long run, because the

Founder will make sure that peace and order are restored."

"And how can this Founder fellow ensure that?" I demanded. "What if the reunification kills everyone? Have ye considered that?"

"It won't," said Kiriah. "The Founder said the reunification will be better for everyone on both worlds. A few people might die, but not everyone. There will be enough people leftover from both worlds to allow us to rebuild a better society, a society where we can all live in peace as one."

"It sounds to me like your Founder has his head in the clouds," I remarked. "In any case, I cannot support this endeavour, even if ye do, sister. I fear the possible consequences of this decision, for merging two separate worlds sounds to me like a deadly thing even if Dela and Xeeo can be merged at all."

"You don't need to support it," said Kiriah. "All you need to do is stand out of the way while we put the final phases of the plan into action."

"Is that why ye broke my legs?" I said, gesturing at my legs 'neath mine blanket. "So I would not get in your way?"

"I am sorry, brother, but it was necessary in order to ensure you wouldn't try to escape," said Kiriah. "But we can heal you, if you would like. If you would agree to work for Reunification, then we could have our doctors fix your legs, even make them better than they originally were. You can then serve alongside me to build a better society after the reunification of Xeeo and Dela is complete."

'Twas a tempting offer, to be sure. I knew not how long my legs had been broken, but I doubted it would do them any good to remain broken for much longer. It would be better to have

Kiriah's doctors fix them up so I would not suffer any long term pain or injuries from these broken legs of mine.

On the other hand, I did not want to serve Reunification, for I still had doubts about their trustworthiness. There was too much I did not know, which did not even factor the fact that they had already tried to kill me twice.

Yet if I rejected the offer, I would certainly die or at least be crippled for life. Not to mention I would also likely be separated from my sister again, my sister who I had spent so many years searching for with great urgency.

But I wondered if that was truly a loss, for Kiriah had already shown herself to be completely different from the sister I had grown up with and loved. Allying with her would only reinforce her own changed behavior, and I did not wish to make Kiriah think that her own behavior was good, right, or noble.

But the pain ... oh, how the pain in mine legs burned. If Kiriah's doctors could indeed remove the pain in my legs, then it might be worth it, throwing in my lot with them.

I prayed to the Old Gods for guidance and wisdom. I asked them to show me what to do, to let me know what the wisest course of action to take was. And I asked them to hurry, because I did not have much time in which to make this important decision.

"Come on, Rii," said Kiriah, tapping her foot impatiently against the tiled floor. "Will you or won't you stand with us? That is all that I need to know."

"What will happen if I refuse?" I asked, mostly in an effort to get more time, because I already had an idea of what they would do to me if I said no.

"We will kill you," said Kiriah. Then she frowned. "No, wait.

Not kill you. Just throw you in the dungeons of this facility, where you won't be able to communicate with anyone outside of the base. Of course, this all depends on what the Elders say. They might just want you dead, seeing as you know more about us than any non-Reunification member has any right to."

"I face death, then," I said, "or imprisonment. Not much of a choice, is it?"

"That's just the way Reunification works," said Kiriah. "If we didn't adopt such stringent measures against people who rejected our offers, then we would not have gotten nearly as far as we have."

"It is a barbaric thing," I responded. "I believe that any organization like yours that operates in the shadows is not to be trusted."

"Is that a rejection, then?" said Kiriah. She folded her arms over her chest. "Are you saying you don't want to join?"

My legs burned so horribly that I could barely think for a moment. 'Twas enough of a sign from the Old Gods to confirm my decision for me, as much as I wished I did not have to make it.

"No," I said, shaking my head. "I am merely saying that I do not agree with Reunification's methods. As for the offer ... I accept it."

Kiriah clapped her hands together in excitement. She looked so happy about my decision, just like how she had looked when she was a young girl. It almost made me think that perhaps things were not going to be so bad now, as Kiriah would no doubt have her doctors repair my legs right away.

Nonetheless, I could not join in Kiriah's happiness, because I still had one question that I needed answering.

"This is great," said Kiriah. "I am so happy that you've decided to work with us. Because despite everything that's happened, brother, I still would rather have you on my side than against me."

"That is good, sister, but I do have one more question I needed ye to answer for me before anything," I said.

"What is that?" said Kiriah.

"Resita," I said. "What will happen to him now?"

Kiriah's happy smile vanished suddenly. It was replaced by an annoyed look, as if she considered my question to be irreverent. "He's going to remain in the dungeons of this place until we purge every answer from him that we're looking for. After that … well, we won't need him anymore."

"But ye will spare him?" I asked. "Ye will let him go free after you are done with him, at least?"

The coldness in Kiriah's eyes made me shiver with fear. "I'll talk with the Elders about what we should do with him. Fair warning, though; I can't guarantee he'll still be alive after we are finished with him."

Once again, the woman who wasn't my sister showed her true self through that mask that resembled Kiriah's face. Yet I did not argue against her, for I knew that that would be useless. 'Twas not as though I could threaten these 'Elders' she spoke of to convince them to let Resita go, after all.

Hence, I nodded to show that I understood and said, "Fine. In the mean, will ye summon your doctors to fix mine legs now?"

"Sure," said Kiriah, her smile returning to her face as if it had never disappeared at all. "I'll send someone to take you down to the medical room, where you'll be treated. This room we're in right now isn't supposed to be used for medical purposes."

"All right," I said. "What shall we do after my legs are repaired?"

"I will get you initiated right away, obviously," said Kiriah. "I can't wait."

She sounded so excited about it that I almost forgot that this was the same organization that had sent gene-spliced lizard men to eradicate their enemies and nearly killed me and Resita, as well.

But I did not, because despite what I had said earlier, I did not truly support Reunification or its goals.

No, I only said what I said in order to gain the knowledge and information I needed to take down this organization from within.

Because despite my sister's assurances that these people were good and noble, I knew that her allies were not. And I also knew that I was perhaps the only person in both worlds right now who could stop them before their misguided attempt to merge the worlds ended in utter catastrophe the likes of which have not been seen in the histories of either world before.

The only question was if I was too late to stop them. There was only one way to find out.

Chapter Eleven

The facility in which Reunification was headquartered was even larger than I thought it was. I discovered that when a couple of floating robots came to my room and transported me out on a flat, floating metal board, which they pushed along through the hallways of Reunification's facility toward the room where the doctors would work on me.

'Twas a well-kept facility, with spotless walls, ceiling, and floor. It was clearly Xeeonite in design, for only the Xeeonites designed buildings with such sleek interiors. We passed many doors on the way down, but I could not see through the windows on the doors because we went too fast and most of the windows were covered with white curtains that were too thick to see through.

We did not go down very far, only about two floors or so, at which point I was taken into a room on the right side of the hallway. Kiriah, who had been following us, told me she would wait outside until I was fixed, which did not please me, as Kiriah was the only person I knew in this place.

Nonetheless, when I entered the medical room, I was soon distracted by all of the elaborate Xeeonite medical instruments that I had never in my wildest imagination would have thought of on my own, such as a flat table with strange mechanical arms sticking out of it and a dazzling variety of screens that showed images I did not understand in the slightest.

Oddly, I did not see any actual doctors of any sort. Indeed, it seemed to me as if I was the only living, breathing organic creature in the room, as I saw no hint of anyone else. Then I realized that I hadn't seen any other people on our way down here, either, though perhaps all of the Reunification members were busy working elsewhere at the moment.

The two robots that had transported me to that room immediately (though gently) placed me on the flat table and strapped me down securely using the straps on the table. Before I could even ask what they were going to do to me, one of the mechanical arms rising out of the table jabbed a needle in my arm. 'Twas like being stung by a bee, but as soon as I felt that needle pierce my skin, I lost all consciousness.

It was perhaps a moment later that I awoke. At least, it felt like that, though I knew how quickly time passed when ye were unconscious.

When my senses came back to me, I realized that I was sitting in a room, at a comfortable temperature that was neither too hot nor too cold, a room which 'twas very similar to the room I had found myself in earlier. The only main differences being that there was no bed and none of the walls were glass or indeed had any windows for me to look out of at all.

Additionally, I found myself sitting in a reclining chair that

213

was quite soft, though I did not recognize the material that it was made out of (probably some synthetic Xeeonite substance, as the Xeeonites detested anything crafted by nature). A blanket had been spread over my body, a rather heavy one, but it was a comfortable weight that made me want to lie down and sleep forever.

Then I noticed that my legs no longer hurt even half as badly as they used to. There was no pain in them at all, though they did feel slightly stiffer than normal; nonetheless, I preferred the stiffness to the pain.

And then I realized that I was not actually alone in here. Kiriah stood in the doorway at the other end of the room, seemingly unaware that I was watching her, arguing with someone I could not see. All I saw of her conversation partner was a flickering blue light, though that was not much of a clue to his identity.

"No, I understand," said Kiriah, her frustrated tone quite familiar to me, even though it had been years since I last heard her use it. "But just because Rii just got here doesn't mean he can't be trusted. If I show him the Secret, I'm sure he'll be more than happy to help us."

Then Kiriah went silent, as if her partner was talking. But I did not hear any voice speaking from the blue flickering light. That made me wonder if the speaker was silent or perhaps Kiriah was somehow communicating with him in ways I could not tell.

In any case, I listened hard without making a sound, for I did not wish for Kiriah or her partner to know that I was awake yet. I thought that, by eavesdropping on their conversation, I might learn more about this 'Secret' mine sister spoke of, whatever it was. For it did not seem likely that they would explain it to me later, if Kiriah's argument was any indication of her conversation partner's feelings on the subject.

Then Kiriah raised her fist, but lowered it, as if she thought better of hitting her partner. "I guess you're right. But I can still initiate Rii into the organization, can't I?"

More flickering of that strange blue light. I thought I heard a low buzzing noise from outside the doorway, in the hallway, but I could not even begin to guess what might have been making that noise. There were likely many Xeeonite machines that could make such a sound, but what this one was, I did not know.

Once again, Kiriah spoke, saying, "All right. Just tell the other Elders what we talked about. Also, make sure to keep that damn robot in your sights. He's a tricky one and we can't afford to have anyone stopping us, not when we're so close to success."

'Twas no response, as before, but the flickering blue light did vanish. As soon as it did, Kiriah turned around. Before she lay her eyes on me, I looked down at my chest to prevent her from seeing that I had been listening. For I was under the impression that mine sister had not wanted me to listen in on that conversation, which did not make me feel well about my current situation, to put it lightly.

"Rii?" said Kiriah. "Are you awake?"

Yawning falsely (for I had to continue to make Kiriah think I had just awoken), I looked up at her and said, in a tired voice, "Yes, sister, I am awake. I just awoke, in fact. How many hours have passed since my surgery?"

"One," said Kiriah. "The doctors put your legs back together in about ten minutes. Isn't that amazing?"

"Indeed it is," I said. I rubbed my legs, just to be certain they were in one piece, and they did indeed feel that way. "Whilst I've never been the biggest supporter of Xeeonite technology, if it is capable of feats such as this, then perhaps it is not as bad as I thought. Still, I consider Delanian magic to be better, as I know that a truly skilled wizard could have healed my legs even faster."

"Perhaps, but what matters is that your legs are better and you should be able to walk on your own now," said Kiriah. She clapped her hands together again. "That means that I can now initiate you into Reunification. After all, you're one of us now, so that means that you need to go through the same things that we did before anything else."

Something about her words made me mightily uneasy. "What, exactly, must I do now that I am a member of Reunification?"

"If you are ready to walk, I can show you," said Kiriah. "Do you need me to help you up?"

I shook my head. "Nay, sister. I believe I can walk of my own accord now."

Thus, I took my blanket off my body and looked at my legs more closely. They looked as normal as ever, which did not surprise me too much because I had already suspected they would. Still, I bent my knees and moved them around anyway, just to be certain that they functioned as they ought to be.

Once I was certain that my legs would not give out on me, I looked up at Kiriah again and said, "Now, let me try to walk. If I need your help, then I will ask for it."

Kiriah nodded as I put my hands on the arms of the chair and pushed myself up. 'Twas difficult as first, for despite my legs being whole again, I did not feel entirely normal. I figured that

that my legs merely needed time to recover, however, so I did not worry much about it.

It was only when my feet touched the ground that I realized that I was wearing shoes. They were soft and comfortable and fit my feet perfectly. They weren't much to look at, but I was so glad to have shoes again for the first time in a long time that I did not complain about their plainness.

"I had the machines put shoes on your feet when you were sleeping," Kiriah explained. "I noticed how hard and scratched your feet were, so I thought you would appreciate it."

"Thank ye, Kiriah," I said, though I still held onto one of the chair's arms to help me stand. "I greatly appreciate the gesture. Ye know not what it was like to go without shoes for so long."

"You're welcome, brother," said Kiriah. "Now, can you walk on your own or do you need my help?"

I could stand just fine, but I did not know if I could walk. I was hesitant to try, but then I let go of the chair and took a step forward. When I did not fall flat on my face, I looked at Kiriah and said, "It appears that I can walk just fine, sister, though these shoes will take some getting used to, I think."

"You'll get plenty of opportunity to practice walking in those shoes, brother," said Kiriah. "Now, follow me. If you're going to be supporting Reunification, then you need to understand what we're doing better than you already do. And that means you have to participate in the Ceremony."

"The Ceremony?" I repeated. "What might that be?"

"It's the initiation ceremony that all new members of Reunification must undertake when they join the organization," said Kiriah. "We would have put you through the Ceremony right away had your legs not been broken."

I noticed how carefully she worded that last sentence. 'Had your legs not been broken' ... what a joke. After all, hadn't it been Kiriah who had ordered her men to break my legs? Of course it had. Did she think she could make me forget her involvement in my broken legs by refusing to take responsibility for it?

Nonetheless, I did not bring it up, because I was trying to stay on good terms with her. If Kiriah continued to believe that I had had a change of heart, if she believed I had forgiven her for breaking my legs (despite her not even asking for forgiveness from me in the first place), then taking down Reunification from the inside would be that much easier.

"Well, what are we waiting for, then?" I said. I stretched my arms and legs, for they were still quite stiff from me sitting in that chair for an hour. "Lead the way and I shall follow ye, as always, my sister."

Kiriah smiled, like I had just said exactly what she wanted to hear. She then turned around and gestured for me to follow her, which I did, albeit slowly, as my legs, while rapidly returning to their original limber form, were still stiffer than they appeared.

Upon exiting the room, we found ourselves in the empty hallways of the facility. I still saw no one else in here but ourselves, although I did hear the sounds of workers and construction equipment outside, which brought to mind that crane I had seen before. Nor did the hallway have much of a smell to it; 'twas slightly sterile, as if the people who maintained this place had put an obsessive amount of work into keeping it clean. I did not understand why they would, but Xeeonites in general were far more obsessive about cleanliness than we Delanians were.

Perhaps that was all there was to it.

In any case, I asked Kiriah, "Where are all of the Reunification members? Why is this place so deserted and empty? I thought your organization would have many more people in it."

"The facility we're in is largely maintained by robots," said Kiriah. She gestured at a camera hanging from the ceiling, which I had not even noticed had been watching us silently the entire time. "They're a lot more dependable and trustworthy than organic beings, for one. There are probably only a dozen or so organic, living beings here at any one time; we can't have more than that."

"Why not?" I asked. "I thought Reunification was much larger than a dozen or so members."

"The more people you let in on the Secret, the more likely it becomes that someone will spill that Secret out to the public," Kiriah explained. "And we don't want the public—whether on Dela or Xeeo—to know about us, at least not until the Reunification process is complete and the two worlds are one again."

"What is the exact number of members in your group, then?" said I, folding my arms over my chest.

"I can't tell you that, mostly because you're still not technically a member yet," said Kiriah, shaking her head. "Also, because the less we know about each other, the less useful any of our captured members become to enemies who may kidnap them."

"I see," I said. "That is how ye control the flow of information in this group, then? By determining what your inferiors deserve to know?"

"What they *need* to know," Kiriah corrected. She wagged a finger at me. "And don't make it sound like that. It's not like I know everything going on around here, either. I know more than most, but it's the Elders who know everything, and above the Elders is the Founder."

"I thought ye said ye were the leader of Reunification," I said, frowning. "Sounds to me as if ye are in fact just another subordinate in the chain of command."

"But I *am* the Leader," said Kiriah. "I just handle the day-to-day stuff that the Elders and the Founder don't have time for. That's all."

She sounded more than a bit offended by what I had said, but I did not apologize, though I probably should have. Knowing the exact chain of command in this organization did not make me respect my sister anymore than I already did; indeed, I had less respect for her now than before, if only because it was now clear to me that, despite her protests, she was indeed just another subordinate, albeit one higher up in chain of command than most.

That would make taking down Reunification from within that much more problematic, as I could not simply defeat Kiriah. Nay, I would have to deal with these 'Elders,' too, whoever they were, and the enigmatic Founder, whoever he was.

That knowledge made this task of mine seem far more insurmountable than I thought, but I did not show my worry. I knew Kiriah well enough to know how to hide my true thoughts and feelings from her, and as I could not allow her to suspect my true intentions, it was imperative I keep them to myself.

"Well, whatever," said Kiriah. "Come on. I have to take you

down to the Ceremony Room."

"Ye have a room devoted for the purposes of the Ceremony here in this place?" I asked. I looked around at the sleek Xeeonite interior architecture. "I did not think that Xeeonites cared much for ceremonies."

"Reunification is neither Xeeonite nor Delanian," said Kiriah, shaking her head again. "We're both, and neither, and more. We have Ceremony Rooms in all of our buildings and facilities for exactly this kind of situation. We need to be able to induct new members into the fold quickly, after all, no matter where they join."

"What is the Ceremony like?" I asked. "Is it painful?"

"You'll see once we get there," said Kiriah. "Follow me. The Ceremony Room is underneath the facility, so we will have to take you down there right away."

Kiriah began walking down the hallway. I followed, listening to the sounds of construction equipment and workers outside, wondering still what they were working on. These noises were quite foreign to mine ears, but I paid them little attention, partly because Kiriah did not seem likely to answer any questions about them, partly because I was more distracted by the new shoes on my feet than anything.

How comfortable these shoes were! Granted, they were not the fanciest of shoes, nor even the best pair I had ever worn; however, after having gone so many long days without shoes, even this simple pair 'twas better than nothing. I felt as though I could wear these shoes for the rest of my life; indeed, I wondered if I could keep them or if Kiriah had only given them to me until I could buy a pair of mine own. I would have to ask at some point.

I expected us to walk down a long series of stairs to the Ceremony Room, or perhaps take one of those infernal 'elevators' that the Xeeonites seemed to have installed in every building they had ever made.

But instead, Kiriah stopped in front of a door and pushed it open. Whilst I was no expert on Xeeonite technology, I thought that this door did not look anything like the door to an elevator or stairs. Wherefore, then, were we going?

I followed her in anyway, for I trusted that she knew where she was going. And what I saw was an odd sight that I had not expected to see in any Xeeonite building.

The room was almost completely empty of all furniture, save for a large stone platform in the center that had the symbol of the Old Gods carved into it. There was no mistaking that full moon symbol for anything else, though what 'twas doing here, of all places, I dared not say. A hint of ancient stone entered my nostrils, while my ears caught no sound aside from Kiriah's step against the tiled floor. Even the sounds of the construction equipment and workers outside seemed distant now, as if this room was inside another universe entirely.

"This is the main teleporter in this facility," said Kiriah, gesturing at it as she walked up to it. "It will teleport us to the Ceremony Room."

"Why does it have the symbol of the Old Gods engraved on it?" I asked, after my speaking abilities had returned to me, for I had been temporarily rendered mute by the sight of the symbol. "Does Reunification serve the Old Gods?"

Kiriah stopped, as if I had asked a question that she had not considered before. Then again, perhaps she was thinking of the best way to answer that question, although it seemed a simple one to I. After all, ye either served the Old Gods or ye did not; there was none of this 'gray area' that some liked to speak of when it came to whether they worshiped King Una or not.

Then Kiriah said, without looking at me, "Oh, well, that isn't just a symbol of the Old Gods. It's a symbol of reunification, too. That it resembles the symbol of the Old Gods is just a coincidence."

"I dare say that it appears to be appropriation and even mockery of the Old Gods," I said. I folded mine arms over my chest. "I thought this would offend ye, sister. After all, ye and I both grew up in the Old Religion together, did we not?"

Kiriah still did not turn to look at me, though that did not make me doubt myself, for I had said the whole truth. Our parents had indeed raised all three of us—Kiriah, Sura, and I—in the Old Religion, because they believed it was their duties as parents to do so. I could not be certain whether Sura still followed the Old Religion, as Kiriah's disappearance had shaken his faith and we had not spoken in years, but I thought that at least Kiriah would still show faith in the Old Gods.

Then Kiriah shrugged. "We can talk about this later. Right now, we need to get you through the Ceremony. After that, we can talk more about religion."

Though her tone was light and casual, as if this was an incredibly trivial and inconsequential thing, I sensed more than a hint of danger in her voice. It was the danger I had sensed earlier, when we had spoken prior to my surgery, a danger that I had never heard in my sister's voice before. I suspected she must have picked it up from her fellow Reunification members, which gave me yet another reason to hate this group.

Kiriah stepped onto the teleporter and gestured for me to join her. I did not want to, as I wanted nothing to do with what I considered to be a mockery of the Old Gods. Nonetheless, I knew I had little choice in the matter, so I climbed up next to Kiriah.

"All right," said Kiriah, looking up at me as she spoke, "I don't know if you have ever teleported before, but it will be a little disorienting at first."

"Will it be painful?" I asked. "I have heard stories of teleporters turning people who used them inside out."

"That's what the earliest teleporters did," said Kiriah, waving off my concern as if it was childish, "because teleporters were so new and no one really understood them. Nowadays, they can teleport a whole group of a dozen or more people without any trouble."

"Indeed?" I said, scratching my chin as I looked down on the teleporter under my feet, which felt sturdy and solid. "I have to admit, Xeeonite technology can be rather magnificent at times, though it is still no substitute for good old Delanian magic."

"I know," said Kiriah. "It's why I'm happy to be here. Xeeonite technology is simply amazing, sometimes even more so than our magic."

I frowned. "Now, sister, that is a bit strong, wouldn't ye say? As good as Xeeonite technology can sometimes be, Delanian magic is still the preferred practice of the Old Gods. Don't ye remember what our parents used to teach us before we went to bed every night?"

Kiriah scratched the back of her head. "I don't really remember. It's been so long. Was it something about magic over tech or something?'"

My frown turned into a smile as I quoted what our parents used to tell us at bed time so many years ago, "'Always appreciate the magic of old, for it is a gift from the Old Gods that keeps ye safe and secure at all times.'"

"I'm surprised that you remember that," said Kiriah, looking at me in surprise. "Then again, you are older than me, so that's not surprising."

"Indeed," I said. "Now, how does this teleporter work?"

Kiriah tapped her thin wrist. A holographic image of a keyboard rose from the spot she had tapped, a keyboard with Xeeonish letters I could not read. My sister's fingers danced across the keyboard as quickly and easily as if she did this every day, typing up what might have been a password of sorts as she did so.

I shuddered when I saw the hologram appear above my sister's wrist. I did so because it meant that Kiriah had indeed received implants just like every other Xeeonite. It disturbed me that my own sister had done that, which made me wonder again just how much she had changed since her disappearance so many years ago.

But I said nothing about it, because I doubted that Kiriah would listen to me. Xeeonites in general, I noticed, did not like anyone criticizing their implants, as if their implants were an integral part of their identity. I did not understand it, as these implants always seemed disgusting to me, but then, there was much I did not understand about this world and its people. Kiriah was not a native Xeeonite, but she certainly acted like one nowadays.

As soon as Kiriah finished typing on the holographic keyboard, everything around us began to shift like the water in the ocean. I looked around in panic, but then Kiriah grabbed my hand and held it tightly, like a reassuring grip, and said, "Stay still."

Though she spoke, her words became slurred and hard to understand, as if whatever witchcraft that was making the world around us shift and churn was affecting her, too. Still, I listened to her anyway and tried to calm down even as the walls melted and the platform under us turned into mush.

Just as I began to think that our surroundings were going to envelop us like a slime ball, everything returned to normal immediately. The abrupt transition—if you could even call it that, for it had not been much of a transition to me—made my stomach churn and my head hurt as if I had been clubbed by an angry dwarf wielding a hammer. My vision, too, was blurry, which made me hesitate, for I was unsure just how much longer my vision would remain this way.

"Here we are," said Kiriah, who I heard standing next to me. "The Ceremony Room. Can you see?"

Eager to see where we were, I rubbed my eyes in the hope that that would help clear them up more quickly. Rubbing my hands against my eyes did make them burn somewhat, but it must have worked, for when I lowered my hands, I could see them as clearly as anything else.

Then I looked up at the chamber we had teleported into and looked around to see where we were.

'Twas not a very large room, though it was bigger than any other room I had seen in this facility so far. Aside from its size, what struck me most about it was how it looked completely unlike any other Xeeonite room I had seen so far. There were no tiles on the floor, ceiling, or walls. Instead, there was stone, very old stone by the look of it, as if this room had been built ages ago by the Old Gods themselves.

And on the walls, floor, and ceiling were images I did not understand, especially due to the poor lighting from the florescent bulbs above. Two spheres were a common image I saw on much of the room, as well as a third, much larger sphere that was in between the worlds (for I soon realized that that was what they had to be). Ancient weapons—swords with serrated edges and axes with large, flat heads—were strung along the walls, but I did not know where any of those weapons might have been from, for I did not recognize their design at all.

In the center was some kind of strange machine I had never seen before. Its metallic surface was at complete odds with the ancient stone appearance of this room, as if whoever had built this chamber had not considered how the machine would look against the rest of the room. The machine looked like a box of some sort, with several blinking green lights on its perimeter, which made me hesitant, as I did not trust those lights. There was also a keyboard—a physical one, not a holographic one like the one that Kiriah had used—just to the right of its door, but aside from that, the machine looked quite plain and unremarkable, noticeable only because of its sharp contrast with the rest of the room.

Indeed, if I had not known any better or seen that odd machine over there, I would have foolishly believed that I had teleported back to Dela. This room certainly did not look like something from Xeeo, which did not make me feel quite comfortable.

"Why does this place look so … ancient?" I asked, looking at

Kiriah with a puzzled expression on my face. "It does not look like the sleek design of most Xeeonite rooms."

"That's because it's not," said Kiriah. She gestured at our surroundings. "This room is actually one of the last surviving ruins from before the splitting of Dela and Xeeo. We built the facility on top of it to keep it safe from prying eyes, though as you can tell, we've made more than a few adjustments to bring it up to modernity."

I considered that. If Kiriah was telling the truth, then this was indeed quite an old room, far older than anything on Dela. It made me wonder how something like this could have survived for so many years, but then, the works of the ancients were said to have been even greater than the works of us modern folk, so perhaps its good condition was far more believable than I first thought.

In any case, I pointed at the strange machine in the center and said, "What is that machine right there? What does it do? I have never seen anything like it."

"It's part of the Ceremony," Kiriah explained. "You have to sit inside it. Then we'll hook up your brain to the machine and it will ensure that you are loyal to Reunification."

When she said that, I was forced to hide my true feelings. Right now, Kiriah still seemed to think that I was on her side; still, I did not like what she said about that machine 'ensuring' that I was loyal to Reunification, whatever that meant.

So, in as casual a tone as I could muster, I said, "Say, sister, what do ye mean that the machine 'ensures' that I am loyal to Reunification?"

Kiriah smiled, which I took as a sign that she did not sense anything out of the ordinary from me. "The machine—which is a

Brain Editor—was originally designed for use by Xeeonite neurosurgeons to detect damaged or ill parts of the brain in their patients. What we learned, however, was that, with a little modification, it could be used to rewrite someone's memory and personality at will."

I had never before, in mine whole life, felt more threatened by the word 'rewrite' than I currently was. I looked at the machine again, which though silent no longer looked quite as benign as it once did.

"Basically, what happens is that we take you and hook your brain up to the Brain Editor, as I said," said Kiriah. She gestured at the back of her head, perhaps to indicate where the wires were supposed to go in my head. "The Brain Editor then, well, reads your brain. It looks for any sign of deceit or doubt and rewrites it accordingly."

I kept a casual demeanor, but it was hard to do because all I wished to do now was run for mine life. "Interesting. I am guessing ye have had trouble in the past with enemies attempting to infiltrate Reunification?"

Kiriah nodded. "It was before I joined. There was this guy … well, you don't need to know about him. He's long dead. The Elders bought and modified this Brain Editor to ensure that nothing like that would happen again."

"Good riddance, I say," I said. And even though I put on as good a show of genuineness as I could, in truth, I was disgusted at her short tale about the man, for I doubted that this infiltrator had been a truly bad man. "May I ask how permanent the rewrite is?"

"Completely," said Kiriah. She patted the back of her head. "Once the Brain Editor rewrites someone's brain, there's no changing them back. Sometimes all it does is take away someone's memory of their traitorous plans so they don't remember their original schemes, but more often than not it completely alters someone's personality."

"Did ye go through the Brain Editor when ye joined Reunification?" I asked.

Kiriah's smile never wavered as she said, "Yep. I still remember you, though, brother, and most of our past. The Elders told me I only needed subtle changes, so I don't think it really caused any lasting damage to my brain."

Except make ye crueler and less empathetic towards others. 'Twas what I thought, anyway, but I did not say that aloud because I was now thinking that I would need to find a way out of here if I was going to avoid getting my personality 'rewritten' and my memories altered.

"Don't worry," said Kiriah, resting one of her small hands on my arm. "I doubt it will do much to you. And if it does, it will be for the better; after all, the Brain Editor is supposed to make us more loyal to Reunification, which is always a good thing."

She said that as if it were a self-evident truth. It did not help that she was looking at me with her green eyes as she said that, like she thought I would agree with her.

To keep up the ruse, I said, "Why, of course, sister. The Brain Editor is indeed a noble machine, if a machine can be called such."

"Great," said Kiriah. She took her hand off my arm and began walking toward the Brain Editor. "Now just come along here. I'll get the machine started, which shouldn't take long, because despite its age, it works really well."

REUNIFICATION

I hesitated for a split second, for I had two choices before me now. One was to go along with the ruse a little while longer, maybe even sit in the chair and allow the wicked machine to change who I was. It certainly would not arouse Kiriah's suspicions, but it began to seem to me that the cost of pretending to be a loyal member of Reunification was far outweighed by the cost of sitting in the Brain Editor.

So, rather than follow Kiriah, I turned and ran back to the teleporter. I heard Kiriah calling for me to stop and come back, but I did not listen to her. I simply jumped onto the teleporter, which activated as soon as the soles of my shoes landed on it, and then the Ceremony Room vanished and melted away, although I knew that even this escape did not mean that I was free just yet.

Chapter Twelve

When I had teleported back into the original room I and Kiriah had been only moments prior, I dashed toward the door, though I soon regretted the hastiness of that action, for my stomach lurched and almost made me throw up. However, as I had not eaten much if anything in a day, I did not barf anything (though I felt awful nonetheless).

I made it to the door, however, and slammed it open with my shoulder. I then looked both ways down the hallway, trying to determine which direction I should go in, but I was still as ignorant of the layout of the building as ever, so I did not know which way lead out and which way would simply take me deeper into the bowels of hostile territory.

But I had no time to simply stand around and think, for I knew that any minute now Kiriah would be back, and once she was, I would likely be forcibly placed in the Brain Editor. 'Twas a terrifying thought.

Hence, I turned to the left and ran down that hallway as fast as I could. My shoes slammed against the tiles, making loud echoing noises, but I did not care because I knew that mine cover was already blown and that it would only be a matter of time before Kiriah or one of Reunification's other members found me.

I dashed by a camera, but as soon as I did, it detached from the ceiling and flew after me. I glance over my shoulder at it in surprise, watching as it flew with the speed of a humming bird, though it had what appeared to be a tiny rocket speeding out of its behind rather than wings. A bothersome and loud alarm shrieked from its body, which only made me wish to turn around and break the stupid machine like the toy it was.

I at first wondered why it chased me until I realized that it was trying to keep an eye on me. Perhaps Kiriah had sent a message to Reunification's security or perhaps the camera was designed to automatically chase anyone who seemed suspicious. Whatever the case, I knew I could not shake it easy.

Hence, I continued to run, almost literally flying above the tiled floor, hoping against hope that the stairs at the end of the hall would take me down closer to the exit. Of course, I hardly had much of a chance of survival even if I escaped the facility, but I pushed that thought from mine mind so I could focus on what was truly important at the moment.

And thus I ran until I reached the end of the hall. I found double doors at the end which I managed to push open without much difficulty, but before I could close them, the annoying flying camera swooped in after me, though I succeeded in closing the doors afterward. Then I barred them with a chair I found leaning against the walls, sticking it under their handles, though I had no idea for certain how long that chair would hold the doors shut.

The camera's alarm was even louder in the tiny room I found myself in than it was out in the hall, almost deafeningly louder. But I still lacked something to throw at it, so I would have to tolerate it slightly longer than I liked.

As annoying as that alarm was, I was happy that I had managed to make it in here without being caught. I turned to run down the stairs, but stopped when I saw that there were no stairs for me to run down. 'Twas simply an empty room, with a platform on the floor similar to the teleporter I had used to escape my sister in the first place.

I thought a thousand curses to the Old Gods, but then stopped when I realized that Kiriah was likely still coming after me. She might not have been alone, either, for this facility could have all kinds of security systems that I did not even know about. Therefore, I would have to figure out how to use the teleporter in this room to escape, which now seemed to me to be the way that the Reunification members traveled through this facility.

So I jumped onto the teleporter and expected it to teleport me away to wherever I was supposed to go. That was, after all, how that previous teleporter had worked. Why would this one not behave similarly?

Unfortunately, the teleporter did not send me anywhere, even though I had made certain to land on it. I stomped on the teleporter in frustration, but it still refused to teleport me anywhere. I wondered briefly if it was broken, which would be just mine luck, but decided that instead there must have been something else to it that I did not know.

I looked around the room frantically, but I did not see anything that looked like a control panel or anything. How did these Reunification members use these teleporters if they had no control panels? Was I missing something? This was another reason I utterly loathed Xeeonite technology, for it so rarely made sense.

The camera continued to blare its alarm, which made it even harder for me to figure out how to use this teleporter than before, for its sound distracted me greatly. 'Twas like someone screaming in my ear, and I had no way to shut them up.

It seemed to me as if all hope was lost, for if the teleporter did not work and I had no way to figure out how it worked, then I would inevitably be captured by Reunification. And then mine personality would be rewritten like the incoherent scribblings of a scribe.

'Tis then I noticed a vague holographic keyboard hovering above the front of the teleporter, the end facing the doors. How had I not noticed it before? Ah, I see. It was so transparent as to be almost invisible.

Nonetheless, I ran up to it and looked down at it. The keyboard resembled Kiriah's wrist holographic keyboard, but unfortunately, as with my dear sister's keyboard, the keys on this one were etched with Xeeonish letters.

Whilst I was not much of an expert in Xeeonite tech, I understood that I needed to input some kind of code in order to operate this teleporter. That did seem like a simple task, but unfortunately, I did not know what code I had to input.

At this point, however, I was desperate enough to try anything, so I raised my fingers to begin typing at random until I found the code when I heard the doors budge.

I froze in place and looked up. Through the tiny windows in

the doors, I saw Kiriah banging her fists against the doors. She was screaming, too, but what she might have been saying, I did not know, because the doors muffled her screams. I could guess, however, and it did not endear me much to her, that was for certain.

But Kiriah was not alone. Though the windows were too small for me to see much detail, I saw something large and metallic also beating against the doors. It was probably some kind of robot—everyone on this gods-forsaken world seemed to have one—but I doubted it was a mere service clicker. I could imagine what it would do to me once it got hold of me, which snapped me out of my paralysis.

Having never typed before, I found it hard to input letters and words into this keyboard. 'Twas especially difficult for me to focus because of the sounds made by Kiriah and her robot friend as they tried to tear down the doors, not to mention the alarm made by the damn camera, which now circled my head like an annoying insect that was destined to be swatted.

And then there was the texture of the keyboard itself. It was clearly not solid, but when my fingers awkwardly danced over its surface, I had no problem whatsoever with touching the keys. I kept expecting my fingers to pass through it with every stroke, but they never did, for which I was thankful, as this was mine only way of escape.

But every time I entered in what I thought was the correct word and hit the large button that I had learned through trial-and-error to be the enter key, a red 'X' would appear in front of me. There was no doubting what that meant, which is why I kept typing away anyway, hoping that the luck of Walnak would save me.

Yet as the red 'X' came up again and again, I began to lose hope. Especially when the doors were almost knocked inwards; the chair holding them back almost crunched under that blow. All Kiriah and her robot friend needed was one more blow like that, and then I would truly be dead.

That thought was by itself almost enough for me to cease typing and simply accept my fate. Yet I did not, because I was still a Knight of Se-Dela, and Knights of Se-Dela did not give up no matter how grim the situation was.

Then the doors burst open. Their sudden opening sent the chair flying over my head, striking the camera and sending it crashing to the floor near my feet. I paid it little attention, however, because I was still pecking my way across the keyboard, still hoping that Walnak would bless me.

Nonetheless, I looked up anyway, just in time to see Kiriah and her robot friend enter. Their combined bulk blocked off the doorway, so there was no way I could run around them if I wished. Not that I had ever seriously considered that plan; I noted it only because I now had one less way of escaping this place alive.

The robot that had entered with Kiriah was not as slim as Assassin. It was shorter and bulkier, built more like a battle ax than a rapier. It had round fists like boulders, with pistons behind them that were clearly what gave its attacks their punch.

"Rii," said Kiriah, her voice far deadlier—and hurt—than it had been before. "Why did you run? I thought you were loyal to Reunification."

I did not answer, because I was still typing madly across the holographic keyboard before me. Besides, I knew that Kiriah already knew why I had run; she was no idiot, even now, after having her personality irrevocably altered by that hateful machine, that machine I would someday destroy, assuming I lived long enough to do that.

"I guess I forgot to tell you what happens to people who try to back out of Reunification at the last second," said Kiriah. She gestured at her robot. "Usually, they wind up broken and in pieces across the Dead Lands, generally by Guard here. We can't have any flip-floppers on our team running around telling everyone who we are and what we're up to."

"But I am your brother," I said, briefly glancing at Kiriah before looking back down at the meaningless gibberish I typed away in a fury in order to strike gold. "Does this organization and its secrets matter more to you than the life of your own brother?"

As I suspected, Kiriah hesitated. Perhaps her personality had been rewritten by the Brain Editor, but she still seemed to care about me. If I could just take advantage of that for a little while longer, then I would be fine.

But then Kiriah stepped aside and said, addressing her robot companion, "Guard, teach my brother what happens when he tries to trick his sister."

Guard slammed his round fists together and ran at me much faster than a robot of his size should have been able to. He swung his fists through the air like the wrecking balls of a Xeeonite crane.

I should have run, but what good would that have done me? After all, there was nowhere to run to. Still my best hope lay in deciphering the secrets of this accursed teleporter, which now seemed to be intentionally keeping me from discovering the code word I needed to escape.

But I had little time in which to do so, because Guard was rapidly approaching. I estimated I had less than six seconds before it smashed its fists into my skull, which prompted me to type faster and faster, even though my increased speed did not help me find the password any more quickly than before. All I succeeded in doing was making the large red 'X' appear again and again, without any indication, not even a slight one, to let me know if I was any closer to escaping this place alive.

Guard's fists were so close now that I could feel the wind that followed them, like the strong gusts of the Cyclone Mountains. I had no more time. This was it. I was going to die, and all of my striving would be for naught.

Just as Guard's fists came within range of my face, just when I was absolutely certain that I was going to die, I inputted the last word I knew I would ever get to type.

And rather than another wicked red 'X' appearing to steal away mine hope, the entire keyboard glowed a bright blue, followed by a dinging sound that even I, someone who knew virtually nothing about Xeeonite technology, understood to mean that I had successfully found the right password.

As before, the world shifted around me. Guard's flying fists slowed down and became like mud, but soon they faded away and I found myself standing alone in a room identical to the one I had just been standing in moments before.

Still, mine heart raced, for I understood that I had just narrowly avoided death itself. 'Twas such a shocking feeling that I merely stood there, unable to comprehend completely my own success and the magnitude of that action, not even thanking the Old Gods for their help. I almost wanted to scream, even though I was currently in danger from nothing at the moment.

Then a loud beeping noise, like a siren's wail, made me jump. I tripped over my feet before regaining my balance and looking down at whatever had made that siren.

It was that security camera from before, the cur, its awful smoke filling my nostrils, the one that had chased me down and annoyed me with its loud alarm. I assumed it must have teleported with me, likely because it had been lying in the teleporter when I had teleported, but that did not make me at all happy about it.

Instead, I kicked the damn thing, but 'twas much heavier than it appeared, for as soon as I did, pain exploded in my toes. I grabbed my foot and hopped around, shouting a thousand different curses, whilst the camera continued to lie there as if I had not touched it at all.

The pain in mine toes subsided quickly, however, allowing me to lower my foot back onto the teleporter I stood upon. Nonetheless, I glared at the smoking, wreck of a machine, but shook my head and turned away. 'Twas no threat to me anymore; for what purpose, then, did I have to waste time punishing it, even though, were it a human being, I would say that it rightfully deserved to be punished, in accordance with the Six Laws of Justice laid down by Jakonal, the Old God of Justice, at the beginning of time?

So I stepped off the platform and walked over to the double doors. I hoped that these next few floors would offer even less of a challenge, even though I knew that that was naught but wishful thinking of the highest order. Still, perhaps Walnak's luck would strike again, and I would face no obstacles on my way out of here. Stranger things had happened, after all.

Thus, I pushed open the double doors, confident that I could handle whatever lay beyond … and then a sword flew from the opened doors and slashed across mine chest.

Chapter Thirteen

By all that was heavenly! My chest burned as blood poured forth, staining my clothes and spilling all over the floor, though I managed to step backwards in time to avoid getting a much deeper and far worse cut.

Still, the pain was so awful that I had to grasp my chest, feeling the hot blood that flowed like a river. Then I looked up at my assailant, who now stood in the doorway holding one of the double doors open with one hand, the other hand holding a bloodied silver sword with blinking lights running down its length.

"Apakerec," said Assassin, its harsh, grating metallic voice sending shivers up my spine. "Long time, no see. I received the Leader's message that our newest recruit had gotten yellow-bellied and wanted to drop out at the last minute. I am guessing that *you* are that newest recruit?"

I grit my teeth, mostly because I knew that if I spoke, I would scream. All I did was nod and continue to walk backwards until I was back on the platform, leaving a trail of blood along my path as I did so.

"I see," said Assassin. "Well, I'm glad you confirmed that for me, even though I already suspected it would be you. Let me guess, are you going to try to throw another trash can lid at me again? Then again, there aren't any trash can lids around here, so I guess you'll just have to make do with nothing, huh?"

Assassin spoke far too casually for a robot, made even more disturbing by his featureless face. Not that I focused much on that, however. Instead, I began praying fervently to the Old Gods for their aid, though I knew not if I would get it.

"Anyway, I can see you're in no mood for conversation," said Assassin. He raised his sword, my blood dripping from its blade onto the floor below. "Why don't we pick up where we left off? I've since recovered from that nasty little electromagnetic shock that those idiotic Foundation members used on me. Indeed, I even studied the technique and figured out how to use it to my advantage."

Assassin took his other hand off the door—which swung closed behind him as he did so—and aimed it at me.

A lightning bolt lanced from his finger tips toward me. I ducked to avoid it, but the action caused me to slip on my own blood and fall flat on my back. The lightning bolt struck the wall behind me, leaving a sizzling black crater that smoked as much as the camera.

"Do you like it?" asked Assassin, lowering his hand. "I developed the Touch of Zaunas all on my own."

Hearing the name of the Old God of Lightning uttered forth from this obvious heathen's lips gave me enough strength to gasp, "How dare ye use Zaunas's name like that! The Names of the Old

Gods are not for us mortals to toss around so lightly."

"Good thing I'm not a mortal, then," said Assassin. He began walking toward me, looking as terrifying as a lion about to devour its prey.

Normally, I would have stood up and fought, but mine chest still bled without end, which sapped my strength as rapidly as a sponge wiped across a wet surface. Of course, what also took away my strength was the knowledge that I could not defeat Assassin, at least on my own and in this terrible condition.

But I did not wish to give up, even though that would have been the most logical and rational course of action to take in this situation. For I was a Knight of Se-Dela, which meant that I would have to get back up and fight to the bitterest of ends. 'Twas better to die standing on one's feet than to die lying in one's own blood.

Yet how was I supposed to fight? I had no weapons; not even my energy knife, which likely had been taken away from me after Resita and I had been captured. I did not have even the tiniest of weapons—nay, not so much as a rock—to defend myself from this evil machine.

Then my eyes flickered over to the destroyed camera which lay on the teleporter next to me. It smoked and was clearly in no condition to fly anywhere, but it was the only thing around that I could possibly use as a weapon. I was no great improviser, but even I knew the importance of making do with what one has on hand, rather than crying that ye do not have what ye wanted or needed.

Hence, I grasped the security camera, which was hot to the touch but thankfully not as heavy as it appeared. I pushed myself to a sitting up position, but gritted my teeth when more blood poured from my chest, though I told myself to ignore it for as long as it took me to defeat Assassin (though whether I would be able to summon that much willpower, I did not know, though I was determined to try).

"Is that one of our flying security cameras?" said Assassin, watching as I staggered to my feet. "Well, that's an unusual weapon, I will admit, but hardly a threatening one. What, do you think I'm camera-shy or something?"

In truth, I had no idea what I could do with this smoking, wrecked machine. 'Twas nothing like any weapon I had used before; indeed, I doubted there was any way I could use it as a weapon. It had no blades, nor did it appear to have any lasers or projectiles to fire at Assassin. The best I could hope to do with it was to perhaps throw it, but even if it hit Assassin dead on, I doubted it would hurt him very much.

Nonetheless, I held the security camera with one hand, gripping my bloodied chest with the other, and tried to look as threatening as I could, even though I knew I looked more pathetic than anything. Assassin did not seem impressed or frightened, for he kept walking toward me, holding his sword at his side as if he was taking a nice stroll through the Fertile Plains.

"Well, it was nice knowing you while you lived," said Assassin. "I thought you might put up an actual fight, but if your best weapon is nothing more than a silly little broken security camera, then I can see I will not be getting the fight that I expected."

I prayed to the Old Gods, as I always did, for guidance. That they would show me how to use this camera, though I was beginning to think that perhaps the reason that the Old Gods hadn't listened to my prayers recently was because this was how I was destined to die.

Moving far more swiftly than any robot should have the ability to, Assassin raised its sword and ran at me with ferocious speed. I recognized the attack, because it had been a technique that Sir Lockfried had taught me during my training. If it hit, I would surely be dead.

Thus, with no time left to think, I did the only thing I could: I hurled the security camera at Assassin with as much strength as I could gather in my weakened state. The movement made my chest burn even more, but I could not allow myself to be distracted by the pain or the blood, for I did not have the luxury of worrying about it at the moment.

Much to my shock, the camera did indeed hit Assassin in the head, even before he had a chance to dodge it. 'Twas an amazing thing to see, watching as that damaged little machine crashed into Assassin's plate face, and caused him to veer off course, staggering to the side from the blow.

This was my opportunity. Without waiting, I dashed toward the doors and pulled one of them open. It was difficult, for I was so weak from the bleeding, but I succeeded in opening it just wide enough for me to slip through. Even so, I could hear Assassin already recovering, if the sound of the security camera being smashed to pieces behind me meant anything.

And thus I ran, heading straight down the hallway, blood flowing freely from my chest. I had lost so much blood by now that I wasn't running nearly as fast as I normally did, but I pushed myself to keep going anyway. Because to give up in this situation was to die for certain.

Even worse, however, was how my senses were rapidly fading in and out the further I ran. Most likely was the blood loss, trying to steal my consciousness from my grasp, but I had no intention of letting myself sink into the darkness that awaited me. I could survive ... I could survive ... I could survive.

But then, without warning, my legs gave out underneath me. I fell down on my hands and knees, though in truth I only supported myself with one hand, for with the other, I grabbed my bloody chest to keep it from bleeding too much, even though that gesture did little to help.

Oh, by the names of the Old Gods ... this was too much. As a Knight of Se-Dela, I had never been in such a horrible situation before. The blood loss almost overwhelmed for me by itself, though in truth, it was my sister's betrayal that brought me pain more than anything. Or perhaps it was both the blood loss and betrayal ... Ah, what did I know? I was beginning to lose consciousness anyway. Nothing made much sense anymore.

I fully expected to feel Assassin's sword dig deep into my back and finish me off, but I did not even hear him approach me from behind. Perhaps he understood that I was going to die and there was no reason for him to waste time and energy killing me himself.

Then I heard footsteps coming before me at an even, easy pace. Despite the terrible pain I was in, I managed to look up to see who was walking toward me, to see who would take my life.

'Twas some sort of humanoid being, wearing a long, flowing golden wizard's cloak, striding down the hall toward me. I almost mistook him for a Sage, but then noticed that his hands were mechanical and metallic plating poked out from under the skin of his face. He looked like no being I had seen, either on Xeeo or Dela, but even in my weakened state, I could tell he was not a friend.

"Another villain?" I gasped, as the figure continued to walk toward me. "What is your name, you cur? Are ye associated with this evil organization that stole my sister's brain?"

As the figure drew closer, still not saying a word, I smelled a powerful fragrance—like oranges, almost, though it could have been my blood-deprived brain inventing that for all I knew—wafting off his frame. He stopped before me and looked down at me as if I were a pitiful child in need of help. His face was half-mechanical and half-human, a face straight from my darkest nightmares.

"Young man," said the figure, his voice deep and masculine, but not unkindly, despite his strange appearance. "You are injured. And broken. Like Xeeo and Dela. Allow me to help you."

I had no time to respond to that, because when the man placed his mechanical hands on my face, I immediately lost all consciousness.

Chapter Fourteen

Brother, brother, are you awake? Brother, brother, can you hear me?"

That voice ... it took me a moment or two to recall, but I remembered it as the voice of Kiriah, my dearest sister, who I had not seen in years. Yet how could that be her? After all, she had gone missing so long ago that I had not thought I would see her again. Perhaps I heard someone else's voice, another woman who sounded like Kiriah.

The only way to know for certain was to open mine eyes and see. She sounded as if she was close by, perhaps even close enough by that I could see her.

Slowly, I opened my eyes. The lids felt heavier than normal for some reason, as if I was awakening out of a deep sleep. And indeed, my whole body did feel as stiff as a metal pipe, though why that 'twas, I could not remember.

When my eyes fully opened, I saw Kiriah's face staring at me. It was slightly older than when I had last seen it, but there was no mistaking that small nose or those distinctive, thin eyebrows for the features of anyone else but my sister.

"Kiriah?" I said, the word sounding weak from my mouth, the back of my head pounding for some reason. "What are ye doing here? I thought ye had been missing for six years."

"I was missing, but now we're back together again," said Kiriah, putting her hands together in happiness. "All we need to do now is get Sura back and everything will be back to normal again."

I smiled a grand smile, the grandest smile I had smiled in years, at her words. Yes, there was no mistaking this woman for anyone other than my dearest sister, Kiriah. We were reunited at long last. Praise the Old Gods!

Then I noticed I was sitting in some sort of strange, cramped box. The interior was lit by a white light, while mysterious little mechanical instruments, such as knives and needles, hovered over my head. It smelled as sterile as a Xeeonite hospital, though as far as I could tell, I was not in one of those buildings at all. 'Twas a door hanging open, too, a thick, metal door, with a white glowing interior much like the interior of the machine I sat in.

"Uh, sister?" I said, looking around at the strange machine I was inside. "What is this thing? Where am I?"

"You were injured," said Kiriah. She gestured at the machine. "And we brought you here, to be repaired. This is a Xeeonite healing machine. It regenerated your skin, mended your broken bones, and even gave you blood that you lost. Isn't Xeeonite tech amazing?"

I nodded, but then felt a sharp pain in the back of my head, in the part that pounded, like an insect had stung me there. Instinctively, I reached behind and grabbed it, but there was nothing to feel save for my hair and what felt like stitches, though I had no idea where those had come from.

"Headaches?" asked Kiriah in a sympathetic voice. "That's all right. Everyone who uses this machine has them. They'll only last a little while, though. Then they'll be gone for good and you'll be all better again."

My sister spoke so sweetly that I had no reason to disbelieve her. I didn't even ask her about the stitches. Most likely, those were the remains of the work that the machine had done on me and would be removed as soon as they were not needed.

"I am glad to hear that you are whole again, Rii," said another voice, one I did not recognize, but which stirred up feelings of unease in me immediately. "Because there is still so much for us to do and we need every last bit of help we can get."

Then a tall, humanoid figure appeared behind my sister. He wore golden, flowing robes and had mechanical hands, which were put together as if in prayer. His face was hideous; half mechanical, half organic, he made the Xeeonites, a people obsessed with mechanical implants, look positively normal by comparison.

Kiriah stood up and turned to face him. "Oh, Founder, there you are. Yes, Rii is all better now, but he says he has headaches."

"I heard that, Kiriah, but thank you for informing me anyway," said this 'Founder' character, whoever he was. He rested one of his large mechanical hands on Kiriah's shoulder. "I do not believe there is a kinder or more devoted sister in the two worlds than you. It is what I most admire about you, for you give me hope that there is still some good in this fragmented world."

Though Kiriah's back was to me, I could imagine her blushing at the compliment, because she always used to blush whenever she was complimented by anyone. 'Twas another good aspect about her, for it showed her purity of soul, which was what I had always loved about her.

Whilst I hated interrupting these moments, I nonetheless held up a hand and said, "Whilst I do agree with ye about my sister, I do not believe I have met ye yet, sir. What is your name?"

Founder pushed my sister gently aside, but even before he did so, Kiriah scrambled to get out of his way. He then stepped forward, looking at me with his eyes. The left eye, the organic one, glowed a natural blue, while the right eye, his mechanical one, glowed an artificial red.

"You can call me the Founder," said the man. "For reasons, I am certain, you already know."

I did not understand that cryptic speak, but then without warning, the Founder no longer seemed unfamiliar to me. When I looked at him, I recognized him as the leader of Reunification, on a holy mission to reunite Dela and Xeeo, to restore what was lost … but more importantly, I saw him as *my* leader, who I could not afford to question.

Where and whence did these thoughts come from? I did not know. They seemed to come from the back of my head, where those stitches were, but I soon stopped pondering deeply about this, because the undeniable truth of those ideas held me as firmly as the fangs of a vampire on my throat. I felt awful for questioning these ideas at all.

"Yes," said the Founder, nodding. "I can see in your eyes that you understand. Are you willing, then, to do what I say, when I say it, if it will aid us in reuniting what is divided?"

I should not have known what that meant, but I did, and so I said, "Yes, Founder, I am."

"Good," said the Founder. "Now rise, Rii, brother of Kiriah, for it is now time for us to begin the final process of Reunification. And there is no one now who can stop us."

Now available:

Two Worlds #2:

Alliance

Your allies are not always who they seem to be.

When J997, a law enforcement robot who rarely takes things at face value, travels to the magical and mystical world of Dela after a wanted criminal from his homeworld of Xeeo, he has only one, very simple mission in mind: Find the criminal, arrest her, and bring her back to justice for her crimes.

But when J997 is drawn into an ancient conflict between two secret organizations that he cannot trust, he struggles to avoid getting caught in the crossfire. His new objective is to return to Xeeo in one piece, yet he may be unable to return to his home, much less capture the criminal he came to arrest, if the two organizations have anything to say about it.

Now available in ebook and trade paperback wherever books are sold!

Other books by

Timothy L. Cerepaka

Prince Malock World:

The Mad Voyage of Prince Malock

The Return of Prince Malock

The New Era of Prince Malock

The Coronation of Prince Malock

Mages of Martir:

The Mage's Grave

The Mage's Limits

The Mage's Sea

The Mage's Ghost

Standalones:

The Last Legend: Glitch Apocalypse

All of the above novels are available in ebook and trade paperback wherever books are sold!

About the Author

Timothy L. Cerepaka writes fantasy and science-fiction stories as an indie author. He is the author of the Prince Malock World fantasy novels, the Mages of Martir fantasy novels, and the science-fantasy novel *The Last Legend: Glitch Apocalypse*. He lives in Texas.

Find out more at his at www.timothylcerepaka.com.

www.ingramcontent.com/pod-product-compliance
Lightning Source LLC
Chambersburg PA
CBHW021959170626
46808CB00001B/222